THE LONG WAY HOME

A Samantha Church Mystery

by
BETTA FERRENDELLI

For Robert E. Cox
You were a wonderful man.
You have traveled on, but you will always be in my heart.

ONE

S amantha Church shifted in the saddle of her stationary bike, trying to find a more comfortable position.

But the seat was hard and unforgiving and her new position wasn't any better than her last.

It was New Year's Day. Sam had purchased a spin bike as a Christmas present to herself. April and Sam had wrapped it together on Christmas Eve and placed a large red bow in the center of the box before situating it next to the tree to open on Christmas morning.

Sam had gone through the trouble and the time to research bicycle seats to replace the narrow one that had come with it for a better, more expensive one that she hoped would make the ride a bit more comfortable. She and April had sat together under the soft light at the kitchen table, drinking Howard's hot cocoa and reading so many online reviews for bicycle seats that they finally had to stop after all the narratives started to blend together.

The final few they read had glowing five-star reviews and promised the seat would be cushioned and comfortable. The extra wide, soft, gel-padded seat was great for indoor cycling, the description read. *"Great seat!" one person wrote. "Best thing about it is I didn't fall off the bike!"* The memory foam bike saddle was also waterproof and dust-resistant, and would maintain its comfort throughout the ride.

"Mommie, Mommie, this one!" April had said and pointed to the computer screen. "You said you wanted a seat that was extra wide."

"You're right, April, extra wide is perfect!" Sam said and read the description once more before she let April click *add to cart*.

Howard had helped her set up the spin bike in the barn the day after Christmas. He had wanted to clear out the extra room in his carriage house so she could exercise indoors where it would be warmer than the barn, but Sam refused.

"The cold will make me work harder to stay warm, Howard," she had told him.

For good measure she bought an exercise mat and a smattering of weights, five, ten, fifteen pounds. She had set them up next to her exercise bike. She also bought a pair of twenty-pound weights. It would be, however, some time before she could work up to those. She could barely lift the fifteen-pound weights over her head.

Her new bike faced the window so when she pedaled, she could stare out across the open fields until a small grove of Evergreens, perhaps a hundred yards away, came into view.

The day was raw and the sky, the color of iron, was thick with heavy clouds that threatened more cold weather. The field beyond the framed window was covered in freshly fallen snow and earlier that morning the sky was a radiant blue and the sun shone fully on the ground that glittered as though it were covered in diamonds.

She checked the timer on the spin bike, certain she had been pedaling at least twenty minutes.

"Ugh," she muttered and her head dropped heavily below her shoulders. *Ten minutes. Is that all I've been on this stupid thing?*

She sat up in the saddle holding her backside with both hands, her butt already aching. *Gotta keep going.*

She gripped the handlebars, hunkered down in the bicycle seat and kept pedaling. She closed her eyes, trying to stay focused on the country playlist April had created for her. The male singer was singing about 'what ifs', *what if I kiss you ... what if the world stops turning ... what if this is it, what if it's meant to be?*

Men. What's the point of them anyway? Sam thought. *All they do is let you down.* Jonathan, April's father, came to mind. She'd thought that had been love, but no, that had been, well, she didn't know what that had been, and then there was the pregnancy scare with Trace.

No more, she swore. She was better off on her own.

Another five minutes passed, she was swallowing gulps of air, but she refused to stop. Her lungs burned like fire, but she kept going, pushing down firmly on the pedals with one leg and then the other. As hard as she pedaled, she could hardly get her speed up and the bike's resistance was already at its lightest level.

But every time she wanted to stop, his memory kept her going.

When she thought of Hunter being hit by the truck, she pedaled faster. She closed her eyes and replayed the same scene over and over, just as she had since the September evening it had happened. She could see them running away from the construction site like thieves, the truck racing after them. Hunter ran like a track star, and quickly left her behind. Sam tried to yell at him, but she was so out of breath, she struggled to form the words. "Hunter! Wait! You're getting too far a— ahead of me!"

It was my fault. If only I'd been fitter, if only I'd been faster. She grimaced and lowered her head, making herself push through the pedals, her legs ready to give in to exhaustion. She remembered how he had turned and seen the truck bearing down on her, and how he had come back for her, pushed her aside. Saved her. And she remembered the look in his eyes when the truck barreled into him instead, twisting and breaking his young body.

My fault. Howard had told her not to think like that. Howard, Wilson, everyone had, but she couldn't help it. So many what ifs.

What if?

What if they had never gone to the construction site? What if Sam had insisted they had stayed in the station wagon? What if she had ignored the anonymous letter about money laundering and undocumented workers that had started everything?

What if, what if, what if?

The timer on the bike rang sharply, taking Sam from her muddled thoughts. She exhaled deeply, relieved that her first thirty-minute ride was over. She took a long swallow of water, the chill immediately cooling her down.

She got off the bike so slowly she felt as though she was having to peel herself off piece by piece. She wrapped the towel around her neck, looking out the window. It was dusk. The sun had made another brief appearance shining through threadbare trees that lined the sides of the field. The long, thin shadows falling in the open meadow in perfect, parallel lines.

She started for the barn door on wobbly legs, patting her forehead with the tip of the towel. She left the barn and followed her breath toward the ranch house, thoughts of Hunter filling her every step.

She was always thinking of him.

Always.

Through the dark and light of every moment of every day.

And she knew that no matter how hard she pedaled, how far she rode, how many *what ifs* came to mind, or how fast she could learn to run, nothing would ever bring him back.

Two

S am woke the following morning well before dawn and looked toward her bedroom window. The blinds were open, the way she always kept them. She could not yet see a hint of daylight in the darkened sky. The clock on her nightstand showed a few minutes before six a.m. She didn't like rising early in the winter when the morning light was stingy. She always felt as though she was getting up in the middle of the night.

At least she had finally started to sleep through the night again. The days, weeks and months after Hunter's death, she had only stared up into the darkness and waited for dawn.

Sam closed her eyes and listened. She could hear the muffled movements outside her bedroom door. She guessed it had to be Step, his nails clicking against the hardwood floor in the hallway. The lab-chow mix, dark as an inkwell with a spotted tongue and a square of white on his chest, was devoted to April. When she was home, he hardly ever left her side. Step was leaving or returning, perhaps, to April's bedroom. Sam listened as the sound of his footsteps faded toward the kitchen.

She reached for the lamp on her nightstand and shielded her eyes as she turned it on. Light filled the room and illuminated a small framed wooden photograph beneath the shade. Since Sam had brought the picture home, she'd made a point to look at it every time she entered her bedroom. It was the last thing she looked at before she went to bed and the first thing she saw when she opened her eyes in the morning.

She picked it up and held it with both hands. She ran her thumb over the front of the glass. She knew Hunter had kept it on top of his refrigerator in his apartment. He had told her one of the first things he did when he'd come home and entered the kitchen was to hold it and scrutinize every inch of it as though he had to commit every detail to memory and remind him of his promise.

She studied the photo under the soft light by her bed. She knew it was the only one he had of himself and his little sister—a photo taken only one week before the car accident that claimed their parents' lives.

Sam's face softened and she felt herself starting to smile, the kind of soft smile one has when they think of someone they love. Hunter and Jenny were sitting next to each other on the couch, his little sister leaning into him, both freshly bathed and wearing pajamas. Hunter was grinning into the camera. Jenny's hand was in the air as though she was waving at their parents. There was a small lilac-colored stuffed animal resting against Jenny's leg that Sam thought looked like an elephant.

During the few months she and Hunter had spent working together, he had often told her of the last time he saw his sister. How he longed to find her again and reconnect. Jenny was the only family he had left and desperately wanted to hold on to.

"But even if I found her now, she probably wouldn't even know who I am," Hunter had told Sam during one of their stakeouts.

He didn't have the means to look for her as a boy. Even as a teenager, he had no idea how or where to begin. Now that he had graduated college and had landed his first newspaper job, now that he had his place and his part of his parent's life insurance money, he had told Sam he could finally start to search for her.

But he knew nothing about her, what she looked like or where she lived.

He only knew that Jenny had been a few months old and they were living in the west Texas town of El Paso when their parents were killed by a drunk driver on the interstate as they returned home one Sunday afternoon. Hunter had been gravely injured. He had spent several weeks in the hospital and turned nine years old while in a coma. Jenny was in her car seat and hardly received a scratch.

El Paso was the only home he had known, but once his parents were gone, he and Jenny lived with their aunt, his mother's sister, in *Ciudad Juárez, Mexico* for over a year. One day his aunt told him he was returning to the United States.

"The day they brought me back was the last time I ever saw my sister," Hunter had told Sam. Recalling the yearning and sadness in his voice brought tears to her eyes now as it did the first time he'd told her.

She felt the chill in her bedroom on the tip of her nose. She nestled deeper under the warm, inviting covers and fell back to sleep, the lamp on and the photo still in her hands. Her alarm sounded twenty minutes later, dragging her unwillingly from sleep and her dream. Sam reluctantly got out of bed, trying to remember the hazy images of her dream.

She showered and got ready for work. She looked in on April. Her daughter was sleeping peacefully with Step now back at the foot of her bed. She couldn't see Morrison, save for the tip of his long black tail, which was sticking out from beneath April's bed.

The house was still when Sam entered the kitchen. She made coffee for her travel mug as she looked out the kitchen window over the sink. Under a blanket of stars, the sky was easing into daylight. Nearly a foot of new snow had fallen overnight, covering the distant trees in winter white. Sam could see that the snow on the gravel road from the house had already been cleared. She put on her winter coat and stepped out on the deck. She wrapped her scarf around her neck as frigid air touched her face.

She could hear the distant sound of the puttering motor of the old International Scout. Howard Skinner had put a blade on the truck and she knew he was clearing the road all the way to the main gate so she could get out with ease. The two-tone brown Chrysler station wagon was already parked in front of the house, the snow removed from all the windows and the interior now cozy and warm. Howard was taking care of her, of April and Nona. As he always had. She felt a happiness flow through her like a river and she hoped she never had to find out what it would be like to live without him.

Sam made the thirty-minute drive from the ranch into Grandview, a suburb on Denver's west side.

It was a few minutes after eight when she was unlocking the door on the lower level of the *Grandview Perspective* newspaper that led into the kitchen. The moment she stepped into the newsroom she remembered her dream.

THREE

In the dream Hunter was sitting at his desk, his hands poised over the keyboard. Sam threw her hands up and covered her mouth, her eyes wide with exhilaration and disbelief at the sight of him.

"Hunter! You're back! I am so happy to see you—you don't know how much I've missed you!"

He turned to face her.

"Why didn't you come to the ranch for Christmas dinner?"

As she neared him, she saw his mouth was tightly closed as though it had been zipped shut. She saw he had been staring at the wooden photograph of him and his sister he had kept in his kitchen. When she reached him, he picked the photo up and showed her. No matter how many times she called his name, he couldn't answer her.

Then her alarm sounded.

She walked slowly toward her desk, feeling the usual lull between her shoulders. Her desk and the one Hunter once used were no longer touching. Shortly before the new reporter started in late October Wilson told Sam he was going to rearrange Hunter's desk so that it was no longer facing hers. She did not protest. There were little reminders of him everywhere and this was just one more. It had been enough for her to come to work in the days after his death to see his empty desk.

As she reached her desk, she took note that managing editor Nick Weeks' office was still dark and the only other light on in the newsroom emanated from Wilson's office. She set her bag down on her chair, took her coat off and placed it over the top of her things.

As she neared his office door, she could hear him typing on his computer. She was continually amazed at how well he had mastered using his prosthesis to type. Well, to do everything, for that matter. He had told her early on in his recovery, nearly two years ago now, that he hoped only being able to type with one hand wouldn't interrupt the flow of his thoughts or slow him down. It was clumsy in the beginning. He initially had to hunt and peck at the keyboard with his device, almost as if he was learning to type all over again. It didn't take him long, however, to get used to typing mainly with his right hand and using the index digit of his Myoelectric hand to type the other letters.

She hesitated near the door, waiting for a pause in his typing before she knocked.

"Good morning, Wilson." She was standing at the threshold.

He looked up as he removed his reading glasses. They exchanged even glances. Their collective joy at seeing each other was like a mirror.

"Welcome back, Sam," he said and pointed at the two chairs in front of his desk. When she sat down, he said, "How was the rest of your holiday?"

Wilson Cole Jr. was the publisher and owner of the *Grandview Perspective,* a large community newspaper that published weekly on Fridays. He made every effort to treat his employees with kindness and respect, but raises were scarce and when he was able to give his employees an increase in pay, it didn't amount to much. So, Wilson tried to make it up to his staff in other ways. During the holidays, he always gave them a small bonus and the week between Christmas and New Year's off with pay. Save for two reporters on call, Wilson was the only employee who came in the office that week to open mail, monitor the police scanner and cover any potential breaking news.

Sam couldn't help sighing. "I'm not going to lie, Wilson, it wasn't the easiest few weeks to get through, especially with the anniversary of my sister's death and everything else. April and I put a wreath on Robin's grave on Christmas Eve. If it wasn't for Howard, Nona and April, it would've been much harder to get through. They fill my days completely. I know sometimes it's the only way I make it through. And thank you again for coming on Christmas. It was such a lovely day to have you with us."

"I enjoyed it, too, Sam. The food, watching April open gifts, the warmth from the fireplace, everything was great." Wilson stroked his beard. He was dressed smartly in a black turtleneck sweater that accentuated his full beard, which seemed grayer and whiter than she remembered. "April really likes my beard, doesn't she?"

Sam laughed as she gave him a sideways glance. "Whenever she knows you're coming the next thing she asks is if you still have it."

"Did Howard help you set up your exercise bike in the barn?"

Sam laughed again. "Yes, he did and," she tapped the top of his desk playfully as she leaned into it. "I did my first full thirty-minute workout yesterday afternoon."

He gave her a thumbs up. "I guess that new seat worked better, too."

"Well," Sam said, leaning back in her chair. "I wouldn't go that far. It was pretty uncomfortable when I finally got off, but it's better than that skinny one."

"Planning another thirty minutes tonight?"

"I don't know how my backside is going to feel about that, but absolutely I'll be on the bike tonight," she said, folding her hands lightly in front of her. She had told Wilson during Christmas dinner how she and April had researched the extra wide seat, but she hadn't told him how much time she had spent researching exercise bikes in general. The stationary bike she ultimately selected was top-of-the-line, with multi grip handlebars and an upgraded heavy flywheel. It had a weight limit of two hundred and seventy pounds. She wasn't anywhere near that, thank goodness, but if she wasn't careful, she could gain eighty more pounds just as easily and nearly unnoticeable as she had gained the rest.

17

The look on Sam's face turned serious as she changed the subject. "I had a dream about Hunter this morning as my alarm was going off. He was holding the picture of him and Jenny."

He shook his head slightly. "It doesn't seem to have gotten any easier for you since his death, has it?"

"He's always on my mind." Sam shrugged and her hands were still folded in front of her. "I can't help it, but I replay those last few days of his life over and over and over." She squeezed her hands tightly and shook her head, trying to dismiss the sinking feeling in her stomach.

She considered herself with a grim, hopeless look. "You can see why I couldn't keep up with him."

"Sam, no matter the situation, Hunter would've always been able to outrun you."

"Maybe, but that's not the point."

"Then what is?"

"That if I had been able to keep up with him or at least not fallen so far behind, then we would've been able to get back to the station wagon…" she hesitated briefly before she could bring herself to add, "in one piece."

"Sam, please. It would've been no different if it was me, or Nick or anyone else from this office running alongside him. He would have left us all behind; the kid was a picture of physical strength."

"But it wasn't you, it wasn't Nick. It was me."

Wilson held up his prosthesis and the device produced its usual mechanical noise as he opened his hand. "You're making this harder on yourself than it is has to be. What can we do to try and get beyond this?"

She knew the first thing that would be on his mind. "You don't have to worry, Wilson, this hasn't and never will affect my sobriety." She scooted toward his desk for a better look at the New Year calendar. "In fact," she said, tapping the day's date of January second, "Today marks eighteen months since I took my last drink and that won't change today, tomorrow, or ever." She pressed her lips firmly. "As long as I am alive and breathing, no one will *ever* take April away from me again."

He gave her a sure smile. "We should celebrate by going to a noon meeting tomorrow."

Sam nodded. "Of course, and I'll tell you what else I'm planning to announce at the meeting." There was a sparkle in her blue eyes.

He considered her, letting his gaze travel the length of her face, allowing himself a moment to take in her lips, the color of red wine, how she had pushed her hair, shades of winter wheat, behind her ears to reveal delicate gold loop earrings. "What's that?"

"I've never read the AA Big Book from beginning to end, only bits and pieces here and there. Tonight, after dinner and my ride, I'll start reading it and I won't stop until I've read it all the way through."

Wilson gave her another thumbs up. "That's a great idea, Sam. It'll help give you some guidance and a good perspective."

"There's something else I have to do, too." The conviction in her voice was unmistakable.

He gave her a serious look over the top of his folded hands.

"I know this may sound foolish, at best, but I want to take a week's vacation and go to El Paso."

"El Paso?"

"Yes, El Paso. I want to try and find Jenny, and it's the best place to start." She gave him her full attention, holding her breath, expecting him to rebut.

To her amazement he said, "It would be the only place to start."

Sam exhaled a deeply satisfied breath. "I expected you to tell me no."

Wilson gave her a patient laugh. "Sam, I know this has affected you deeply, and if you think going to El Paso will help, then I'm all for it. So much so that I'll throw in two days of pay since you will be working after all."

Her smile was full of gratitude. "Who knows if anything will come of it, Wilson. Maybe nothing, but I feel like I have to do something. It's not going to hurt if I spend a few days there, walking around his old neighborhood or visiting UTEP where his father taught, to see if anyone remembers anything, or maybe I'll get lucky and find someone, a neighbor or someone, who knew Hunter's family. It may go nowhere, but honestly I don't think I can go on not knowing, not trying to do something that Hunter wanted more than anything."

"When were you planning to go?"

"Next week, if that's okay with you and Nick, too, of course. You know how he is when I want to take a few days off. He'll act like the sky is falling."

"He knows you were one of the reporters on call over the holiday."

"Yeah. Maybe he'll see it that way, too, and cut me a little slack. Also, I'll need to get a few other things lined up as well."

"What other things?"

"Tomorrow when I go to city hall, I'm going to visit the police chief. I'm hoping he'll be willing to do an age progression photo of Jenny so I'll have something to take with me at least. I have Hunter's picture." She rose from her chair. "I'll show you," she said as her shape retreated from his desk. As she left his office remnants from the soft floral scent of her perfume stayed behind.

She returned moments later holding her cell phone. Muted sounds of the police scanner and reporters chatting in the newsroom filtered into the office as Sam scanned her phone. "I want him to see this photo of Hunter. It's the one April took of him when we had your sixtieth birthday dinner at the ranch."

She showed him the photo. Hunter was looking into the camera, his head tilted slightly toward the right, his hands folded loosely in front of his chest, his cheeks glowing in the firelight, his sandy mane skimming the tops of his shoulders. He was smiling evenly and comfortably. "I want to show him this one. Maybe that will help some since they were siblings. It's a long shot, but worth a try."

"That's a great idea, Sam," Wilson said and nodded his approval. "I'm sure James Page will be very happy to see you."

FOUR

Before Sam headed to Grandview City Hall the following morning, she stopped at a print shop and made several photos of Hunter off her cell phone. When she was scanning in his image, it asked for a name for the file. She stopped momentarily, thinking, her fingers floating lightly over the keyboard. She entered his full name, *Hunter John Hollingsworth*, staring at it for what seemed a long time before she tapped return.

She also brought the framed photograph of Hunter and Jenny with her that she kept on her nightstand and made several copies.

She didn't like to think about how impossible, how unfounded, perhaps, this venture to El Paso likely was. It didn't matter. Even if it went nowhere, she at least had to try for Hunter.

Their conversation about the last day Hunter saw Jenny had stayed with her: *"My aunt always said she never had kids and she had grown so accustomed to having Jenny and raising her that she didn't want to give her up. So, she kept her."*

Sam remembered staring at Hunter with one long blink, her mouth partially open. *"She took the baby with her?"*

Sam put the photos in a large white envelope, not knowing what to expect when she visited police chief James Page for her appointment at eleven a.m. She could only hope he would be willing to help with an age progression photo.

She was sitting in the Chrysler outside Grandview City Hall ten minutes before her appointment. She stared unblinking at the tan-colored building which housed the police department, watching people come and go through the automatic double doors. Nearly everyone had their thick winter coats and jackets pulled tightly against the cold.

The sky was cast in a deep pall. She had her window partially down, feeling the curt wind and watching dense storm clouds stampede across the sky. Sam wrapped her scarf around her neck and got out the station wagon. She followed several police officers through the double doors. The officers paid her no heed and she was glad to walk through the lobby largely unnoticed. When she had been married to Jonathan Church, a Grandview police detective and also the department's public information officer, she knew nearly everyone on the force, and came and went from City Hall nearly every day. After his death, she stayed away from city hall as much as possible, thankful the city beat wasn't hers to cover.

She had, however, spent a great deal of time at city hall early last year, training Hunter, a cub reporter who had been hired by the *Grandview Perspective*. He was the city hall and police beat reporter, one of the more unique, challenging positions at the newspaper. Reporters hired for that beat typically stayed a few years before they would leave for the same reason talented reporters often leave community newspapers, for larger metropolitan dailies. Sam was certain Hunter would have been no exception.

She had hoped when the new reporter took Hunter's place Wilson wouldn't ask her to be a mentor again. One afternoon the publisher had told his newsroom staff the new reporter, a new college graduate who had majored in criminal justice, but wanted to be a reporter, would be starting soon. After the meeting, Wilson called Sam in his office. She feared he would ask if she'd be willing to help with training. Of course, she wouldn't have told him no, but to her relief Wilson had told her he couldn't expect that of her. He only asked her to be available if the new reporter had questions. She had told him she was more than willing.

At two minutes after eleven Sam was knocking at the police chief's door. She poked her head inside. James Page was on the phone, but he motioned her in. She selected a chair directly in front of him and studied him while he talked. Clean shaven, with a firm jaw and sharp blue eyes, he looked the same as ever. She guessed James was in his early forties. With short dark hair, fit, trim and boyishly handsome, he was the perfect showpiece to head the Grandview Police Department. His sleeves were rolled up to his elbows and he wore a watch with a large dial and thick silver and black band on his left wrist. He gestured with his right hand, and as he spoke, the bright green custom silicone wristband he wore slid up and down.

Sam and James were mavens in their respective professions, who had come to mutually respect each other. James had allowed Sam to work with him to help solve the murder of a baby girl found in a Dumpster in an apartment complex, a cold case more than a decade in the making. It had been his first major case as a young police officer. James Page was a detective when Sam first met him. Initially he had been reluctant to have a reporter look at the child's cold case files, but he quickly learned that Samantha Church wasn't like most reporters. She was certainly more stubborn than anyone he knew, a familiar trait in himself he knew too well.

He hung up the phone and Sam reached across his desk to shake his hand. His grip was strong and warm. He cocked his head slightly and pointed a playful finger at her. "I know by now when you want to see me, Sam Church, you've got something on your mind."

"You know me well, Chief Page," Sam said, trying to keep the smile off her face.

"What's going on in Grandview that I've missed and you're going to bring to my attention?" he asked.

"Well, it's not exactly Grandview," she said. "I came to ask a favor."

James raised an eyebrow. "That all depends, you know."

"Of course," Sam said and cleared her throat quietly. "I was doing research online about age progression photos of people who have been missing for years."

"Who's missing?"

Until Sam heard James' words it didn't fully resonate with her Jenny wasn't missing. She looked out the tall windows behind his desk to an expansive view of a park and water feature framed by mature Cottonwood trees. She loosened the scarf from around her neck. "Honestly, James, no one is missing in the true sense of the word. I guess it's more of someone who hasn't been seen for some time."

"How long is some time?"

Sam tapped her index finger lightly against her chin as she did the math. "I'm thinking around a dozen years, maybe closer to fifteen, sixteen years."

"And you think this person's here in Grandview?"

"Let me explain," Sam said, and she told James about Hunter's sister.

"Oh, yes, I liked that kid. An unfortunate end for such a promising young man. So, his sister, Jenny, was still a baby when she was taken to Mexico, and Hunter never saw her again?" James said, confirming Sam's story.

Sam nodded, biting the inside of her bottom lip.

"How long did Hunter stay in El Paso as a boy?"

"He lived there until the car accident. He was seven, eight years old then. After his aunt brought him back to the US, he went into foster care, first with a couple who was returning from El Paso to Denver to live. Hunter never returned to El Paso after that except for a brief visit shortly before he started at the *Perspective*."

"What makes you think Jenny's there now if she went with the aunt to another town in Mexico as a baby?"

Sam shrugged, still biting her bottom lip. "I don't even know if she is, James. It's the last place Hunter knew, the only place, really, he thought she could be. We spent so much time talking in the station wagon during our surveillance and Hunter said at his first chance to start looking for his sister he would've returned to El Paso."

"Makes sense in that everything needs a starting point," James said. "So, you're going to do a little poking around down there. See if you can turn up something?"

Again, Sam nodded, feeling a knot form in the pit of her stomach at the improbability of her success. "I thought an age-enhanced photo that might resemble how Jenny could look today would be helpful to show those who might remember Hunter and his parents."

He pointed at her envelope. "Do you have photos?"

Sam dug them out and handed them to him.

James went back and forth between the two photos, letting his gaze settle for several minutes on each one, then he looked across his desk at her. He wasn't smiling. "Sam, I don't want to dampen your spirits, and your intentions are certainly commendable, but…"

"But?"

"But do you know how many people go missing every year in the United States?"

When Sam didn't respond, James said, "More than six hundred thousand people annually. Though most of those missing from that number are runaways, that number does run the gamut from younger children to older individuals. And of that number…" James' voice faded as he opened a desk drawer, his attention drawn to the files as he sifted through them.

He removed one file nearly three inches thick and opened it to the first page. "These are the latest stats I have." He spoke without looking at Sam. "In the United States, sixty percent are male, and women make up the other forty percent. The average age of people who go missing is around thirty-four years old. Since we're talking about a young girl in her teens now, according to AMBER Alert Reports, there are more than one hundred missing children currently in this country, who were younger than a year old when they disappeared."

"Jenny could be one of those statistics," she said.

"Anything's possible, Sam."

"Does age-rendering progression work?" Sam asked. "I've read pros and cons."

"It's called age progression technology," he said. "And, yes, it does work and police departments are relying on it more and more."

James put his desk phone on speaker and dialed a number from memory. A woman with a pleasant voice answered before the first ring ended.

"Elsa, James Page, how are you?"

"Good, sir, how are you?"

"Very good, are you busy at the moment? I'd like to stop by for a few minutes." He and Sam locked eyes. "And I'm bringing a reporter with me."

FIVE

B ecause Sam had been in and out of the admin area for so many years, she had a good idea where they were headed when they walked across the lobby to a set of locked double doors.

James flashed his laminated ID badge against a small brown box near the entrance and the red light changed to green. He pulled one of the doors open and allowed Sam to enter the crime lab first.

A young Black woman, a civilian, greeted them as they stopped at her desk. James smiled politely. "Hi, Joan, mind if we pop in to see Elsa for a few minutes?"

The woman nodded and smiled at Sam, handing her a clipboard and a plastic visitor's badge. Sam scribbled her name, time, date and clipped the badge on the outside of her scarf. She waited as James placed his ID badge against another locked door and then she walked in before him.

An entire wall nearly filled with photos and accolades of accreditations and accomplishments the Grandview Police Department had acquired over the years stood before them. Sam caught sight of one photo that

27

showed a chubby Latino police officer standing with a tow-headed six-year-old boy that Sam knew was the recipient of the department's award honoring Grandview residents who go above and beyond. The little boy had called 911 when his mother had fallen in the bathroom, hit her head and lost consciousness. The child was able to respond to all the commands and instructions the 911 dispatcher had asked of him and waited patiently by his mother's side until emergency crews arrived. Sam remembered Hunter taking the photo when the boy was honored during a city council meeting.

They walked the full length of the main hallway. Sam knew on the other side of that long wall was the property and evidence room. They turned another corner and James stopped at the second door on the right. It was open and Sam could see a woman with long, silver blonde hair pulled back in a decorative clip bent into her computer screen. James tapped lightly on the threshold.

"Elsa, we're here," he said and stepped back to allow Sam to enter first.

Elsa sat in front of two large computer monitors. The overhead lights were off and two floor lamps on opposite sides of the desk illuminated the room. A smaller lamp was situated next to Elsa's phone, casting a dull shadow over the desk. The windowless room was vastly smaller and darker than the police chief's corner office.

Elsa stood and extended her hand toward Sam and the women greeted each other warmly. She was pencil-thin and taller than both James and Sam. She wore a drapey reddish-purple V-neck blouse with two button cuffs that accentuated her long neck and marquise diamond necklace.

James was looking at Sam and extending his hand in her direction. "Elsa Greer, this is Sam Church, she's a reporter with the—"

"*Grandview Perspective*," Elsa said, nodding at Sam. "Nice to meet you, Sam, I see your name in the paper all the time."

Sam could feel her face flushing. "Thanks, I guess that means I'm doing something right."

"Elsa used to work with the National Center for Missing and Exploited Children and came to work for us a few months ago. She's a forensic artist who has already done considerable work for this state

28

and police departments around the country," James said, giving Elsa a nod of admiration. "I recruited Elsa for months before she finally came on board. As I told you in my office, Sam, we're increasingly using age progression technology and I wanted to be one of the first departments west of the Mississippi to have such a skilled artist on the team."

"Well, Sam, I hope I am as good as James says," Elsa said and she smiled over a set of perfectly polished teeth. "So, what brings you to see me?"

James told Elsa of Sam's intentions and ended by saying, "Sam brought these photos of Hunter and Jenny."

As James handed Elsa the envelope, Sam noticed a large marquise diamond on her left hand that elegantly complemented her necklace. As James did in his office, Elsa spent several minutes poring over the image of Hunter in front of the fire at the ranch and the other of Hunter and Jenny as children.

"I'm sure there'd likely be no resemblance between Hunter and his sister now," Sam said. "But I thought it was important that you see what he looks like, or, well, I should say looked like."

Elsa shook her head sadly and clucked her tongue. "He was nice looking. So unfortunate what happened, but no, Sam, this is great, even if there's not much similarity between siblings, it's great to have as a reference."

"It's pretty amazing what Elsa can do with a few photos and the accuracy of it," James said.

"May I keep these?" Elsa asked.

Sam extended her right hand at her. "Yes, please, by all means."

Elsa returned the photos to the envelope. "Any chance you might have photographs of his parents, that would be most helpful before I start anything."

"I do have some of Hunter's boxes that I took with me when we cleaned out his apartment. I can look through those tonight when I get home."

James was watching the exchange between the women with his arms lightly folded and resting against her desk. "Do you have some time tomorrow, Elsa, 'bout this same time?" he asked. "We can come back then so we can see what you can come up with."

"Can you do it that quickly?" Sam asked, wonder showing in her eyes.

"An initial rendering, yes," Elsa said. "You can sit beside me and watch tomorrow, if you'd like."

"Yes, of course, I'd love to, if your boss says it's okay," Sam said and looked at James. The grin he gave her revealed a dimple in his cheek.

"Great, then I'll see you both tomorrow," Elsa said, confirming.

James saluted Elsa with two fingers and followed Sam out of her office. They walked together through the main lobby, parting ways as Sam reached the automatic double doors and James returned to the police department.

Sam drove straight back to the *Perspective*, aware she'd have to hurry in order to be on time for the noon AA meeting. She saw Wilson's Honda Accord as she drove into the back lot, parked in its usual place. She glanced quickly at his personalized license plate—Page 68—as she did almost every time she entered the lot. She made her customary mental note to ask him the significance of the plate.

She was in the newsroom less than ten minutes when she and Wilson hurried out of the building to attend the meeting. Wilson opened the car door for Sam and caught a delicate scent of her perfume as he waited for her to get inside.

The AA meeting was already underway with the serenity prayer when Sam and Wilson entered the room, but they managed to find two seats together in front of a wall poster that recited the twelve steps.

Sam waited for her opportunity to address the room. When the group leader, a woman, said, "Would anyone else care to share this afternoon?" Sam raised her hand. The woman nodded at her and smiled. Wilson and Sam's elbows touched lightly as she rose to address the room. She started by telling them she had marked eighteen months of sobriety as the New Year began. Those in the room nodded with approval.

She extended an open hand toward Wilson. He was sitting with his leg crossed and his hands comfortably resting over one knee, his right hand covering his prosthesis. "My dear friend is one reason I can be standing here before you today to say that with confidence."

The room filled with light, sustaining applause.

"He's been my sponsor all this time even though I know men and women are not supposed to sponsor each other. My friend here isn't even an alcoholic, but he's been there for me every step of the way."

Sam glanced at Wilson as he shifted slightly in his chair, keeping his eyes on the group leader.

"He always seems to know what to say to me when I need to hear it the most," Sam went on. "And, honestly, I almost don't want to jeopardize that by finding a new sponsor."

More light applause filled the room.

"But it hasn't been without its challenges, which I can certainly say I've dealt with in other ways," Sam said and did a quick inventory of her attire. The red blazer she wore over a black sweater dress did a less than decent job of hiding her weight. "As you can see there's more than enough of me to go around."

She hesitated a moment and went on. "But this holiday season was particularly challenging as I lost a dear friend, a young man, in the fall, who had been looking forward to spending Christmas day with my family and me at our ranch. He had been in foster care most of his teen years and never had much of a chance to celebrate the holiday. So, when I invited him to come for Christmas day, you would've thought I was giving him the moon." Sam shook her head and smiled to herself as she struggled to hold back tears. Everyone waited for her to continue.

She took a deep breath and went on. "But he passed away following an accident in September and, well…"

The group made sorry noises and Sam stopped to find her voice.

"As you might imagine, I nearly lost it. One evening after work, I had found myself sitting outside the liquor store where I always went, staring at the doors with my hands gripping the steering wheel harder than I can ever remember. My cell phone started to ring and when I saw it was my friend calling, I cried with relief. I don't know what I would've done had he not called."

Sam folded her hands in front of her and found strength in squeezing them. "I know life goes on, and one of my constant thoughts during this holiday season was 'what can I do to come to terms with his death and not lose sight of myself?'

"One night I was in bed looking up into the darkness when I thought about the AA Big Book and reading it completely." Sam brought a hand and clutched her chest. "As I told my friend, at more than five hundred pages, I've only read bits and pieces. I've never been able to get through the entire thing, but I am planning to read every page, starting tonight. It'll take a little while to get through the whole book, but tonight's the night."

The room filled with boisterous applause and encouragement as Sam took her seat.

After dinner, Sam changed into a pair of sweats, went to the barn to exercise, carrying her water bottle and wearing a towel around her neck. It was day two of her friendly bet with Howard of how many days in a row she would ride the bike. Her guess, ten days; his, one week.

Before she got on the bike, she stood before the half-dozen boxes they had taken from Hunter's apartment. They had been on a shelf in the barn since she and Howard had put them there. Sam kept them in the hopes of someday giving everything to his sister.

The first box was filled with books, and to her amazement, the lilac-colored stuffed animal that was next to Jenny in the photo of the two of them sitting on the couch. It was an elephant and looked brand new. She tucked it under her arm and looked at the lid on the second box. The words Mom & Dad, were written in Hunter's familiar script. She pulled the box off the shelf and placed it on Howard's workbench, beneath the long fluorescent light. She removed a hodgepodge of keepsakes including a silver Timex watch with an expandable band that Sam guessed had been his father's. Time had stopped. She took out a pair of rosary beads made of sterling silver that she folded in the palm of her hand, certain they had been his mother's.

On the bottom of the box was a photo album. Sam lifted the book out with such reverence she felt as though she had found a treasure. She set it on the workbench and flipped through each page. On the last two pages, she found what she was looking for. The first photo showed

Hunter's parents. They were in a hospital room and his mother was in bed holding a baby in a bundle of cream-colored blankets. They had fresh jubilant faces that looked so youthful and vibrant that Sam had to believe the baby in her arms was Hunter.

The other photo had to be one his father had taken. Hunter and his mother were sitting on the tailgate inside their small pickup. Their legs were dangling and she was holding Jenny in her arms. Hunter was leaning in and had placed his arm over Jenny and his mother. He seemed to be glaring at the camera with a stern look as though it was his job to protect them. The backdrop behind them, the Franklin Mountains in El Paso.

This couldn't have been that long before the accident, Sam thought and she placed her hand lightly over the photo. She closed her eyes and felt her heart wither like a prune. Hunter, you don't know how much I wish you were still here.

Movement at the barn door captured her attention and before she could turn around, April was beside her and had her arms wrapped so tightly around her mother's midsection that Sam gasped. Howard was standing next to April. Step trotted in behind them and was busily sniffing every corner.

"It's been more than an hour, so we came looking for you," Howard said and his blue eyes were shining behind his glasses.

"Yeah, Mommie, whatcha doin'?"

Sam showed them the elephant and then the two photos. "This is exactly what Elsa will need for the photo enhancement of Jenny."

"How's she gonna be able to find her?" April asked, pointing at the photo of Hunter and his mother.

"Well, Baby, she's not going to be the one to find her, she's just trying to help me. Mommie's going to try and do that when I go to El Paso."

Howard cocked his head slightly. She had not told them about her plans to go to Texas. She looked at him and said, "I was waiting to say something to make sure I knew I'd be able to go before I told you."

"Wilson thinks it's a good idea?" Howard asked, looking unconvinced, but knowing she would have discussed the venture with him.

"I don't know if he really does or not, Howard," Sam said. "I think he senses it is something I need to do."

Howard stuffed his hands in his back pockets and looked over Sam's shoulder at the photos. April jumped on her mother's bike and started pedaling. She rode with such fluidity it made Sam stop and marvel at how effortless her daughter made it look.

"I haven't made it that far yet," Sam said and took the towel off her neck. "Honestly I don't have the strength or the energy to get on that thing tonight. So, you win!"

She glanced at Howard for his reaction, but when he didn't respond, she pointed at the fifteen-pound weights. "I'd have to use two hands to even pick up one of those darn things."

"No, sense in doing it now, Samantha," Howard said. He motioned with his head toward the house. "There's a strong fire in the fireplace and we were getting ready to watch a movie. April and I came to get you."

"Yeah, Mommie, Nona's making popcorn!" April said, still pedaling with ease.

Sam glowed with happiness. "Well, I certainly wouldn't want to miss that for the world!"

Six

Twenty-four hours after leaving Elsa Greer's office, James and Sam were returning armed with the photos of Hunter's parents.

James was smartly dressed in a midnight blue suit, matching print tie and black Oxfords. His hair had been freshly cut, trimmed to a straight even line along his neck. As they walked toward the crime lab, he tugged at his suit jacket and gave Sam a sideways glance. "I have a meeting with the governor this afternoon."

"If it's big news, I hope you'll remember your favorite reporter," she said in a lighthearted voice.

James winked and gave her a wry grin. "You're the first person I'd call, right after I call the *Post* and W. Robert Simmons," he said, knowing how she felt about Simmons, her former coworker at the Denver daily.

"Very funny," Sam said and shook her head.

In the admin wing, Sam signed in and received her visitor's badge. They made their way to Elsa's office. She had turned on the overhead lights and was standing in front of her large desk.

Sam gave her the photographs. She seemed as happy as Sam was to have found them. "These are perfect and will help immensely," she said, giving Sam and James a hearty smile.

Elsa spread them out across her desk. The two photographs Sam had brought yesterday were directly above the ones she brought of Hunter's parents. James and Sam stood on both sides of her like bookends. She studied each print closely passing her slender hands and neatly manicured nails slowly back and forth over the tops of them. She stopped more often on the photo Hunter's father had taken of him, his mother and sister.

"Sam, do you know, by chance, the span of time between Hunter's mother in these photos?" Elsa asked not looking up.

"Hunter was seven years old when the drunk driver hit them," she said. "He had a birthday while in the hospital."

Elsa shook her head slowly. "Eight years."

"His parents, John and Rita, were in their early thirties, I think, when they were killed. I'm guessing this photo was taken a few weeks or so, maybe a month at the most, before the accident." Sam motioned toward the photo of Hunter and Jenny sitting on the couch. "This one, too."

"It's good to have something that shows the difference in years, especially of his mother," Elsa said, still captivated by the pictures. "And Hunter would have been how old on his last birthday, which you said would have been in October?"

"Twenty-four."

"So, the best guess on Jenny's age now would be..." Elsa's voice faded.

Sam shrugged looking at James. They did the math together and James answered by saying, "She's probably close to eighteen now."

Elsa picked up the photo of his parents in the hospital room and held it at arm's length, taking in their sweeping smiles. She used a magnifying glass to amplify different parts of their facial features as Sam and James looked on with interest.

"They really were an attractive couple," Elsa said. "Hunter certainly was a handsome young man, just like his father."

Sam looked with Elsa at the photo of Hunter by the fire, feeling a faint ache running along her ribs, remembering his fashionable facial stubble, full head of tousled curly locks the color of a lion's mane and how tall and well-built he was. "He was at the ranch on Labor Day when my daughter took this photo. The next day he was struck by the truck."

Elsa clucked her tongue. "Makes me sadder each time I hear the story."

Sam nodded tightly. "Yes, I know what you mean."

Elsa studied the frame a moment more with her magnifying glass. "I can only imagine that Jenny will also be just as beautiful as her parents and brother."

Elsa collected the photographs and returned to her chair. She settled in and invited James and Sam to join her in the two chairs she had provided. As soon as Sam sat down, she noticed a five-by-five-inch white framed photograph under the lamp on Elsa's desk of a young girl who was sitting in the last seat in the back of a school bus. It was as though the photo called to her and Sam couldn't help picking it up. Up close, she could see the photo had faded over time. The girl was looking and smiling softly into the camera. Her face was round like the moon and her dark hair was thick and stopped in a collection of curls about her shoulders. Both her hands were resting over the seat in front of her.

"Is this your daughter?"

Elsa looked at the photo with Sam and shook her head. "That's the first age progression photograph I did of a child. Her name was Theresa and that was the last day anyone saw her alive. She got off the school bus a few blocks from her house. The bus driver said he saw her cross the street, but she never made it home."

Sam shook her head and her mouth turned down at the corners. "How old was she in this picture?"

"Twelve when she disappeared," Elsa said. "At the time I did the photo, it had been a dozen years and that was almost ten years ago."

"And she's never been found?" Sam asked and she returned the photo to its place on the desk.

"Unfortunately, no," she said. "I've done so many of these over the years that Theresa's case and just a few others are the only ones I still regularly keep track of."

Elsa took each of Hunter's photos and started to scan them into her computer. The first image to unfold bit by bit down her large monitor was Hunter by the fire. His parents in the hospital room took up the entire screen on the other monitor.

Elsa studied the photos, her hands resting in her lap. "Hunter had the lighter coloring and more of his father's looks and features," she noted. "He looked very much as his father had at the same age."

Sam nodded. "Rita was born in Mexico. She met John when she came to El Paso to work as a housekeeper for John's parents. They were in their mid-teens then and John was a few years older. To hear Hunter tell the story of how they met and fell in love, it was almost immediate. Hunter was fluent in Spanish, too, and he told me he spoke it better than his father ever did."

"About the only thing, really," Elsa said and paused for a moment in thought. "We can't guess or accurately foresee how a person's hair will look in an age progression photo."

"And you can't guess on the hair for, I assume, obvious reasons," Sam said. "The way it's cut or the color could be different, for example, or they might not even have hair."

"Precisely," James said. "And for obvious reasons, a person's face changes gradually as they grow and age."

"It's also difficult or nearly impossible to predict how a person's facial features will develop under extreme stress or in captivity," Elsa said. "So, I'm going to guess, then, for the sake of my work here that Jenny will have more the look of her mother, her darker skin, the eyes, the nose, the lips, everything."

Elsa scanned in the photo of Rita sitting with her children on the bed of the pickup. She enlarged Rita's image. At this magnification, her oblong face loomed before them on the screen. The look on her smooth face was alluring, almost angelic, her smile small and nearly unnoticeable. Her eyebrows were full and the right one seemed to be in a perpetual arc. Her brown eyes were round and deep-set.

Elsa noticed Sam seemed to be drawn in by the shape of her nose and she drew a red circle around it. "Because of its location and prominence on the human face, it can be the most recognizable and distinctive feature of an individual." She pointed to it with her mouse, the arrow highlighting each feature, her long, thin bridge, narrow nostrils, how the

38

tip came to a point.

"She really is quite stunning," Sam said, unable to take her eyes off the screen.

"Since Rita's hair is pulled away from her face, for the sake of our photo, we'll make Jenny's hair straight and long and the same brown color as her mother's. I'll make it fall evenly below her shoulders, as though it will come to a stop near the center of her back."

Elsa drew another red circle around Rita's entire face. "You say they died in their early thirties?"

Sam nodded when Elsa looked at her. "She hardly looks twenty-five in this picture," Sam said.

Elsa scooted her chair closer to her desk. "Let's see what we can come up with."

Within the hour Sam had what she needed, an age progression rendering of what Jenny could look like now as a teenager. Elsa put a few finishing touches on the final version, tweaking Jenny's image around her eyes and mouth, making her lips slightly fuller, her nose shaped like her mother's. She made her hair a slightly darker shade of brown.

Sam and James stared at the computer image. "Wow," they said in unison.

Sam felt the dull pain around her ribs return. "What I wouldn't give for Hunter to be here so he could see this."

The room fell silent. Elsa printed several copies of the rendering, the whine of the printer filling the quiet spaces between them.

She put the images in a large envelope and handed it to Sam. "Good luck."

Sam accepted it with a sense of falling and appreciation.

"Hopefully James can keep me posted on your efforts," Elsa said. He nodded when she looked at him.

"Hopefully I'll have something to report," Sam said.

They started for the door and Elsa called to Sam as she reached the threshold. "It's great what you're doing, Sam, really a noble gesture."

Sam turned to face her. "Honestly, I'd rather Hunter still be here so he could look for his sister himself." She shrugged deeply. "And who knows what Jenny knows? She was just a baby when all this happened. She never knew Hunter or their parents. Thank you, though, for everything because I'm going to need the luck."

James walked with Sam from the crime lab to the automatic double doors in the main lobby. He wished her luck, too. "Keep me posted," he said.

Sam buttoned her coat and pulled the envelope closer to her chest. "I will, and thank you for doing this for me. I greatly appreciate it."

James gave her shoulder a firm squeeze and she smiled. "I know a few detectives with the El Paso PD. I can put you in touch with them if it ever comes to that."

"Thanks, James, I'll let you know."

James stayed at the automatic doors and watched her walk toward the Chrysler, her head tilted toward the left to avoid the wind and snow that had just started to fall.

SEVEN

It was near the end of the day and Sam was in Wilson's office, showing him the age enhancement photo. They were standing in front of his desk so close the distance between their shoulders was razor-thin. Their backs were to the door and their arms were folded like mirrors as they viewed the image.

"That's remarkable," Wilson said. "I wonder how close Elsa has come."

"I'd love to find out," Sam said.

Their heads were still bent into the photograph when they turned toward a sharp knock at the door. Managing editor Nick Weeks stuck his head around the corner. "Hope I'm not interrupting," Nick said.

Wilson stepped away hastily from Sam and motioned Nick into his office. Nick came to the desk and looked at the photo. "Who's this?" he asked, looking beyond Sam as though she was an apparition to Wilson.

Wilson removed his reading glasses. "I'll let Sam give you the details."

Sam answered begrudgingly. "I don't know if you remember that Hunter had a sister he had lost track of after his parents were killed."

She could tell Nick was processing the information by doing his usual—twisting the right corner of his mustache as he mulled over her words. "Yeah, yeah. I heard Hunter mention something about it. He went into foster care and the sister ended up with the aunt somewhere in Mexico."

"That's right," Sam said coolly.

"What was his sister's name?"

Sam told him.

"Is this what she looks like now?" Nick asked, pointing at the image with a number-two pencil.

"We hope so, at least close anyway," Sam said. "But we don't really know how she looks given, that it's been so long."

Nick looked at Wilson as he filled him in on what Sam was planning.

"But she's not a missing person," Nick said when Wilson finished.

Sam kept her attention on the paper clip she was fidgeting with, trying to keep from saying something she shouldn't. "No, Nick, of course she's not, and that's how we're treating this. Hunter had every intention of looking for Jenny when he was alive, but, well…"

"Yeah, yeah, I get it," Nick said. "No need to say any more."

As Nick gave the rendering another look, Sam took a moment to study Wilson and Nick, who she knew cared for her very little, if at all. He was almost as tall as Wilson, but not nearly as attractive or distinguished. Nick was in his mid-forties, a decade older than she was. Though he was tall, his frame looked as soft as white bread, which aged him and made him appear out of shape. His belly protruded slightly over his belt buckle, and when he sat down, the bottom buttons were constantly taut. He had a full head of curly brown hair sparsely mixed with gray. His mustache was so thick it was hard to see his upper lip and his glasses seemed permanently etched on the tip of his nose.

Most of the time Nick's manner was abrupt and abrasive, and he was crotchety more days of the week than he wasn't. He had been the managing editor for nearly a decade when Wilson purchased the *Grandview Perspective*. Wilson kept Nick on staff because he knew the community well and Wilson needed someone with depth, experience, and knowledge if he wanted his new venture to thrive. Nick had a good command of what it took to keep the newspaper competitive without losing its community edge, and Wilson liked and needed that quality. Nick also had a better handle on the financial costs and obligations of running a community newspaper than anyone in the industry, save perhaps Wilson himself. Especially with escalating printing and mailing costs, and as sales were constantly migrating to digital media, if there was a way to save a dollar here and a dime there, Wilson was confident Nick would be sure to find it.

Wilson Cole Jr. was a tall, handsome man with a thick shock of silver hair and a voice that resonated as deep as a bass note. The gray and black in his full beard and the midnight blue dress shirt and light print tie he wore made his hair appear rich and more defined. He looked like any other businessman, yet managed to project something more comfortable. Perhaps it was his face. At sixty, it had begun to fold softly with gravity's pull. Perhaps it was his manner, described by those who knew him as direct, but low-key and most of all, calm. Community leaders, business owners, elected officials and residents were attracted to Wilson because his style was thoughtful and methodical. He had tact and knew when and how to use it. Being overbearing, callous or rude were not parts of his collective personality.

Sam couldn't help her bias, but there were times she felt like they could be on the bow of the Titanic, heading straight for the iceberg, and Wilson Cole Jr. could be trusted to calmly and efficiently take control of the situation and steer them clear of disaster. Nick, on the other hand, could likely have a coronary if he discovered someone was overcharging them for the hand soap in the bathroom.

"I'll let you guys get back to whatever you were doing," Nick said. "But I was actually looking for you, Church."

Sam forced herself to keep a straight face, she hated when he called her by her last name.

"Can you cover a grand opening next week of that new office complex? It's Tuesday. We'll need photos and a short write-up. It's one of those chamber-of-commerce-kind-of-stories, but it's really big news for the city and county with all the jobs and revenue it'll bring."

Sam shook her head. "I'll be out of the office next week."

He frowned firmly at her. "You're gonna be gone? Did you run that by Wilson and me?"

Wilson answered with a slight impatience. "Yes, Nick, remember I told you Sam was taking a few days' vacation and going to El Paso." He pointed at Jenny's rendering. "That's what this photo is all about. She was also one of the reporters on call over the holiday."

"Humm, oh, yes," Nick's face flickered with recognition. "Yes, that's right. Sorry, Wilson, it slipped my mind for a moment."

Sam pursed her lips, fuming as she watched Nick start for the door.

"Not a big deal. I'll assign it to another reporter," he said and grumbled something else unintelligible at the door, and then he was gone.

Sam waited until Nick was out of earshot. She tried to keep from sounding sardonic. "He loves trying to assign me those fluffy stories. I've told you, Wilson, that no matter what, even if I won a Pulitzer, that man is never going to like me or appreciate the work, *the award-winning*," she added with emphasis, "reporting and writing I've done."

Wilson's smile was playful, but serious. He touched his chest with the tip of his prosthesis. "And I've told you, Sam, as long as I am happy with your work, it doesn't matter what Nick thinks."

An hour later Sam was turning off her computer, looking at the desk that used to be Hunter's. It was a habit she had fallen into shortly after his death. She gathered her coat and bag and walked to Wilson's office. She noticed he was holding his suit jacket as she tapped on the door jam.

"Hi. I was just coming to say goodbye since I won't see you again until after I get back from El Paso," Sam said. "Are you leaving, too? We can walk out together."

"Not yet, Sam. I've finished my column, but I want to sit on it a bit before I send it to Nick so he'll have it in the morning. The ending needs a little punch." He was taking Thursday and Friday off, allowing for a long weekend after he had worked the week following Christmas.

He put his jacket on and straightened his tie, which still took effort with his prosthesis, but he managed. "You're leaving Monday morning?"

"Yes. It's April's first day back to school, too, and I want to at least take her that morning. Howard is going with me, and then he's taking me to the airport."

"You'll be home on Friday, right?"

"Yes, late Friday. I want to be home for the weekend. It's enough that I'm going to be away from home and April all week that I don't want to be gone any longer than I have to." She adjusted her coat and bag over arm. "April's birthday is the following Wednesday."

"Yes, the fifteenth," he said.

She nodded. "We're having a party for her on Saturday. She's having a few schoolmates and some of her softball teammates over to celebrate. Nona and I will be cooking up a storm, of course, homemade chocolate cake and ravioli. April asked me last night if you could come, too." Sam smiled slightly embarrassed. "I certainly understand if you have other plans, but she was sure excited asking about you."

Wilson couldn't help the broad grin that covered his face. "Sam, I wouldn't miss April's party for anything. Thank you for inviting me, and you tell April I'll absolutely be there."

"Wonderful! She'll be so happy."

"How far have you gotten with the Big Book?"

"After all those forewords, I'm finally in the middle of chapter one."

"Bill's story," Wilson said. "Bill Wilson, or Bill W. as he is referred to in the AA book. He's one of the AA founders. He died in the early seventies."

"Yes, he has an interesting story, though I am not sure how much more I'll read before I leave, but at least it's a start."

"Keep it up, Sam, and you'll have it finished in no time. Good luck in El Paso. You have my cell. I'll be curious to see how things go."

"I'll call you and let you know."

Thirty minutes later Wilson put on his overcoat and turned out the light in his office. The rest of the newsroom was dark and the only light came from the security light at the top of the stairs and green neon EXIT sign by the kitchen. He stopped at Sam's desk as he headed toward the kitchen to leave, accompanied by the chatter on the police scanner. He wondered if she had caught on that he seemed to know so much about

Bill W. If it did register with her, she gave no indication.

He picked up a small framed photograph of April on the corner of Sam's desk by her computer monitor. April was sitting on the open tailgate of the Scout, her legs dangling and her arm around Step with a vast cloudless blue sky as a backdrop. She was grinning widely into the camera.

He knew why, of course, April liked his *Santa Claus* beard so much. He stroked his chin, thinking of the connection he had with April, a connection Sam still knew nothing about.

And.

And the secret that he had asked the little girl to keep—that he, too, was a recovering alcoholic.

Beyond this moment that wasn't the only thing that had been on his mind. He'd been thinking endlessly about what Sam had said during the AA meeting.

"He's been my sponsor all this time. ... My friend here isn't even an alcoholic, but he's been there for me every step of the way. He always seems to know what to say to me when I need to hear it the most..."

He locked the door to the building and climbed the stairs to the parking lot, the security sensors illuminating the darkened area as he passed under it. He stopped at the back of his car and looked at his license plate: PAGE 68, wondering, as he often did, what it would be like to build a life with her.

He still hadn't told her that he was a recovering alcoholic and had been sober now for more years than he could remember. All these years he had practiced the anonymous part of Alcoholics Anonymous. He had often wondered when the time would come and she finally learned he had been where she is now, whether he had told her or she learned of it by another means, if she'd be disappointed he'd kept his secret from her for so long.

Knowing her as he had come to know her, however, he guessed not.

He had often wondered how she would find out. Now, it was safe to say he knew. It wouldn't be long before she'd reach page 68 of the Big Book, and a revelation she was about to come to on her own.

EIGHT

It was late Sunday afternoon and Sam and April were in Sam's bedroom. She had just finished another thirty-minute workout on the stationary bike. The ride was made a little easier and seemingly passed a little faster as she watched April outside the barn window build a snowman. Step was by April's side and she would stop every few minutes and throw a stick for him to fetch in the open field.

Sam shook her head, admiring how well and how far her little girl could throw. Unlike Sam, who had been informed by her daughter on numerous occasions she threw like a girl. April had an arm like a rocket. A natural athlete, she had a laser-focused throw. From her position at shortstop, whether April was throwing to one of the girls at their base or the catcher, she seldom missed the center of their gloves—no matter what position their glove was in, up, down, or near the ground.

After her workout ended, Sam trudged through the snow with April to put the final touches on the snowman's face. They even stuck one of Howard's old pipes in its mouth. Sam took a photo on her cell phone of April and Step standing next to Frosty, who matched April's height perfectly.

Back in her room, they were dressed in sweats and Sam still had her towel around her neck. Her suitcase was open on the bed in front of them.

"Mommie, what're you going to do if you find Jenny?" April was sitting with her legs crossed on the bed helping her mother fold their laundry. Step was lying at the foot of Sam's bed, fast asleep, and Morrison was sitting in the threshold of the open door, his eyes cast down the hallway.

Sam was putting a collection of white and black sport socks and green and blue crew socks, the color of April's Catholic school uniform, together. April would match the colors and then hand them to her mother. Sam stopped and stared beyond April to the wall behind her. In the fading light of a winter afternoon, fragments of hazy sunlight were splintered through the blinds.

She'd had the same thoughts a thousand times, of course, but until she heard April give voice to the words, she hadn't admitted to herself that she didn't know what she would do.

"I honestly don't know," Sam said and drew in a deep breath. "Tell her about Hunter, but beyond that, I just don't know."

April watched her mother put two work outfits in her suitcase, folding each one carefully to avoid wrinkles. As she placed a pair of dress shoes inside, April asked, "Will you be home for my birthday?"

Sam tilted her head and gave April a confident smile. "Baby, of course. I'll be home on Friday. Nothing is going to keep me from celebrating your special day. Remember, Wilson's coming."

"I remember." April nodded, beaming with enthusiasm.

They separated and folded more sport socks in silence. They could hear the television emanating from the living room. Howard and Nona were watching a drama in front of a roaring fire, and the scent of burning wood filtered into the bedroom.

When April handed Sam the last pair of socks, she said, "Mommie, when are you and Wilson gonna get married?"

April's words hit Sam like a hard splash of icy water and she couldn't help the small gasp that escaped her mouth. She pressed the socks she had been holding closely against her chest and stared in near disbelief at April. It took her a few seconds to find her voice. "Baby, whatever gave you the idea Wilson and I were going to get married?"

April shrugged. "I dunno."

Sam managed to collect herself. "Wilson is a very good man who has helped me so much that I don't know what I'd do without him. He's one of the most kindhearted and caring men I've ever met, and a wonderful boss, too, but that doesn't mean I am going to marry him."

"I think he kinda likes you."

Sam chuckled and tapped April playfully on the nose. "Well, I like him, too, but not enough to marry him. I'm happy being single and being here with you, Howard, and Nona. You're what's most important to me now, April, nothing else is as important to me now or ever more than you."

"His hair is gray, so maybe that's too old for you anyway."

Sam cupped April's face in her hands and lightly kissed her forehead. She smelled faintly of the outdoors, of open fields and Evergreens. "Yes, April, he's a little older than I am, but age really doesn't matter when you love someone. Lots of people get married who are decades apart in age and live happily ever after."

"Mom, I already know that. And I already know that you and Wilson could live happily together."

Sam nodded as her eyebrows drifted up and down. "Oh, you do, do you? And how do you know that when you're just a little girl?"

April shrugged as she jumped off the bed. Step sat up immediately. "I dunno. It's just something I know."

"Good that you were able to confirm that for your mother," Sam said.

She removed her towel and tossed it in a pile of dirty clothes. She put her hand out and April slipped hers inside. "Come on," Sam said. "Let's go see what Howard and Nona are watching."

NINE

“**W**hat the *hell* am I doing here?” Sam was sitting in her rental car, gripping the top of the steering wheel with both hands.

She brought the car to a stop on the fringes of the El Paso International Airport. In the rearview mirror she could see the colorful greeting signs on opposite sides of the terminal doors in Spanish and English, *bienvenido, welcome.*

She looked left then right, scanning an unfamiliar skyline that stretched off from the Franklin Mountains toward a hazy flat horizon. Sweeping, paper-thin white clouds floated endlessly across a sky so blue it looked as though it had been painted in place.

She only knew they were called the Franklin Mountains because Hunter had told her of them and how often he had hiked the hillsides along Scenic Drive with his mother and father. She knew the airport was about four miles west of downtown and that she would take Interstate Ten to get there only because she had done a map quest of the area as she planned for her trip.

It had been so long since Sam had been anywhere different or out of her element that she hadn't realized how much unfamiliar surroundings would make finding even the simplest things, like the hotel she had booked, more difficult. All the easy roads at home, to the ranch, the office, April's school, were so clear in her mind now that she easily navigated them without even thinking.

She sat with the car, idling. In those quiet moments, James Page's comment returned to her, clear as crystal: *"Makes sense in that everything needs a starting point."*

She'd always had a good sense of direction and was good at finding any place she had to visit. She had to be. As a reporter she had done so many interviews and covered so many stories at so many different locations that she quickly had to learn how to navigate a map to find her way.

"A starting point, yes, James, but where now?" she wondered aloud. She rolled down the window as a light, warm breeze drifted inside. She had, happily, she had to admit, left the usual January cold and snow behind in Denver. The ten-day weather forecast she had done of the El Paso area had shown mostly sunny skies with daytime highs in the mid-fifties. She closed her eyes and turned toward the sun, welcoming its warmth.

Sam inched the car onto the interstate and blended in with the light mid-day traffic toward the city center, reaching the downtown exits in a matter of minutes. An attendant, a tall, tidy Latino, greeted her warmly at the hotel off Santa Fe Street and Mills Avenue. She checked in and from her window on the fifth floor she saw a glimpse of *San Jacinto Plaza* in the *Las Plazas* Arts District. She also knew from listening to Hunter's stories about his hometown that the border with Mexico was within walking distance of the city center and the thin blue ribbon of the *Rio Grande* and *Ciudad Juárez* could be seen from almost any rooftop.

Sam checked her watch, nearly three p.m. There was still enough light in the day that she gathered her bag and returned to the car. The map quest she had done from her hotel to Concordia Cemetery showed it was less than four miles away. She had wanted to visit the cemetery where Hunter and his parents were buried. Knowing nothing else about the area, she thought it would be the best place to start.

She reached her destination within ten minutes and parked just beyond the cemetery's skinny wrought iron gates, one of several entrances. Sam had worked with the funeral director at a mortuary in El Paso when it came to getting Hunter's remains back to Texas. The director had told her there were two extra plots with his parents' lot and she had made sure his wishes were carried out to have his ashes placed next to them.

Hunter had told her his parents' graves were located near the center of the cemetery and these specific gates served as the best landmark. They were buried by a small grove of trees, near large twin yucca plants so tall and thick they were hard to miss.

"What kind of trees, Hunter?" Sam had asked him during one of their long hours of surveillance in the station wagon.

She remembered he shrugged deeply with uncertainty. "I dunno, Blondie, just trees."

"Blondie," Sam said out loud and smiled at the moniker Hunter had so proudly given her. She was blonde, of course, but she was not a fan of nicknames and would not have allowed anyone else to call her that, yet it sounded so natural and well-meaning coming from him that she never protested.

Sam got out of the car and shielded her eyes with the flat of her hand as she looked around. Most of the cemetery was surrounded by a thick stone wall and the parched grounds were vast. She stood in a place where time no longer had meaning and listened. Nothing; silent and empty, as quiet as still waters. On her second sweep, she spotted a collection of robust-looking yucca plants in the distance. Just beyond was another small collection of trees, naked now in mid-winter.

She pointed toward the sword-shaped leaves. "They've gotta be the ones he was talking about," she said to herself.

She started toward them, walking over the patchy, sandy terrain, traversing between thick weeds and shrubs, feeling the rocky landscape crunching beneath her tennis shoes. She walked slower than usual. Over the last few days, she had started to feel the full effects of her exercise regimen. Since she had been riding the bike and lifting the smaller weights, she'd become so stiff and sore that getting out of bed, a chair or the car took effort. And trying to bend over to pick something off the floor was nearly impossible.

She headed toward the markers, passing a hodgepodge compilation of gravestones, makeshift crosses of sticks or metal, contemporary, traditional and grandiose cement and stone upright markers and pillows. Other graves were still adorned with temporary markers, some so old and battered the names had faded with time and the elements.

She reached the graves in a matter of moments and stood in front of them with her head down. Her hands were clasped in front of her, and she prayed silently with her eyes closed. She opened them and looked at the names of his parents; first Hunter's father, John Hunter Hollingsworth and the date he came into the world, and then Rita Hollingsworth, and the date she was born. She looked between the two unadorned markers at the date of death, the same day. Hunter had told Sam he was still in the hospital when his parents were buried, and that it was his aunt who brought him to the cemetery to see their graves for the first time. She was holding Jenny in her arms and he stood beside her.

"The next day *mi tía* took Jenny and me to Mexico and I never was able to go back to them again until I returned last year." It had been during one of their many vigils that Hunter had told her of that day.

"And you're with them now, Hunter," Sam said quietly, her words carried away by a light wind.

She walked back to the car and returned to the hotel. She had stumbled onto *La Dolce Vita*, a shabby-chic, quaint café serving coffee and pastries, just off the Plaza, a block from her hotel. She purchased coffee and was settled at a table in front of the windows when she called April. "How was your first day back to school, Baby?"

"Good, Mommie! I already have homework, but I was happy to see all my friends."

"I bet they were happy to see you, too."

"Yeah! It was warm enough and we played outside at recess."

April's voice sounded sweet like a drop of honey and Sam wanted nothing more than to reach through the phone and wrap her arms around her.

"Did you find Jenny yet?" April asked and Sam could hear the expectation in her voice.

Sam laughed as she cradled her cell phone with both hands. "Not yet, but I'm going to keep looking and if I do, you're the first person I am going to tell."

They talked another ten minutes and Sam ended their conversation by saying, "Don't forget bedtime is eight-thirty, and remember to brush your teeth."

She ended the call, thinking of April dressed in her school uniform that morning, her long brown hair pulled back in a ponytail, the crew socks they had folded the evening before, a blue and green plaid pleated skirt and blue sweater that covered her white blouse.

What April had said to her about Wilson had been on her mind since their conversation. Sam traced the rim of her coffee cup remembering her words, *Mommie, when are you and Wilson gonna get married?*

She took her last sip of coffee, enjoying the deep, rich taste of the dark roast as she looked out the long windows of the café. It was dusk now and amber lights that lined the street had begun to shine.

She took her time walking along *San Jacinto Plaza* on the way back to the hotel, beside trees covered in a golden glow of lights, thinking. *What would ever give her the idea that Wilson and I would marry?*

Of course, Sam knew Wilson and April had formed a bond during the days they spent together in captivity. Both of them had offered bits and pieces of what had happened during their time together, but she knew much was left unspoken.

She waved at the same attendant at the hotel who had greeted her earlier that afternoon, and went inside the lobby.

What else could she hope for?

Only that over time she would come to know more about those words left unspoken between April and the man her daughter thinks she should marry.

TEN

S am was looking at herself in a full-length mirror in her hotel
room as she dressed. She wore black slacks and covered her
camel-colored turtleneck sweater with the black V-neck poncho Nona
had crocheted for her.

She had taken her time this morning, walking back to *La Dolce
Vita* for coffee before she got ready. She talked to April on the phone
while Howard drove her to school. She also did another map quest from
downtown to the University of Texas at El Paso, UTEP, where Hunter's
father had taught history. It showed just over a mile, a four-minute drive
to the university, which was situated between the US/Mexico border and
the Franklin Mountains and Chihuahuan Desert. One benefit of staying
in the city center was even though she didn't know the area, it appeared
to be close to everything.

She took another quick look in the mirror, slipped on a pair of black
leather ankle boots and headed for the lobby. As she walked to her car
she waved to a new attendant, a young, slender woman with strands of

blonde hair sticking out from beneath her round dress cap.

It was just after ten a.m. when she was driving around the Centennial Plaza Circle on the UTEP campus, looking for the liberal arts building. The campus was bustling with activity, but Sam managed to find metered parking close by.

She blended in with an eclectic mix of students and educators as she entered the building. Her college days began to inch back into her thoughts, but by then she had already been drinking heavily, so she pushed them away. She found the history department on the directory and adjusted her tote over her shoulder as she headed in that direction. Inside her bag she carried several pens, Reporter's Notebooks and the photos of Hunter and Jenny.

She wandered the hallways until she passed an empty classroom and saw an older man standing in front of the teacher's desk, his head bent into the paper he was reading, his index finger pressed against his lips.

Sam knocked hesitantly at the door. He looked up at the sound.

"Good morning," she said pleasantly and stayed at the door.

"Morning. Can I help you find something?"

"Well, I hope so," Sam said, taking his words as an invitation to enter. She stopped at the front row of the desks and offered her hand as she introduced herself. He was slim and medium height, and Sam guessed he was near retirement. His fine silver hair was parted toward the right, skimming his wire rimmed glasses. His face was lined with folds of wrinkles around his eyes and mouth. His turkey neck slightly covered the top of an elegant deep-red tie. The sleeves of his white shirt were buttoned at his wrists with white gold cufflinks that revealed bits of turquoise.

"Nice to meet you, Sam, Martin Ball. What brings you to El Paso, specifically to UTEP?"

"Well, specifically, I was hoping to find someone, a teacher here who might remember John Hollingsworth."

Martin visibly took a step back. "Oh, my goodness, I haven't heard that name in years. Of course I knew John. I taught with him for several years. His concentration was the US/Mexico border region and the US West. The university was so excited to have him, a wonderful man and a

56

true educator. Had a great rapport with students, I think because he was so young himself."

"Did you know his wife and Hunter?"

"Rita, yes, of course, and Hunter, and their daughter…" his voice trailed off. His attention flickered toward the hallway as he tried to recall her name.

"Jenny," Sam said.

Martin's face lit up. "Yes, Jenny. John was so happy the day she was born. He called me from the hospital, crying. And then just a few months later they were gone." He shook his head. "Still unfathomable to me when I think about it."

"Yes, I know the story," Sam said.

"Oh, you knew John?"

"I knew Hunter."

His head tilted slightly. "Knew?"

Sam clutched the long straps of her tote with both hands. "Hunter's the reason I'm here, Martin."

She took a deep breath and told him about Jenny, the undocumented worker's story and what had happened to Hunter. She ended by telling him, "Hunter never had the chance to do what he really wanted."

"To find his sister," Martin said. He had been shaking his head the entire time Sam had been talking.

Sam opened her bag and pulled out the envelope that contained the photos and renderings. "If you have a few minutes, I'd like to show you these."

Martin stepped away from the desk and opened his hand. Sam placed the photos of Hunter and Jenny over a stack of student papers. Martin studied each briefly before he collected the one of Hunter. He held it lightly with the tips of his fingers, as though he was holding lace.

"He looked just like his father," Martin said.

Sam smiled. "Yes, he always told me he had more of his father's features."

Martin cleared his throat; for a moment he was unable to talk. He kept shaking his head. "It's like, like looking at John again as I remember him. I can't believe how long it's been."

57

Sam looked at the photo of Hunter with him, biting back tears, but unable to help her smile. "My daughter took that photo of him at our ranch in September." Her smile fell. "He was hit by the truck the next day. He would have been twenty-four in October."

Martin set the photo down and picked up Jenny's, holding it the same way. "She'll be as beautiful as her mother." He smiled as though he had recalled a distant memory. "I remember Rita as being very shy. When we had our holiday parties, she'd never leave John's side. She was a beautiful woman, and you could see they loved each other very much."

"Hunter said the same thing," Sam said.

"What makes you think Jenny's here in El Paso?"

She shrugged. "I don't know where she is, Martin. This is the place Hunter said would have been his starting point, so that's why I came and I guess I'd be like him and hope I could find someone who might be able to help."

Martin looked between both photos and started shaking his head again. "May I keep these, Sam?"

Sam nodded enthusiastically. "Yes, of course."

"I'll ask around," he said and gathered the photos. "Almost everyone who was here when John was is still here. I can't make any promises, but I'll start asking. Someone might know something."

"Any help at all would be wonderful, thank you," Sam said and she felt a sense of relief float up in her like a small balloon. "I'll be here through Friday."

Sam and Martin exchanged contact information with their cell phones. She left the classroom and walked out of the building into a mild midday sun.

Sam returned to her hotel and the coffee shop, where she spent an hour scrolling through her notes until she found the address of where Hunter had lived as a boy. Her cell phone showed the drive would take less than fifteen minutes. She started for the area, finding it easily and turned down the street thinking of what Hunter had told her when he returned to El Paso shortly before he started as a reporter at the *Grandview Perspective*.

It was the first time he had been back since he left as a child. He had told

Sam he'd gone to many familiar places he knew growing up, but he could not return to his old neighborhood. Part of him wanted to see it again after so many years, another part of him, more of him, wanted to remember it as it was, without the passage of time—the way it looked from the distance when he and his father had climbed the hillside, the way it looked when he could see the driveway when they were returning home.

Sam drove slowly down the street, looking right, then left, checking addresses until she reached the house, a large stucco two-story home with white trim, a two-car garage and Spanish-style roof. She confirmed the address, which ran down the front side of the garage, and continued down the street. She turned around, headed back toward the house and stopped in front of it. An expansive living room window allowed her to see through the house to a swing set in the backyard.

She got out of the car and listened, quiet, save for the rise and fall of traffic passing on the main street beyond the neighborhood. She walked from one end of the street to the other. Despite that the blinds and doors were shuttered on both sides of Hunter's old residence, she knocked at the doors. No one answered. She was walking back toward her car, when she decided to visit the house directly across the street. It looked the same, closed and uninviting, but she knocked anyway and waited, but no one came to the door.

The afternoon light was beginning to slant. She took a longer way back downtown and the hotel deciding she'd visit the neighborhood every day until she left on Friday in hopes of catching someone at home.

It was almost dark when Sam entered *La Dolce Vita*. The moment she walked in the scent of freshly brewed coffee took her back to the ranch and home, and sitting at the kitchen table sharing a cup with her grandmother in the morning, or on the porch together in the late afternoon. She ordered an Americano and found a table near the window. She dialed Wilson's number from memory to share the news about Martin Ball. She checked her watch as the phone rang, certain he would be finishing up for the day. He answered just before it rang a fourth time.

"Hi, it's me," she said. "Did I catch you at a good time?"

Wilson was getting in his car. "Hello, Sam. Anytime is a good time. I was just thinking about you."

"How was your day?" she asked, feeling a small smile form.

"Good. I'm just leaving the office now for a meeting," he said. "Any luck?"

"Well, it just so happens, I may have some," Sam said and Wilson could hear the lift in her voice.

He listened as she told him about her day and ended by saying, "That sounds like a great start, Sam, and it sounds like Martin would really like to help."

"Yes, if he could," she said. "It may not amount to anything, but you know how it is, Wilson, a lead is a lead and you know how I am, I'll be optimistic about any possibility until I hear otherwise."

"Indeed," Wilson said. "I know how you are."

They both laughed.

"How's work?" she asked.

"Good, but not the same without you in the newsroom."

She smiled and April's words about marriage bubbled up in her like a quiet creek. Suddenly she could see the newsroom clearly, the way the afternoon light would filter in through the tops of the windows and fall silently on the distant wall, the way the desk chairs were scattered here and there, the calm voice of a 911 dispatcher coming from the police scanner. The countless times Wilson would stop at her desk on the way to the kitchen or coming down the stairs from the reception area.

"Well, I don't want to keep you from your meeting, Wilson, I was just calling to say hello and quickly tell you about my day."

They chatted a few more minutes and he told her to be careful. Wilson was staring at the large Cottonwood tree in the lot adjacent to the *Perspective's* as they ended their call. The tall empty branches were stretching toward the sky, swaying in an even rhythm in the late afternoon breeze.

He had to laugh quietly at himself for telling Sam he was just thinking about her.

Just thinking about her?

When, in fact, the thought of her hadn't left his mind all day.

ELEVEN

S am returned to the neighborhood shortly before ten the following morning. The houses were shuttered and the street looked and sounded the same, quiet and empty.

She went to the door on both sides of Hunter's old house and knocked. Silence. She went to the sidewalk and glanced up and down the street before she walked to the house directly across the street. The blinds were closed, but Sam could see a light on in the kitchen through the slits. She knocked. A minute passed, but no one came. She knocked harder a second time. There was a narrow red sign with gold lettering that read, NO SOLICITING in the middle of the screened door that Sam didn't remember seeing yesterday.

Moments later, she thought she heard someone talking and leaned closer. It sounded like a woman's voice. Sam heard a chain rattle on the other side and took a step back. The door seemed to be opening by itself until an old woman with a full head of curly white hair stuck her head out. She scrutinized Sam over a pair of smudged reading glasses that were propped at the end of her nose.

"Yes?"

Sam smiled politely and gave a small wave. "Hello, I'm not here to sell anything, but I was in the neighborhood yesterday and knocked at several doors here on the street, but no one answered. I thought I'd try again this morning."

The woman nodded and her glasses almost fell off her nose. "I know. I saw you yesterday, honey, walking up and down the street and I heard you knock, but it took me s'darn long to get out of my chair that you were gone by the time I got to the door." The woman spoke in a tiny voice that was scratchy and dry.

Sam put an open hand against her chest. "I'm sorry, ma'am. I should have waited just a few more minutes."

"Who you lookin' for, honey?" the woman asked, keeping her position at the door.

Sam gave another polite smile and then pointed at Hunter's house. "Well, as a matter of fact, I am looking for someone. I was hoping to talk to someone who can give me some information about the people who used to live in that house across the street." She considered the woman attentively. "Have you lived here long?"

"Been here all my life, honey." The old woman gave her a proud smile.

Sam felt a bubble of encouragement rise in her throat. "My name's Samantha Church. I'm a newspaper reporter from Denver and I used to work with the young man who grew up in that house over there."

The woman rattled off his name. "Oh, yes, yes, little Hunter John Hollingsworth."

Sam almost gasped out loud. "Yes, ma'am, that's right, Hunter."

"I watched him grow from a baby until he got to be seven or eight years old," the woman said. "He was such a sweet boy."

"Yes, I have no doubt he was," Sam said and she clutched the long straps of her tote. "I worked with him at the newspaper for a short time last year. We covered a story together and that's how I learned he lived here in El Paso as a child."

"Oh, he went into newspapers?"

Sam nodded. "Yes, ma'am, he was a reporter."

"He'd see the newspaper in my driveway every morning and whenever he could he'd bring it to the door for me," the woman said. She opened the door a little further so Sam could see her. Her bony hands were stretched outward if she were holding a newspaper. "I'd answer the door and he'd hand me the paper and say, 'here you go, Mrs. Sheffield.'"

Both women smiled, then the old woman looked from Hunter's house to Sam. She continued to scrutinize her and then to Sam's unexpected surprise, she unlocked the screen door and pushed it open. "Come on in, honey."

The woman had turned toward the kitchen as Sam entered the foyer. "I'll put some coffee on and you can tell me why you're here. Maybe I can help."

Sam followed the woman through a living room crowded with old furniture and sundries. Nearly all the walls were covered in knickknacks, generic landscapes or with what Sam guessed were family photos. Two calico cats were perched on top the couch, but ignored Sam. The house smelled stale, of old food and traces of a litterbox that needed to be changed.

A large solid wood curio cabinet consumed most of the kitchen. Sam waited near the cabinet and did a quick survey of the area. Through the glass, she could see more salt and pepper shakers than she could count, which were sitting on top of doilies and consumed every shelf. A scruffy recliner that had sunk so far in the middle Sam could see why it was such an effort for the old woman to answer the door in a timely way. The arms had frayed to the point they had been covered in thin plastic.

The woman motioned toward the large dark wood dining table surrounded by six chairs with cushioned seats and wide, detailed backs. The table was splashed in sunlight and Sam could see that a generous amount of dust had collected on the tops of some of the chairs.

"Sit down, honey," she said.

Sam selected the chair closest to the door and set her bag on the floor.

The woman's house dress was covered with a colorful print apron, the kind Sam's grandmother also wore in the mornings, and she watched the woman move about her kitchen in a slow, shuffling pace. Her frame was bent like the straw from an old broom.

She talked about Hunter as she made coffee. "I remember that boy used to ride his bike up and down the street like a little terror. He never had training wheels, either. One day he just started riding down the street without them with his father chasing him from behind so he wouldn't fall, and that was that." The woman poured water in the reservoir. "He couldn't have been more than five at the time. He never seemed to run out of energy and he certainly never had any fear of going too fast or getting hurt. He'd be out there all day if his momma hadn't come out to call him in. But as soon as she did, lemme tell you, he obeyed and went right in the house."

The woman brought two mugs to the table and set one in front of Sam. A few minutes later she brought the pot and poured coffee in both of them. She set the pot on a sandstone trivet decorated in the style of the southwest.

"What's your name again?" the woman asked as she sat down. She was still wearing her smudged reading glasses.

Sam told her then asked, "And yours?"

"Margaret."

Sam repeated the old woman's name and then asked, "Do you live here alone?"

"My husband's gone and the kids are spread out all over the place, but I have a daughter in Las Cruces who comes down a few times a month," Margaret said and pointed toward Sam with a crooked index finger. "She's like you, a busy gal. Has a pretty face, dresses nice, but is a little too chubby."

Sam cleared her throat quietly. "Well, Mrs. Sheffield, I'll take that as a compliment, thank you. As they say, two out of three ain't bad."

Taking a slow sip of her coffee Sam told Margaret why she had come to El Paso. The woman listened with one hand pressed to the side of her lined face, and like Martin Ball, shook her head sadly while Sam told Hunter's story.

"Oh my. I always wondered what happened to those children," Margaret said as Sam finished. "Such a tragedy for that entire family, and now Hunter has passed without finding his sister."

Sam nodded and grabbed her bag from the floor. She took the photos out and spread them in front of Margaret. "This is Hunter from a photo in September and what we think Jenny might look like now at nearly eighteen years old."

She let Margaret study the photos. In the silence, Sam could hear the soft *tick, tick* of a clock coming from another room.

"Anything you might remember about those early years when the family lived here might be helpful at some point," Sam said.

The woman kept her hand resting against her cheek. "That boy sure looked like his father," Margaret said. She thought a moment more, clucked her tongue and then said, "I remember they moved in shortly before Hunter was born. I didn't associate much with them, mostly hello, holiday greetings, that sort of thing. They were a quiet family, nice folks who kept to themselves mostly, like everyone on the block. I remember knitting a blanket for Rita when she was pregnant with Jenny."

Margaret tapped the side of her face lightly with her hand. "That was shortly before she had her. In late April, I think. I didn't know if it was a boy or girl, but I wanted to do something, so I knitted a yellow baby blanket with booties and mittens. The next time I saw them John was taking a car seat out of the car, so she'd already had the baby. I brought the blanket over a few days later."

"Do you know when Rita had the baby, Margaret?"

"The date? Honey, no I don't, but it was early May when I saw John with the car seat that, I remember. I didn't see them much the rest of that summer and that fall, of course, they were gone. The house was put on the market shortly after the kids went with the aunt to Mexico."

One of the calicos entered the kitchen and walked in and around the bottom of Margaret's chair, her tail high in the air. "Then, of course, I lost track of them," Margaret added. "Even the people who bought their house moved on a few years ago."

"Do you think it would be worth my time to try and talk to the people on either side of the house?"

Margaret shrugged lightly. "That's up to you, honey, but both families moved in well after John and Rita were gone. The same families still live in the houses at the corners, but they didn't associate much with the neighborhood."

The phone on the wall started to ring. "Oh, that's my daughter, calling to check in on me," Margaret said and struggled to get to her feet. "She wants me to get rid of my landline, but I told her as long as I'm livin' in this house I'm keeping it." She finally got to the phone and answered it on the seventh ring.

When she hung up, Sam stood and put her business card on the table. "Thank you, Margaret. I don't want to take up any more of your time." She collected the photos of Hunter and Jenny. "If you think of anything else that might help, I hope you'll call me."

"I wish I could've offered a little more," Margaret said and followed Sam as she started for the door.

"The fact that you opened your door and spent time with me this morning has been helpful, and I appreciate it," Sam said with earnest.

Margaret stayed at the door as Sam stepped out onto the front porch. "Good luck. I hope you can find what you're looking for, for Hunter and Jenny."

"Me, too, Mrs. Sheffield, thank you."

The old woman closed the door. Sam headed back to her car, feeling the warmth of the sun on her back, thinking out loud, "Early May? Jenny was born in early May."

She headed downtown, but before she went to her hotel, she drove around the city center until she found the administration complex for the city and county of El Paso, a tall building made of stucco and glass. She located the county clerk's office on the directory on the first floor. A greeter outside the office doors, a slender Latina Sam guessed was in her early twenties, acknowledged her with a cordial smile.

"Hello, I'm from out of town and I was hoping you had computers here that would allow me to search birth records," Sam said.

The girl nodded and pointed with her pen toward the doors. "They'll be able to help you inside."

Sam mouthed her thanks and entered the area. She waited in line behind two other patrons before one of the clerks behind plexiglass motioned her forward. Sam greeted the clerk, another young, slender

Latina with long fine brown hair that collected evenly along her shoulders. Her name badge read Amber in small caps. Sam told Amber what she was hoping to find.

"Was she born here in El Paso?" Amber asked.

Sam nodded.

"Are you related?"

Sam slid a copy of Hunter's trust across the counter. "I am the executor of her brother's estate."

Amber studied it a moment before she turned to her computer and brought up the public records section of the website. She found *birth indexes*, clicked on it and was directed to *birth records search*. It had a section for first, middle and last name.

"What's her name?" Amber asked.

Sam spoke in a hopeful voice. "Heidi Jennifer Hollingsworth."

As much as Hunter had told her about his life and his sister, he had never told her why they called her by her middle name.

"When was she born?"

"I'm not exactly sure. I just know it's early May," Sam said and gave her the year.

Amber kept her hands placed lightly over the keyboard and Sam noticed long manicured nails painted crimson red. It matched the color of her lipstick. "Let's try the first seven days of May."

"If it's early May, it should come up," Sam said and she leaned as close to the counter as she could.

Amber hit enter and waited as a colorful circle spun in front of her. Seconds later the information appeared on the screen:

STATE OF TEXAS
CERTIFICATE OF LIVE BIRTH
HEIDI JENNIFER HOLLINGSWORTH
DATE: MAY 6 | TIME: 11:35 A.M.

Amber turned her computer toward Sam and she stared at the monitor for a moment, holding her breath. "Yes, that's her," Sam said and smiles appeared on both women's faces.

"How many copies would you like?"

Sam held up two fingers, feeling jubilant at her find, at the slight step forward she'd made, however small. As she waited to pay for her copies, she had to force herself to stop thinking of the possibilities of showing it to Jenny one day.

TWELVE

Sam left the El Paso city and county building and headed back to her car. She was crossing the street when her cell phone started to ring.

"It's too early for April to be calling," she said to herself as she checked her watch. She quickly dug her phone out of her bag and glanced at the screen.

The name in the caller ID forced her to stop in the middle of the street.

Martin Ball.

"Sam Church," she said, feeling her jubilation rise a notch.

"Hi Sam, Martin Ball here, and I think I may have some good news for you."

A car honked and Sam jumped. She realized she was still standing in the middle of the street and waved apologetically at the driver.

She continued to her car. "Martin, that's wonderful."

"Turns out the wife of one of our professors here is a first-grade teacher at Franklin Elementary, where Hunter went to school. She was his kindergarten teacher and she's willing to talk to you at the school tomorrow after school lets out."

Sam wanted to cry. "Yes, yes, of course. I'd love to talk to her. Just tell me what time and I'll be there. Thank you."

"Great," Martin said. "I'll text you her contact information."

They ended the call as Sam got in the car. She sat quietly with her hands on top the steering wheel, staring toward the sky, enjoying a glimmer of hope.

Someone was willing to talk to her, truly a reporter's dream when working on a story.

Perhaps it may be a lead that would eventually go nowhere, but in this transitory moment of time, Sam was going to happily revel in the possibility that it could take her one step closer to finding Jenny.

THIRTEEN

S am was still sitting in the car, watching a flurry of white clouds pass rapidly in front of the sun when her phone chimed with Martin's text message.

Sam, here's the contact info: Sandy Petersen, first-grade teacher @ Franklin Elementary. If you have a chance, please let me know how the visit goes. Good luck.

Martin included the address of the school at the end of the text.

Studying the directions on her cell phone, she could tell the school was about two miles from Hunter's old neighborhood. She checked her watch, nearly four p.m. Though the sun was inching closer to the horizon, it was still high enough in the sky that she decided to drive by the school.

She found her way to Interstate Ten, took the exit and within minutes found herself passing in front of Franklin Elementary School.

She parked across the street to take in her surroundings. The school, a sizable stucco building, sat in the middle of a parking lot, big enough to handle a large volume of cars and school buses. The entire campus was surrounded by tall, decorative, black metal fencing and situated between housing developments on opposite sides. The Franklin Mountains and a vast open prairie provided another perfect backdrop. Sam watched several women exit the building through the main double doors and head toward a collection of cars. They looked to be chatting happily as they were finished for the school day. She wondered if one of them was Sandy Petersen.

Sam was still holding her phone when it started to ring. The vibration made her jump.

"Hi, Baby, how was school today?" Sam said and couldn't help smiling.

"Good, Mommie! We started basketball practice! The coach made us run up and down the court so we could start conditioning training. We did like ten running drills. Only me and Carol didn't have to stop to rest, but all the other girls did. We're the fastest, too."

Sam was soaking up every syllable of April's sweet, endearing voice as it filled the car.

"I remember Carol from your softball team," Sam said. "She's pretty fast."

"Yeah, we're about even in softball, but she's taller than me, so she doesn't have to struggle to make baskets like I have to sometimes."

"I bet you're starved after all that running," Sam said, knowing that April was always famished when she came home from school, and especially after practice. She'd eat a large bowl of cereal (something chocolaty), and then, two hours later, be hungry for dinner.

"Mommie, did you find Jenny today?"

Sam could help laughing. "Not yet, but guess what?"

"What?"

"I'm sitting outside the elementary school where Hunter went when he was a little boy, and tomorrow I am going to talk to his kindergarten teacher."

"Does she know where Jenny is?" April asked and Sam could hear the innocence in her voice.

"It's not very likely, but maybe she can tell me something else

72

important that will help me to look in another place."

"I know what you call that, Mommie."

"What's that?"

"A lead!"

"Yes! You're right, April, a lead! You know how happy that makes your mother when she's covering a story."

"Yeah, I know." Sam could hear Nona's voice in the background. "I gotta go, Nona says my cereal's gonna get soggy."

"Tell Nona and Howard I'll call later."

Sam ended their call, hanging on to the last vestiges of their conversation and the winsome sound of April's voice. She glanced toward the parking lot, the women and the cars were gone now. She hadn't noticed any of them leave the lot.

She started back to the hotel, imagining John and Rita coming after school to pick up their son. She wondered if Hunter, a little boy carrying his backpack, would have been like April, chattering nonstop about his day at school. Sam remembered Hunter telling her school was his escape after he'd gone into foster care and the only thing he liked better was sports and reading.

He was so clear to her now in his absence. How tall and visibly strong he was. How his amber eyes would change color in different and reflecting light, how his hair was always so nicely tousled, and the natural way it complimented his stylish stubble of facial hair he had from time to time.

The way he used to follow her around like a puppy when he first started at the *Perspective*; how much he loved to talk about his mother's cooking; how excited he was when they first started working on the undocumented worker's story, how he'd do a fist pump every time one of their leads would pan out. He was so proud to be fluent in Spanish, and how essential his knowledge of the language was to their story and how he had tried to teach her.

Little did Sam or Hunter realize that his ability to speak and understand Spanish so well would eventually lead to the event that would claim his life—an act so brazen, it still caught her breath every time it crossed her mind.

FOURTEEN

It was nearly three-thirty when Sam arrived at Franklin Elementary the following afternoon.

She parked in the same spot across the street to wait as school was letting out. Children's laughter filled the air as a steady stream of students wearing backpacks and winter jackets filed out of the main doors. Some headed toward two school buses at the far end of the campus, while others walked toward a parade of cars parked on the outside of the school's perimeter. Others waited for a crossing guard to guide them across the street to waiting parents on the other side.

Sam watched recalling the times she was able to pick April up from school. She'd race across the parking lot and jump in the car. She'd often announce on the way home how she planned to go to law school and be an attorney like her Auntie Robin. Other days, often after doing well on an English test, she'd tell her mother she was going to be a journalist like her. Now, as Sam watched the last trickle of students and teachers file from Franklin Elementary, she could hear April telling her

74

what her most recent plans were when she grew up.

"Mommie, I'm gonna be both," April had announced to Sam on the way home from school shortly after the year began in September.

Sam had turned on the gravel road leading back to the ranch. "Both what, Baby?"

"An attorney like Auntie Robin was and like you, Mommie."

"You want to be a reporter?" Sam asked, looking at April. She was still tanned from summer vacation, the tip of her nose full of freckles.

"Yeah, I'm gonna be a writer and go to law school."

"That's a great idea, April, that would have made your Auntie Robin very proud. It's a wonderful way to keep her memory alive."

They drove in silence, passing open fields and oak brush that stretched off toward the valley, red dust was rising from the road and collecting along the sides of the station wagon before swirling off in a northerly direction.

"Can I do both, Mommie?"

Sam gave her daughter a confident nod. "Of course you can, you can do anything you want if you put your mind to it."

"You do fun stuff."

"Well, my sweet little girl, it is a good job, not always fun and you don't always see the best parts of humanity, but always a good job. I think I can honestly say it is one profession where you do learn a little about a lot of things and as curious as you are, it might be the perfect fit for you."

After the school yard had grown quiet, Sam crossed the street under a strong sun. She was assaulted by the pungent odor of cleaning disinfectant when she entered the building. She hesitated briefly at the doors, waiting for her eyes to adjust to the interior before she noticed a custodian mopping the main entry. They acknowledged each other as she stepped lightly on the wet floor and entered the main office. After she checked in, she followed the shiny linoleum floor down a wide hallway lined with lockers toward the last classroom on the left.

The door was open and covered with colorful construction cutouts of farm animals. Sam knocked lightly. "Hello?" She stuck her head inside the room so bright with sunlight the overhead lights were off.

"Sandy Petersen?"

The woman nodded and got up from behind her desk. She carried a pair of scissors and orange construction paper and met Sam in the middle of the classroom. The women shook hands.

"Yes, hi, are you Samantha Church?"

"Yes, please call me Sam."

"Nice to meet you, Sam."

Sandy pointed toward the back of the classroom to a small table surrounded by four brightly colored plastic chairs and they walked toward it.

"When my husband told me that someone was asking about Hunter, I almost fell over," Sandy said.

Sam sat down in the yellow chair and Sandy sat across from her in the blue one. The table and chairs were pint size for elementary students and Sam's bottom filled every inch of the tiny chair. Sandy Petersen, with the lithe body of a yoga instructor, looked slim and relaxed in her seat, but Sam felt clumsy as she tried to find a better, more comfortable position.

Sandy set the scissors and construction paper beside her and went on. "Even though it's been years and years since the last time I saw Hunter, I have to tell you every now and then he still crosses my mind. I'd love to see him again and see what he's done with his life. Of course, I'm sure he wouldn't remember me, but his class was the first class I taught out of college, so those students have always remained special to me." She smiled almost apologetically. "I was kinda learning along with them."

Sam set her bag at her feet. "Sandy, did Martin tell your husband anything else about Hunter?"

She shook her head. "Not really. Just that you had asked about him and were looking for someone who might remember him. He told my husband it would be better if I talked with you directly."

Sam swallowed hard. "Honestly, Sandy, there's no easy way for me to say this, but Hunter passed away in September."

Sandy gasped as she brought her hand to her mouth. "Oh my God, no! That's horrible. What happened?"

Sam explained what led up to Hunter's death and the reason she had traveled to El Paso. As with Margaret and Martin, Sandy shook her head dolefully as Sam spoke. When she finished, Sandy broke eye contact and dipped her head. "You know, I'm not surprised he was an organ donor. I heard that if a transplant had been available his mother may have survived the crash. Maybe Hunter had heard that, too. My husband and I are donors, too. It's a way of going on, you know?" She stared at the cutout she had started with the construction paper. "At least he still lives on in others."

"I know now that Hunter finally had the chance to start looking for his sister," Sam said, changing the subject. "I don't believe he would've stopped until he found her."

"I will help you in any way I can, Sam."

Sam dug a Reporter's Notebook out of her bag. "So, you taught kindergarten first?"

She nodded. "And the next year I went to first grade and had Hunter and the same class again that year, so I guess that's why they're still special to me. In fact, I've kept in contact with two of my students from that class, both are going to be teachers, too." She fiddled with the construction paper. "Of course, you know Hunter never finished his first-grade year. He'd only been in school about a month before the accident."

"Yes, I know," Sam said.

Sandy smiled sadly, shaking her head. "I remember the day Hunter came to school and told me his mother was pregnant with Jenny. He really beamed with pride that he was going to have a new little sister."

"Did you have the chance to meet Jenny?"

Sandy nodded and sat a little taller in her chair. "My husband and I actually became good friends with John and Rita. We sort of had the same arrangement, I guess you could say."

"How's that?" Sam asked.

"Rita was from Mexico and met John when she came here. I was born here in El Paso, and I met my husband when we were both attending UTEP. He's also from Mexico, so it was just natural, I guess, we hit it off. Neither John or I were fluent in Spanish and I'm still not, but I know enough to get by."

Sam made a few notes and then considered Sandy, who had to be near forty, but still had a fresh, youthful face and large green eyes. She wore gold hoop earrings and her flaming auburn hair was piled high on top her head.

"Did you lose contact with Hunter after he went to Mexico?"

"Only for that year or so he was gone," Sandy said. "I had asked to be kept informed if he and his sister were ever to return to El Paso. And the attorney who was handling the estate did let me know that Hunter had come back to the United States, but not Jenny."

Sam drew a cheerless deep breath. "Yes, and this is where we are."

"He went into foster care almost immediately after he returned here and I did ask the attorney if Hunter's new parents would be willing to accept my contact information because I wanted to at least keep in touch as much as I could."

"How did that go?" Sam asked.

"Good, very good, actually," Sandy said, the look on her face becoming more animated. "The mother was great about emailing and we went back and forth for nearly that entire year. She sent photos of Hunter on his birthday and then at Christmas. He seemed to be so happy there, all things considered…" Her voice trailed off and she played with the corners of the construction paper. "Then, one day shortly after that new year, I got an email from the mother with the subject line that said pregnant. She informed me in the email now that she had finally gotten pregnant, they wouldn't be able to keep Hunter, too. And, well, you know what happened. I felt so sorry for that poor little boy."

Sam nodded and folded her hands over her notebook, and the two women sat in a consuming silence.

"Did you lose contact with her after that?" Sam asked.

"Yes, it wasn't long after. I tried sending a few more emails, hoping to stay in touch, but unfortunately one day my email came back as undeliverable."

Sam reached into her bag and pulled out the photos of Hunter and Jenny. "Let me show you these," she said and spread them across the small table.

Their young faces were staring up from the table at Sandy, and she went immediately to Hunter's photo, holding it carefully in her hands. "It's like looking at John again."

Sam nodded knowingly. "Those were almost Martin's exact words."

Sandy reached for Jenny's photo and balanced them both on her legs. "And this would be his sister…" her voice faded as she studied the photo. "She's about eighteen now."

Sam nodded, looking on at Jenny's age progression photo. "That's what we think and that's how the forensic artist drew her picture."

Sandy ran her hand along Jenny's long hair. "I bet she'd look like her mother, too. Rita was so attractive, especially her hair. She never wore it down much when I saw her, but one afternoon, probably a year before Jenny was born, Rita was a chaperone on one of our field trips and she wore her hair in a ponytail and that was the first time I saw how long and beautiful it was. The most natural-looking brown I've ever seen."

Sandy studied the photos a moment more. "Do you have children, Sam?"

Watching April bound toward the school building, her backpack bouncing up and down on her back, on Monday morning before she left for the airport popped into her mind. "Yes, a daughter, she'll be twelve next week."

"Just a little one," Sandy said. "Are you married?"

"Divorced," Sam said. She never used the word *widowed*. She had been divorced from Jonathan a year before he died. "What about you? Do you have children?"

"Two, a son, and we had our daughter in July. My husband and I didn't have children right away."

Sam and Sandy talked until the sun disappeared and the classroom had grown darker. It was after five p.m. when the custodian stuck his head inside the classroom. "Mrs. Petersen, yours is the only room left."

Sandy acknowledged him with a wave. "Yes, of course, sorry, we'll wrap things up here quickly."

They waited a moment for the custodian to leave the area, then Sandy said, "May I keep these? I want to show my husband."

"Yes, by all means." Sam reached in her bag and pulled out two business cards. "Here's my contact information. If you remember anything else, even if it seems trivial, please email or call me."

"All of this seems so consuming, a daunting task, really, if you think about it," Sandy said and there was heaviness in her voice. "It's like trying to find the proverbial needle in a haystack."

"I'm not one for clichés, but yes, it truly is. If I allow myself to think about it deeply, it really can be overwhelming," Sam said, the immensity in her voice a mirror of Sandy's. "Last night I was looking out the window of my hotel room and the city lights stretched out before me, glittering like a huge circuit board. I don't know how long I stood there, Sandy, but it was as though I wanted to look at every single light, as if one of them might be Jenny's."

"Have you thought about hiring a private investigator?" Sandy asked as she scribbled her contact information on the orange construction paper.

"It's certainly crossed my mind," Sam said. "I came here because it's a starting point, but obviously I can't stay. I guess I'll have to wait and see where this takes me, if anywhere really."

"Makes sense that it would have to be someone who lives in this area," Sandy said and she slid the orange paper across the table toward Sam.

Sam folded her contact information and slipped it inside her tote. Sandy walked Sam to her classroom door. "Good luck, Sam. If I remember anything else, I'll let you know and I hope you'll keep in touch and let me know how things go."

Sam acknowledged Sandy with a wave and look of gratitude and left the building through an exit door just outside her classroom. By the time Sam reached her car the sun had slipped below the horizon, the sky had darkened to a deep, dusky blue, and the air had grown noticeably cooler. She slipped her poncho over her head before she got in the car, immediately feeling her grandmother's warmth and love in every stitch that surrounded her.

Within minutes she was on the interstate. She took the downtown exit and found her way, now familiar, to the coffee shop. She bought an Americano and sat at the same table facing the window. She checked her watch and knew it would be too early to call. Nona, Howard and April would be eating dinner, so she'd call before April's bedtime. She imagined everyone at their place at the kitchen table, the scent of a homemade meal and the full glass of milk in front of April's plate. Sam had to laugh at herself because her mouth was watering.

Instead, she dialed Wilson's number and he picked up on the first ring.

"Hi, Sam, good to hear your voice," he said.

"Did I catch you at a good time?" She could hear what sounded like someone was cooking. "Are you home?"

"Yes. You're on speaker if that's okay," Wilson said and there were a few moments of hesitation. "Would you believe I'm trying to make a stir fry?"

"Sounds delicious."

"Well, I wouldn't go that far, I'm not Gordon Ramsay, you know, but it's always been one of my favorite dishes. I have to say it's a struggle to position this big pan with my prosthesis, but I have gotten a little better at it."

"Which hand is better for that?" Sam asked.

"I still have the myoelectric on now, but for something like this, I could use either one."

Wilson's main device was his myoelectric hand, which he mainly wore at work. He had also recently received a body-powered hook. As with many people with upper-limb loss, more than one device was needed to meet all their needs. In Wilson's case, a quick wrist connection system allowed him to easily change out terminal devices so he could transition from one task to another. Both devices seemed to work well for him and had their own unique purposes, which he had continued to master.

Sam listened to Wilson mix and stir the ingredients. The sizzle sounded like bacon frying.

"Do you want to know what's really good about having a prosthesis when you cook, Sam?"

She giggled into the phone. "Tell me."

"You never have to worry about getting burned."

They both laughed.

"That way I wouldn't have felt the nasty burn on my fingers I got earlier when I was heating the fry pan."

"I can call back later," Sam said.

"No, no, this is fine," Wilson said quickly into the phone. "It's about done so I'll let the heat cook the rest of it." He stepped away from the stove and entered his living room. The gas fireplace was on and the lamp on the end table next to the sofa gave the room a soft, warm glow. The large-screen television was on the evening news. Wilson struggled, but he managed to lower the volume. "How was your day?"

"Good, very good actually," Sam said. "I met Sandy Petersen today."

"Oh, yes, Hunter's kindergarten teacher."

"Yes, and as it turns out, his first-grade teacher, too. She had moved to that position the next year and had Hunter's class again."

"How'd the visit go?"

"She was able to keep in touch with the first foster mother Hunter had, but she lost track of her after he went back into foster care."

"Those are some positive developments," Wilson said.

"I'm not sure how much more they'll develop, but I did leave the photos with her, and I've managed to talk to more people here this week than I expected," Sam said.

"That and getting Jenny's birth certificate, sounds like it's been a productive few days," he said.

"I can't complain."

"Are you ready to come home?"

"I'm counting the hours. Every time I hear April's voice all I want to do is reach through the phone and wrap her in my arms. I'll be ready to get back to reading the Big Book, too."

"Did you read any more before you left?"

"Not much, I'm still in the middle of chapter two."

They talked a few more minutes. As Sam ended their call, she caught sight of a couple passing in front of the window holding hands. She followed them until they left her sight. The man looked to be somewhat older than the woman. She thought of April's comment about the age difference between her and Wilson and then her response ... *age doesn't have anything to do with it when you love someone.*

She had been so close to telling Wilson he should make his stir fry recipe for her one day, but she was glad she had stopped short of saying anything.

Sam finished her coffee, thinking of everyone in Denver doing homey things. She thought of April starting homework after dinner with Step resting at her feet. Nona and Howard would be watching television in the living room in front of a roaring fire he had built, filling the house with the welcomed scent of burning wood.

Sam hadn't eaten since breakfast and her stomach was rumbling. She asked the barista for a good place to eat. Sam found the place she recommended, and ate a hamburger with another cup of black coffee. Lemon pie was the dessert special, her favorite, but she resisted.

Back at the hotel she asked the concierge for a place to buy flowers. Before she went to the airport tomorrow, she'd leave them on Hunter and his parents' graves. When she finished packing, she stared out her hotel room window, her padded reflection captured in the darkened glass.

Beyond the window, she took all the lights into view and remembered what she had told Sandy.

I don't know how long I stood there, but it was as though I wanted to look at every single light, as if one of them might be Jenny's.

FIFTEEN

Wilson was the last person to leave April's birthday party early Saturday evening.

It was an event-filled day with April and her friends running and playing all over the house while Sam, Wilson, Howard and Nona happily looked on. Gifts and wrapping paper covered nearly all the living room floor. The dining room table was marked with the remnants of empty plates, once filled with homemade ravioli, bread and chocolate birthday cake.

The January day had been chilly and raw, but the full splendor of sunlight spilled in every window of the house. Sam was putting on her coat to walk Wilson out to his car when April dashed up to them and wrapped her arms tightly around his midsection.

"Thank you for coming, Wilson, and thank you for my gifts," she said and pressed the side of her face into his belly. "It means a lot."

He put his hand gently on her head as he looked at Sam. "You are welcome, young lady."

Sam watched as April pulled away from him. April and Wilson locked eyes briefly as they always did whenever they shared such a moment. It was a knowing look, a meaningful and deliberate expression that Sam knew was only between them.

Sam rested her hands on April's slender shoulders as she stepped away from Wilson. "Go help Nona because she's already started to clean up, and I'll be there after I walk Wilson out."

April waved at both of them and disappeared into the living room.

Wilson opened the door and they were greeted by cold night air as they stepped onto the porch. Sam wrapped her hands tightly around her arms as they walked down the steps and followed their breath toward his car. The sky was clear and scattered endlessly with stars that glittered like crystals.

"Thank you for coming, Wilson, and thank you for the gift card. You know how much April loves that sporting goods store. With that amount, she might be there all afternoon."

Wilson laughed as he fished his keys out of his overcoat. "I told you, Sam, I wouldn't have missed it for the world."

"It means as much to me as I know it does to April."

"What are your plans for the rest of the weekend?"

"Honestly, nothing. I'm going to get back on the bike tomorrow and since snow is in the forecast, I am going to plant myself in front of the fireplace and spend all afternoon catching up on reading the Big Book. I'd like to read at least the first seventy-five pages."

Wilson gave an approving nod. "Sounds like a great way to spend the day."

When he hugged her, she leaned into him. Sam stepped back from the car as he pulled away from her. She watched as he drove from the house, following the car taillights down the long gravel road until it rounded a small grove of trees and disappeared.

A snowstorm on Sunday afternoon did provide the perfect backdrop for Sam and April. She planted herself on the couch with the Big Book open on her lap and a cup of herbal tea on the end table beside her. April spent the first part of the afternoon finishing homework at the kitchen table. Sam had read through to the first dozen pages of chapter four when she stopped to help Nona with dinner.

"Mommie, can we watch the movie after we eat?" April asked as they sat down at the table.

Sam wasn't a fan of the little wizard boy movies April liked so much, but of course she wouldn't pass up an opportunity to watch them with her daughter. After dinner, Nona made popcorn and everyone settled on the couch. April had fallen asleep before the end of the movie with her head in Sam's lap. Howard picked her up from the sofa with ease and Sam followed him toward April's bedroom. Step was close at their heels, his nails tapping lightly as he sauntered across the hardwood floors.

Sam was in bed as she found her place near the bottom of page fifty-six. She read through to page sixty. Words at the top of that page highlighted three pertinent ideas: that alcoholics cannot manage their own lives, no human power could have relieved their alcoholism, and God would help if He were sought.

On page sixty-two she read the often-familiar words she heard at AA meetings—that alcoholics are selfish and self-centered. She read on to page sixty-six, then sixty-seven.

She turned the page. Page sixty-eight.

When she read the sentence, *"Perhaps there is a better way—we think so. For we are now on a different basis, the basis of relying and trusting on God. We trust the infinite God rather than our finite selves,"* she stopped and looked toward the blinds. They were open and the window was draped in darkness.

She read the line again and then finished the rest of the paragraph.

When she read the next sentence, *"We never apologize to anyone for depending on our Creator. We can laugh at those who think spirituality is the way of weakness. Paradoxically, it is the way of strength,"* she set the book down on the bed beside her. She crossed her arms and stared at the open page, squinting at it until the words seemed to blur into one.

Wilson has said those words to me a hundred times.

The revelation made her sit straight up.

Can it be?

She got out of bed and sat on the edge. *Can it really be what I am*

86

thinking? It must be, of course. It's always seemed so natural coming from him. Yes, of course, now it all makes sense. I'm certain that's what page sixty-eight means.

Sam walked on cat feet to April's bedroom and quietly opened her door. Light from the hallway fell into the room, covering her bed. She sat lightly on the bed next to her daughter, her face in shadow, partially obscured by the darkness. Sam rested her hand on her shoulder and listened to the rhythmic sounds of her breathing. She remembered the look on April and Wilson's face this afternoon when they broke away from their embrace—a look Sam had witnessed every time she saw them share a tender moment.

"Oh, Baby, you knew. I'm sure of it," Sam whispered. "You're just like your Auntic Robin. You'd never betray anyone's secret or their trust."

Regret and shame coursed through Sam like ice splitting on a frozen lake as she thought of her daughter having to witness her alcoholism. Her selfish guttural need to put the bottle first—before April, before Jonathan, before her career, before her grandmother and Robin, before, before, before, *everything.*

And yet. April never complained. In many ways, she was precocious, always able to understand, always more advanced, wiser than her tender young years. Sam thought of the life April now enjoyed at the ranch. It was full and happy—and Sam would continue to do everything she could, physically, mentally and emotionally to keep it that way.

When Sam's alarm sounded at five-forty-five a.m., she had been awake for the last hour. She dressed, looked in on April and started for the office, driving past snow-covered fields draped brightly in the morning sun. When she arrived at the *Perspective's* parking lot a few minutes before seven-thirty a.m. she was surprised to see Wilson's Honda Accord.

She stopped the station wagon in front of his car and stared at the license plate.

PAGE 68

A conversation she had had with Hunter floated through her mind. They had been on one of their stakeouts in the parking lot adjacent to the

Grandview Perspective early on in their investigation when Wilson had turned in off Wadsworth Boulevard. As they followed his car toward the parking lot in the back of the building Hunter had caught sight of his plate and asked, *"Blondie, do you know what page sixty-eight means?"*

Sam shrugged. *"I don't and I've always meant to ask him, but unless it's staring me right in the face, I never think about it."*

She kept her gaze on the plate. "Well, Hunter, now it's staring me right in the face. Now I do know what it means."

Sam entered the newsroom through the kitchen and saw the light on in Wilson's office. She set her things on her desk and put her coat over her chair. She headed toward his office, listening to hear if he might be on the phone. But the newsroom was quiet enough that she could hear traffic passing back and forth on Wadsworth Boulevard.

It was almost as if Wilson was expecting her, because he was looking directly at the door when she stopped at the threshold. Her hands were folded lightly in front of her. His hands were on his desk in front of him, his right hand partially covering his prosthesis.

Sam said, "We never apologize to anyone for depending on our Creator. We can laugh at those who think spirituality is—"

Wilson interrupted her and finished the sentence. "The way of weakness. Paradoxically, it is the way of strength."

"Page Sixty-eight."

"Yes. Now you know." Wilson was holding his breath, biting the inside of his lower lip, waiting for what might be on the verge.

"Can I come in?"

He motioned her in and told her to close the door.

She sat across from him and they were at eye level. "Why didn't you tell me?"

"This is not about me, Sam."

"How long have you been sober?"

"A long, long time. You remember the day you took your last drink, Sam."

"Of course I do," she said without pause. "I missed April's softball game and her first homerun."

Wilson touched his chest with the tips of his myoelectric fingers. Sam was staring down at her hands, but looked up as the mechanical movement of his device produced its now-familiar sound.

"I remember mine, too," he said. "I woke up one morning at the edge of the bed in some hotel room, having no idea where I was or how the hell I got there. The woman I went into that room with was gone and so was my wallet. I looked at my clothes scattered all over the floor from the doorway to the bed, feeling like an idiot. I only knew where I was because I found a pack of matches on the floor with the name of the hotel on it.

"I remember I got dressed and walked out of the hotel and into the street. Nothing looked familiar, not the hotel, not the room, not even the street I was standing on." Wilson turned his head in disgust and embarrassment. "I can still see myself as clear today as I could back then, looking up and down that street, searching for anything that might be familiar.

"I had only been with the wire service a short time then. I had been warned by my editor that my job was in jeopardy because of my drinking. He called me in his office one afternoon just before the hotel incident and said to me, 'Son, you're young and you've got your whole life in front of you, but you're this close,'" Wilson held his right index finger and thumb inches apart. "'To running out of chances. I've done all I can to help you not lose this job, but you're dangerously close to ruining your career. If you do, it'll be all your own doing. You're a helluva journalist, and you have great potential to go far. I'd hate to see you throw all that away.'"

"You didn't lose your job," Sam said, but it wasn't a question.

He shook his head. "The moment when I was standing on that street corner, I said to myself 'this has to stop. I am too adamant to let this be better and stronger than me.' So, I stopped drinking that day. Sure, I've teetered a bit over the years, I'm not going to lie to you, Sam. It's not always easy, as you well know, but I've never touched a drop of alcohol since. The first time I read the Big Book and page sixty-eight, it became my mantra, if you will. There's hardly a day I don't say that very sentence to myself."

"You practice the anonymous part of AA."

"Always have," he said. "Very few people know. No one in this office knows."

"April knows."

"Yes, she does."

If he was surprised at Sam's comment, he gave no indication.

"You told her when you were held captive together."

The corners of Wilson's mouth turned slightly upward as he nodded. "Do you want to know one of the first things April said to me in that room where we were being held?" He didn't wait for her response. "She said, 'You look like Santa Claus.'"

He was relieved to see Sam smile.

"By then it had been more than two weeks since I'd been kidnapped and well," he ran his hand over his beard that Sam noticed now had been neatly trimmed. "I was a mess, my clothes were filthy, torn and wet from my failed escape attempt. Since we'd never met, I didn't want to scare her, so I said, 'I'm afraid I'm not as jolly or as clean as he is right now, April.'"

"Why did you tell her you were an alcoholic?"

Wilson sat back against his chair and considered her carefully. "When we were first in that room together and started to talk, Sam, she was very angry with you."

The small smile fell from Sam's face and she nodded with an unfortunate familiarity. She felt as she always did when confronted by her miserable alcoholic failings on her journey to find sobriety— as though she was underwater and frantically about to run out of air, knowing her next breath would be her last. "April thought I had come to her grandmother's house because I was going to bring her home from Canal Island," Sam said. "And not only I couldn't, but I couldn't tell her why because she was too young to understand why her father had put her there in the first place."

Wilson kept his voice low as he continued. "We were sitting on that raggedy mattress, waiting for someone to come and get us out of there and I knew the only way I could get April to relate to you and your situation was to tell her my own story."

He looked at Sam hard for a moment and pointed from himself to her. "How *I* was where you are in a way she could understand. So, I said to her, 'Can you keep a secret?'"

Sam sat in silence with her head down, listening to Wilson.

I told April when I was about your age, I had the same kind of problem you had and once I almost lost my job.

She asked me why.

I told her like your mother I had a very hard time trying to control how much and when I drank. And like your mother I wanted to stop more than anything because it was hurting the people I loved.

I explained to her how even though I didn't know all of your journey, I knew you had tried many times to stop drinking, but you didn't have it very easy because it's not an easy thing to do.

As sweetly and innocently as she could she said to me, 'But you did it.'

Yes, I did, I told her, but it wasn't easy for me, either.

Then she asked if you really wanted to stop drinking.

More than anything else, I told her. It won't be easy for your mother, but I told her what she could do to help you. Don't listen to what other people like your grandmother, your classmates or anyone else says about her. I told her, 'Make up your own mind, April, believe in her and don't give up on her just yet.'

There was a steady silence in Wilson's office after he finished. The newsroom was full with reporters and busy now, bustling with activity that Sam and Wilson could hear through the closed door.

When she finally looked at him, he said, "Are you going to tell April you know?"

Sam glanced toward the ceiling, as if it contained the right answer. She shrugged lightly. "No, I don't think so. At least not right away. At some point I will, though."

"Do what you think is best, Sam. April should know I've told you. You'll know when the time is right."

She nodded and left his office without another word.

A few minutes before three that afternoon, Sam stuck her head inside Wilson's office.

"Would you mind if I took off a little early? I'm going to get April after school, but I'd like to watch some of her basketball practice."

"Of course, Sam."

"I stuck her gift card from you in my purse this morning. I thought we'd make an afternoon of it." There was a smile in her eyes. "After the sporting goods store, I thought we'd grab a pizza."

"Yes, her favorite," Wilson said. "With extra pepperoni, she'll love it."

Sam spotted her daughter the moment she entered the gymnasium. The basketball team was on the court doing running drills and April was leading the pack. They'd touch one line and then run to the next, hustling back and forth, up and down the court, their athletic shoes squeaking against the floor's smooth, shiny surface and all the players jostling into each other. April was concentrating so much she didn't notice her mother until the team had finished and she saw her sitting in the bleachers a few rows up from center court. Sam gave a quick wave and a broad smile covered April's face that was pink with exertion.

The team gathered around their coach. April was standing next to him, her hands on her hips, her head down slightly as she caught her breath.

After being held captive with Wilson April had changed with her mother, it was as though her daughter had grown up before her eyes. No longer cold and aloof, April had become more patient, kinder, more affectionate toward her mother.

Now Sam knew the reasons why.

The coach barked out instructions for another drill. Something about the way April dashed ahead of her teammates with the other players trying to catch up, made Sam feel unsteady. She had to place both hands down firmly on the bleachers.

She could not get over how much April looked and acted like her Auntie Robin. She was still at that coltish young age of her life, still straight as a board, but it wouldn't be long before her figure would begin to blossom. April, like her Auntie Robin, had the olive coloring of their grandmother. Sam had the fair skin, the blonde hair and blue eyes of their mother. She had no doubt April would be as dark and winsome, tall, graceful and athletic as Robin had been.

She would turn heads someday, too, just as her sister had done.

Sam never pretended there was ever anything striking or glamorous about her physical features, no high cheekbones, no deep-set eyes or wide, inviting smile. She had the posture of an old worn-out sofa, and missed the days when Robin would scold her for not standing up straight.

Sam was as plain as a farm girl in every sense of the word. She had long ago come to terms with herself. And she was okay with that.

But her daughter.

Well. That was a different story.

April would rise above, and that's all that really mattered.

SIXTEEN

Sandy Petersen was sitting in the auditorium at Franklin Elementary, listening to the school board president drone on about the city of El Paso's proposed mill levy increase.

Her cell phone was face down on the desk beside her materials when it lit up with a text message. She grabbed it off the desk and turned it over. She saw the photo of her husband and children in the face of her phone and smiled.

Sandy clicked on her husband's text message.

Hola, hola mi amor. Dónde estás, still at the school board meeting?

Sandy put her phone in her lap and typed her return. *Sí, Roberto, it's another one of those marathon meetings. Que paso, my love?*

Mi amor, no tengo leche en la casa.

No milk in the house?! Sandy inserted a shocked smiling emoji in her text and sent it.

Sí, mi amor, los niños drank the very last drop. Can you stop quickly on the way home, por favor y gracias.

Sí, hopefully it won't be much longer here. I'll be home soon. Are the children in bed?

Sí, sí, mi amor, as snug as little bugs in the rug.

Sandy sent a text of rows and rows of colorful hearts and turned her attention back to the school board meeting.

An hour later she was chatting with the other elementary school teachers as they left and walked to their cars in the chilly night air.

It was near midnight when Sandy entered the grocery store. She grabbed a basket at the automatic doors and headed for the dairy section. She put a gallon of milk, eggs and a loaf of bread in her basket and went to the checkout stand.

She was waiting patiently for her turn in line when she heard a male's voice a few aisles over say, "Hey, look at this, Jenny."

Sandy glanced in the direction of the man's voice. He was showing the girl who was standing next to him a photo on the cover of a star-studded gossip magazine.

"She's a really big star here in the United States," he told her. Sandy watched the girl lean in for a better look at the magazine. She nodded, but seemed uninterested.

Sandy was glad she had set her basket on the floor in front of her, otherwise she likely would have dropped it.

She couldn't help gawking at them. He was in his late fifties, but the girl was young, perhaps still in her teens. She was rail thin and the thick, ill-fitting jacket she wore enveloped her entire body. The coat was black and bulky and didn't seem feminine enough for a woman. Sandy noticed the man wore a thin black sweat jacket zipped to his chin and Levi's. His combat-style boots looked clean and crisp, as though they had just come from the box.

She couldn't see much of the girl's attire, only the fringe of her dress, which hung below the heavy jacket. She tried not to stare at her shoes, faded black casual flats.

He flipped through the magazine another few pages before he placed it back in the rack. It was their turn to pay and they put their groceries on the conveyor belt. Sandy caught sight of some of the items, mostly junk food, spicy potato chips, energy drinks, and an assortment of candy bars.

Sandy watched the man pay for their purchase with cash. The girl couldn't have stood any closer to him without climbing into his arms. She seemed to be watching the transaction with interest, paying rapt attention to the clerk's every move. Her brown hair was long and stopped at the center of her back and she had pushed it behind her ears. Even under the store's harsh fluorescent lighting, it had a keen shine.

They were leaving through the automatic doors when the clerk in Sandy's line said, "Ma'am? Are you ready?"

Sandy paid for her groceries and hurried out of the store. She stood in the parking lot and surveyed the area nearly empty of cars, the couple gone.

She rushed to her car and pulled her cell phone out of her bag as she fished for Sam's business card. She checked her watch as she dialed Sam's cell phone. Ten minutes after midnight.

Sam's phone rang three times before it pulled her from a deep slumber. She squinted at the phone, but her brain was thick with sleep, and the number didn't register.

"Sam Church," she said in a raspy voice.

"Sam? Hello, hi, it's Sandy Petersen. I am so sorry to call so late, and oh my gosh, you're probably not going to believe this, but I think I just saw Jenny Hollingsworth!"

Sandy was so excited with the news her words tumbled out in a torrent.

"Wha—?" Sam was still groggy and Sandy was talking so fast she was having trouble processing her words. "Jenny? You saw Jenny? Where?"

"Yes! Here at the grocery store! They were standing in another line, two of them, Jenny and this older man. I only looked over at them because I heard the man say, 'Hey, look at this, Jenny.'"

Sam was awake now, sitting straight up in bed. She turned on the light and the dark room lit up in brightness. "Are you sure it was her?"

"Oh my gosh, yes! One hundred percent! I'd bet my tenure on it," Sandy said and she was still glancing around the parking lot. "And Sam, oh my gosh, that man had to be in his fifties, maybe older, and if it is Jenny then we know it's not her father."

"Without a doubt," Sam said.

"And I am so sorry to say this," Sandy went on. "Because I hate to judge people and rush to opinions about them since we don't know their circumstances, but ugly. On my goodness, Sam, that man was so ugly. He either had greasy hair or it was so fine and he had so little he didn't know what to do with it. He had it parted on one side and had combed it all the way to the other side like he was trying to cover his bald head. And, oh my gosh, he had the jowls of a bulldog and everything."

"I can't believe it. I don't know what to say," Sam said. "If it really is her that'd be wonderful."

"Oh, I'm sure of it. I've kept the rendering you gave me in my purse and I've looked at it almost every day. I wanted to go up to them and see for myself, but, you know, I just didn't feel comfortable."

"I understand," Sam said.

"But I can tell you one thing."

"What?"

"That rendering didn't do her justice."

"What do you mean?"

"It did capture exactly how her hair looks, no doubt, the color looks the same, and it's long, fine and to the middle of her back, but I can tell you one thing it didn't capture."

"What's that?"

"How beautiful she is," Sandy said, and she spoke with conviction and earnestly. "Yes, Sam, I am certain the person I just saw in the grocery store was Jenny Hollingsworth, one hundred percent!"

SEVENTEEN

S am couldn't fall back to sleep after she hung up with Sandy. She tossed and turned while replaying their conversation, especially Sandy's comments and observations about the couple's appearance. Jenny's natural beauty and what Sandy had said about the man who was apparently with her kept her staring up into the darkness.

Sam glanced at the clock on her nightstand, nearly two a.m. She wanted to call Wilson and tell him the news, but forced herself to resist. At five-thirty, she threw the covers aside and got in the shower. She entered the *Perspective's* parking lot before eight a.m. and the station wagon was the only car in the lot.

At nine a.m. Sam was sitting at her desk mindlessly sifting through emails when she heard the door in the kitchen open. She knew it had to be Wilson. They were the only two employees who used that entrance to come and go. She hurried to the kitchen. Wilson was about to turn toward the newsroom when they bumped into each other.

"Sam! Is everything alright?!"

She was nodding, and he could see the jubilant look in her eyes.

"Yes, yes! Everything's fine!"

In her excitement, she grabbed his arm and started to pull him toward his office. "You're not going to believe this…" her voice trailed off and she didn't say another word until they were in his office with the door closed.

She didn't wait for him to remove his overcoat. "Sandy Petersen called me at midnight last night and said she thinks she saw Jenny Hollingsworth in the grocery store."

"I'd say you're kidding, but I know better." Sam's enthusiasm was contagious and Wilson couldn't help wagging his head and smiling. "When and what did she say?"

He rubbed his index finger over pursed lips as he listened to Sam relay her conversation. She ended by saying, "Sandy said the girl was standing so close to him and was watching the entire transaction with such curiosity it was like she was seeing it for the first time."

"This could open up myriad possibilities," he said.

"That's why I couldn't fall back to sleep last night. If it is Jenny, then who was that man with her? A young beautiful girl, a much older man…"

"Let's not jump to any conclusions," Wilson said and watched the euphoric look in her eyes become more subdued.

Sam spread out her hands in front of him. "Obviously, Wilson, there's nothing I can do here to find her."

He nodded knowing he didn't have to ask what she was planning; he was all but certain he knew what her next step would be. He also knew it would be pointless to try and stop her.

He asked in a straightforward voice, "When are you going back to El Paso?"

EIGHTEEN

S am was sitting in a rental car in the same spot across the street from Franklin Elementary School, waiting for Sandy Petersen to emerge from the building.

It had been one week since Sandy's midnight call, and Sam had worked diligently to prepare for her absence from the newspaper. She had filed several news stories for last week's Friday Edition and a fifteen-hundred-word feature spread for this week's paper.

Of course, managing editor Nick Weeks was less than pleased when he learned Sam would be out of the office for at least two more weeks.

Wilson had asked Nick to stay in the conference room with Sam after the staff meeting on Thursday afternoon. He was sitting at the head of the table, Nick and Sam were on opposite sides of him when he told Nick about Sandy's call to Sam and the reason Sam felt it necessary to return to El Paso.

Nick didn't hide the foul look on his face when he scrutinized her across the shiny conference table. "How do we know it really was Jenny she saw?" he asked. "You're taking the word of a woman who wouldn't know her from Eve and believing in her so much that you think you have to race back down there to see for yourself?"

Sam set her folded hands on the table. "Nick, for that matter, I wouldn't know Jenny from Eve, either. If you remember we're going off the rendering made by a forensic artist with the Grandview PD, a rendering done by a professional. A rendering done so well it was apparently convincing enough for Sandy who was willing to bet her tenure the person she saw in that grocery store was Jenny Hollingsworth."

She fidgeted with her pen as she carefully considered her words. "I don't know it about you and you certainly don't seem to know it about me, but I think I have shown countless times with my reporting here that any time there's a credible witness, a credible source, to a story I'm working on I am going to do everything I can to talk to that person. Preferably in person whenever it's at all possible."

Nick turned to Wilson and gave a hard shrug. "And this helps the *Perspective* how, Wilson? There's no story here, and even if there was, it's not a local story. There are no ties to our community, so no one reading it in Grandview will give a shit. Besides, it's not like we're rolling in dough, here. We don't have the financial resources to hire another reporter so Sam can go out on a whim." He started waving his hand wildly in the air. "To go gallivanting off on a wild goose chase somewhere to find someone who means nothing to her and this community."

"This is hardly for pleasure, Nick," Sam said. She couldn't make herself look at him so she directed her comment toward the conference room door.

"Well, it sure as hell isn't for business or for this newspaper."

Wilson held up his prosthesis as if to say *stop*. "You two are going back and forth talking as if there is a story," he said and considered both of them. "I understand where you're coming from, Nick, but we're not talking about a story. When Hunter was alive there wasn't any one thing he really wanted more than to find his sister. Yes, of course, this could end up going nowhere, but I think we, I." Wilson pointed at his chest. "Owe it to a man who died working on a story for us to at least see if this return to El Paso does, in fact, end up going somewhere, namely finding

Jenny. I've given her the okay to take the time she needs in Texas."

Sam leaned into the table; her hand pressed firmly on top. "Just so you know, Nick, this is something I'm doing on my own and I won't be drawing my salary while I'm gone."

If Nick was placated by Sam taking the time unpaid, he didn't show it. "How long do you foresee that being, Wilson?" he asked. "Two weeks now, but I think everyone sitting at this table knows this is not going to be all rolled up into a nice package in fourteen days."

"We'll cross that bridge when we get to it, Nick," Wilson said.

"*If* we ever get to it," Nick said and he didn't bother to hide the irritation and skepticism in his voice.

Sam watched as Nick ignored her, nodded a civil okay in Wilson's direction and collected his pen and tablet off the table. She could almost see the anger steaming from his ears. She knew he was furious, furious with her and with Wilson for seemingly giving her special treatment.

When he left the conference room and closed the door, Sam looked at Wilson. She was shaking her head slowly, her lips tight. "I don't know why he always has to be so crusty to me. He doesn't think I do much of anything when I'm here and then he throws a fit when I am going to be gone."

She shrugged with uncertainty and lowered her head. "Maybe Nick's right, I don't know anymore. If you think it would be better for the paper for me to stay here, I understand. I don't want you to feel like I am pressuring you to let me go *gallivanting* if there are stories here that need me."

"Sam, it's decided," Wilson said and his voice was calm, reassuring. "This is something you have to do and it's the right thing. We owe it to Hunter. Nick will see that way, too, someday. If not, well, that will be on him."

They sat for a time at the table, both silently looking at the whiteboard at the far end of the room. It still had the drawing Hunter had done of Sam and him when they were well into working on the undocumented worker's story. The sketch showed them sitting in Howard's old four-door Chrysler station wagon with its two-tone brown paneling. Their smiling faces framed the windshield. Her blonde hair looked just as it did every day, a shoulder-length bob with a long side swept fringe slightly tousled to the left side of her face. Her gold loop earrings were partially revealed. Hunter was wearing his Colorado Rockies baseball cap, his sandy mane sticking out along the sides and sunglasses shielding his eyes.

Sam got up and Wilson watched her walk to the whiteboard. She stood before it with her hands folded in front of her. When she reached for the eraser, Wilson said, "Sam, what are you doing?" He got up and joined her at the whiteboard.

"There are bits and pieces of Hunter everywhere I look, here and at home, and I don't need to keep being reminded of him every time I come into this conference room."

She went to erase the drawing and timeline, but he stopped her. "Sam, no, not now. No one needs to use this board right now. Leave this alone. It can wait at least until everything with Jenny is over."

NINETEEN

S am's cell phone started to buzz with a text message, pulling her from her thoughts with Nick and Wilson in the conference room. It was Sandy.

On my way, Sam. Sorry! Even teachers get stopped by the principal!

A few minutes later, in the fading light of a winter afternoon, Sandy emerged from the main entrance. She saw Sam and pointed toward a group of cars parked together. Sam gave her a quick wave.

Ten minutes later Sam followed Sandy into the parking lot of the grocery store. They met at the front of Sam's rental car and shared a hug.

"Sam, oh my gosh, I am so glad you wanted to come back," Sandy said and she squeezed Sam's shoulders. "I haven't stopped thinking about Jenny and that night since it happened. I hope you brought more photos of her."

"They're at the hotel. I made twenty copies and I'll be happy to share some with you."

"Oh good!" Sandy said. "I want to show it to friends and co-workers."

They started for the entrance. "There won't be much to see here, Sam, I mean a grocery store is a grocery store. I'll pick up a few things while we're here."

At the door Sandy grabbed a basket and Sam walked with her as she got her items. They were at the checkout when Sandy said, "This is where I was standing when I heard that man say Jenny's name. They were standing in line for that register right over there."

Sam followed Sandy's nod.

"So, you can see with your own eyes they weren't that far away from me," Sandy said. "I told my husband as soon as I got home, but he didn't really believe me."

Sam recalled the conversation with Nick and Wilson at the conference table. "I know what you mean. One of my editors is saying this is a waste of time, but you were able to get a good look at them."

Sandy nodded with confidence. "Like I told you Jenny's enhanced photo is right on. I'd bet my bottom dollar on it."

"You really think Jenny seemed afraid to be in here?"

"More like anxious," Sandy said and she scooted as close to Sam as she could so their bodies were touching. "I mean literally this close. I told you on the phone she might as well have been in his arms."

"I can't help thinking she might have been kidnapped."

Sandy shook her head firmly. "That's just not the sense I got, Sam. I mean, I could be wrong, because obviously I have nothing to base this on, but I really think she knew him. It was darn chilly that night and I'm willing to bet that was his jacket she was wearing, which, for me anyway, begs the question, why didn't she have her own jacket? And her shoes."

"Her shoes?" Sam said.

Sandy nodded. "I mean winters in El Paso are pretty mild and we don't get much snow, but nights are cold, so why was she wearing just flats?"

"Summer shoes," Sam said.

She tapped Sam on the arm. "Yes, well-worn summer shoes."

"There's going to be a lot of questions like that, Sandy, if this ever develops into something more than a sighting at the local grocery store."

Sandy paid for her groceries and they didn't speak again until they were standing in front of the rental car.

"What do you think you're going to do now?" Sandy asked.

Sam surveyed the parking lot with her hands on her hips. "Well, at least for now, I'll find a place to park that will allow me to see the main entrance and the cars that come and go from here."

"Maybe just observe for a few days?"

"For now, yes. If at least one of them lives in the area, hopefully it won't be long before they return," Sam said, her attention now on the grocery store's entrance.

"That sounds like a good start. I only live about five minutes from here, so you're welcome to stop by anytime."

"Thanks, Sandy. That's good to know."

"When do you think you'll start?"

A memory came unbidden.

Their story on the undocumented workers was just beginning to unfold and Hunter had agreed to watch the entrance of the *Grandview Perspective* in hopes their anonymous letter writer would return with another note for Sam.

Wilson had asked Hunter when he wanted to start the surveillance. Sam could hear Hunter's deep voice respond immediately.

She echoed his same reply to Sandy, "Why not tonight. Maybe we'll get lucky."

TWENTY

S am left the grocery store and found her way back downtown as if the route she drove had always been part of her daily commute.

The hotel attendant recognized her and greeted her with a friendly tip of his billed cap as she made her way inside the lobby. She was planning to spend several hours observing the grocery store, and changed into casual sweats and slip-on shoes. She grabbed her bag, left the hotel and walked to *La Dolce Vita* for an Americano to take with her (she shouldn't, but she couldn't resist the homemade lemon biscotti to have with her coffee). She'd buy a premade sandwich from the grocery store once she got settled.

Warmth and the scent of freshly brewed coffee greeted her as she entered the quaint café. She stood behind a woman who was ordering a mocha latte with a long list of special instructions. Sam couldn't see her face, but she looked elegant and refined in a stylish long black wool blend winter coat and matching stilettos. The belted topcoat accentuated her thin frame and highlighted her fine, coiffed silver hair, which stopped in neat curls along the top of her collar.

Sam could hear the woman speaking to the barista at the register in a rapid and surprisingly rude tone. The barista, a chunky young Latina with a full round race, was intently writing the woman's instructions on her cup, trying to avoid eye contact. "Of course, we'll layer the bottom of your cup with mocha sauce, just how you like it, Amanda. Is that heavy cream steamed to one hundred and twenty degrees?" the barista asked.

"Since when do I drink heavy cream?!"

Sam took a step back.

"How many times have you taken my order and you still can't get it right? Maybe if I had a body that looked like *that*." She pointed at the barista. "Cream. Half. And. Half." The lady's snippy voice underscored her words. "And only two pumps. *Comprendes*." She held up two fingers as if to emphasize her request. "And if it's not steamed at the right temperature, I'll send him back until you get it right." The woman jerked her thumb over her shoulder.

Sam couldn't help but turn and look casually over her shoulder in his direction.

She didn't know how she hadn't noticed him standing near the entrance on her way inside. He was so tall and burly that Redwood forests came to mind. He stood with his legs shoulder-width apart and wasn't wearing a coat. His beefy arms stuck out from a tight black tactical T-shirt and were crossed tightly over his compact chest. His ham-sized fists were tucked under his arms as if to enhance his biceps. His right arm was fully covered with a sleeve tattoo. His T-shirt was tucked inside black core cargo pants and revealed a packed, thickly set waist. He was wearing a camouflage ball cap pulled tightly over his brow and sunglasses. His face, covered with a full brown beard, complemented the color of his cap.

Sam wouldn't have been surprised if he was carrying a weapon. She swallowed involuntarily and turned her attention back to the barista and watched the rest of the ordeal with the woman play out.

Moments later the barista at the bar, determined to keep a cheerful face, finished the mocha latte and set it on the counter. The woman grabbed it, ignored the tip jar and turned sharply away from the counter, nearly bumping into Sam. She moved around Sam without saying 'excuse me' and started for the door. Sam and the baristas watched her leave the café in a huff with her beefy friend close on her heels.

Sam reached the counter and said, "I am so sorry for her behavior. She was so rude to you."

The barista waved off Sam's concern. "Oh, don't worry about it, if you did that then you'd have to apologize for her behavior every time she comes in here." Her name tag read Mia. Now that Sam was closer, she could see the girl had a button nose and a soft, pleasant smile. Her friendly face was dotted with acne, her brown hair pulled back neatly in a ponytail.

"I heard you call her by name, so she must come in here often," Sam said.

The other barista, a tall gangling man, joined them at the register. His name tag read Jeff. He looked to be a few years older than Mia with most of his full curly dark hair collected in a man bun at the crown of his head. He wrapped his arm around Mia's shoulder and gave her a quick, reassuring squeeze.

"Whenever we see Amanda coming in, whoever agrees to wait on her gets the tip jar for night," Jeff said.

Mia turned to Jeff and covered her mouth as she smirked. "Did you see her emphasize the number of pumps?"

"Oh my God," he said and Mia started to laugh when he did.

"What was that all about?" Sam asked. "Isn't a mocha already a sweet drink?"

"The mocha sauce is bittersweet," Mia said.

"Yeah, but she thinks it's too bittersweet, so we add two pumps of our classic syrup," Jeff answered. "But *only two*!"

"Is she always that bad?" Sam asked.

"Oh, I got off easy today, you should've seen her yesterday," Mia said. "But we're used to her by now."

"Is she someone important?"

"She likes to think so," Jeff said, looking from Mia to Sam.

"She's Amanda Moore," Mia said. "She's that hotshot personal injury attorney."

"A total ambulance chaser," Jeff said.

"That's the one on the billboards I've seen all over town," Sam said.

"Yep," Jeff said. "The one, the only. Her face is everywhere on television, too."

Mia leaned closer to Sam as if she was about to speak to her in confidence. "Our manager calls Amanda Cruella de Vil. Everyone else here affectionately refers to her as the Devil-Wears-Prada-Lady."

"Yeah, she has the same first name and that same crabby demeanor. She dresses to the hilt and even kinda looks like her," Jeff said and then he fluffed his wavy hair along the sides. "You know, the hair and everything."

"What about the guy by the door?" Sam asked.

Mia and Jeff shrugged almost simultaneously.

"Beats me," Jeff said. "We've both been here about a year and we still don't know his name."

"Yeah, and neither does anyone else who works here," Mia said. "He never comes to the counter. He just waits there at the door. We think he's probably her lackey. Our manager calls him Rambo, only he's not as handsome!"

"We just call him the lug," Jeff said. "He's the only dude I know who wears sunglasses at night."

Sam couldn't help chuckling as she looked at Mia with approval. "Well, Mia, you certainly deserve the tip jar tonight."

Sam got her Americano and put a generous tip in the glass jar.

On the interstate heading to the grocery store, Sam passed three billboards with Amanda Moore's beautiful, yet arrogant face plastered on the front. She hadn't given them a second glance, but after what she had just witnessed in the coffee shop, she paid more attention to each one as she drove by.

The first one read, 'Injured at work? In the car? Workman's Comp? Wrongful death? Amanda Moore can help. Call today!'

The second one she passed read, 'Injured in a car wreck? Expect Moore from Amanda Moore. Attorneys on call all day, every day.'

The last billboard Sam saw before she reached her exit showed a life-size portrait of a stylish Amanda Moore dressed like she was at the café. Her sweeping Hollywood smile beamed at motorists as they passed by. The copy next to her image didn't include her name, only the words, 'Smart. Aggressive. Compassionate.' The number to call and website were listed at the bottom.

Sam took her exit and a few minutes later entered the grocery store parking lot. She drove around until she settled on a spot that allowed her a generous view of the two entrances into the lot and the two sets of automatic double doors.

For nearly two hours she watched cars and shoppers come and go as she finished her coffee and ate her sandwich and the biscotti, the hint of lemon leaving her mouth feeling fresh. She glanced at her watch, nearly eight-thirty p.m. April would be taking her bath soon, so she called home. Her daughter answered on the second ring, excited to hear her mother's voice. They talked long enough for Sam to hear about April's day and that another double-header basketball game was set for Saturday.

"Do you think you'll be home in time to see my game, Mommie?" Sam could hear the hopefulness in her daughter's voice.

"Baby, I'll still be here in El Paso, at least through the weekend. I'm so sad I won't be there to watch you, but Howard has promised to record the game so I can see you play when I get home—so don't tell me who wins!"

"Okay, I won't, but I hope we do!"

"Me, too, but I want you to promise me something."

"What, Mommie?"

"I want you to promise that you'll have fun playing and being part of your team whether you win or lose, just like you were when we came to your game this last Saturday. You promise?"

"Uh huh."

"That doesn't sound very convincing, April," Sam said.

"I like it better when we win."

"Of course you do, everyone does. But what does Nona always say?"

The phone was silent a moment as April thought. "That the best

111

winners are the ones who accept defeat, too?"

"That's right," Sam said, wishing this was a conversation she was having as she was getting April ready for bed.

More silence. "Okay," April said finally. "Cross my heart."

"Sweet dreams, Baby," Sam said and they ended the call.

It was close to ten when Sam felt herself getting sleepy. Sandy said it was near midnight the night she saw Jenny and the man she was with in the store. She wanted to at least make it another two hours before going back to the hotel.

She got out of the car to stretch her legs. The chilly night air awakened her senses.

"Hunter," she whispered and took two deep breaths looking for the stars. The city lights had washed them out. "Why aren't you here waiting with me? I need you here to keep me awake."

They had learned so much about each other during their night-long stakeouts covering the story. She thought about the day he had come to the ranch on Labor Day, a single day before everything changed.

As if she didn't miss him enough, she allowed his memory to take hold.

They had roasted marshmallows in front of a roaring bonfire that last evening they were together. It was after ten p.m. when the fire began to die down. Hunter looked at Sam, their faces reddened by the fire's warmth.

"Thanks for today, Blondie," he had said. "It's been one of the best days ever and thanks for the leftovers."

Sam stood outside the car until a cold winter wind made her shiver. She got back inside and checked her watch, one more hour. At ten minutes after midnight, she felt her head bobbing. She took one more look around. Save for a car parked near the entrance, the parking lot was empty. Only oil spots on the open ground stared back at her.

She shook her head thinking, *two more weeks to go.* How would she fill the long stretch of time before her? She thought of April running the length of the basketball court, shooting baskets from the free throw line. She thought of them sitting together at the kitchen table after dinner and Sam helping her with her homework. Two weeks without any of those moments.

She remembered Hunter the night they were sitting in front of the fire and April capturing that moment of time with a photo she took with Sam's cell phone.

"Two weeks," Sam said.

Thankfully it would pass quickly, as time always does.

She took a deep breath to reaffirm her resolve and started the car. She headed for the interstate and the now-familiar route back to the hotel.

TWENTY-ONE

Eight days had passed since Sam's first night of surveillance at the grocery store.

April had won both her double-header basketball games that Saturday afternoon. Though she wasn't supposed to tell her mother who had won, she couldn't help it. She was so excited, she spilled the beans telling Sam on the way home from the game.

Sam had spent the rest of the week and nearly all weekend parked in the grocery store parking lot at different times during the day. She'd come and go throughout the day, but would end her vigils every night just after midnight.

It was near ten p.m. as she watched a family of four enter the supermarket. The two children looked to be around April's age and Sam couldn't help speaking out loud as she watched them disappear inside. "Shouldn't those children be home in bed?"

Thirty minutes later, Sam was doing her best to stay awake. She looked at her cell phone on the seat beside her. She picked it up and hesitated briefly, her finger over the keypad before she started to dial Wilson's number. She had resisted the urge to call him all evening, but she desperately wanted to make it until midnight, and if she didn't talk to someone, she was certain she'd fall asleep. The last thing she wanted was a stranger knocking at her car window and startling her because she hadn't been paying attention. And she hadn't talked to Wilson since Friday.

His cell phone rang five times before he answered.

"Hi, it's me," she said. "I was about to hang up. I hope it's not too late to call."

"Call anytime, Sam, I've told you that," Wilson said. "I'll be home in about twenty minutes, so this is perfect."

"It's pretty late and you're just getting home. A busy day?" Sam asked and she envisioned a newsroom humming with activity, the police scanner squawking and reporters at their desks filing stories for the Friday Edition.

"Kind of a slow news week so far," he said. "Which is lucky because I'll be handling everything for the rest of this week."

"Where's Nick?"

"Out with the flu. He went home sick yesterday afternoon. He called last night and told me he couldn't even lift his head off the pillow."

"Are you just leaving work now?"

Wilson was waiting at a traffic light and her comment caught him slightly off guard. He hesitated as he thought how to answer her. He was coming from an AA meeting. Until she had learned he was a recovering alcoholic, he had always been vague saying he had been or was going to 'a meeting.' He smiled to himself that this would be the first time he could tell her where he'd really been.

"Honestly, Sam, I had just left an AA meeting when you called."

"Then you should be pretty close to home," she said. "You live so close to the one we go to."

Sam assumed he had gone to the same place off Sixth Avenue near the office she did to attend AA meetings.

"Actually, that's not where I attend my meetings."

"It's not?"

Wilson could hear the wonder in her voice.

"Do you feel comfortable telling me where you go?" she asked, not wanting to be presumptuous.

"For years my AA sponsor lived in Aurora, so that's where I started first attending meetings, which he ran. He died several years ago and I guess since I've attended meetings here for so many years, I never thought much about finding a different place. I come here because this is where I feel most comfortable. Usually, when I attend a meeting, it's before work, otherwise the day will get away from me, which is why sometimes I don't get to work before ten."

"Because you're coming from your meeting in Aurora?"

"That's right," Wilson said. "But since Nick will be out this week, I was at work early this morning."

"It's just as important for you to attend as it is for me," she said.

"Yes, it is. It doesn't matter how long it's been for me either, Sam, the need for me to attend AA meetings is always there. No matter how long it's been it helps me keep things in perspective so I can keep my head on straight."

"I'm beginning to see what you mean."

"And I think it will continue to be more of a revelation for you, Sam, but you have to keep at it. You know as I do how hard it is to resist the urge to drink. Though it's been years for me, at times the urge is still there and as strong as ever. Sometimes it'll just pounce on me like some wild animal that's been waiting in the bushes."

She smiled into the phone. "I only have you to thank, Wilson."

"Only to a point," he said quickly. "You're the one who has to do all the hard work. I'm just cheering you on from the sidelines."

They talked until Wilson pulled into his garage. He ended their call by telling her to be careful.

When she hung up, she sat staring at gray clouds collecting around a pale moon. She was surprised how much she had missed hearing his voice and seeing him every day at the newspaper.

She hadn't realized how often she had poked her head inside his office at random times during the workday to say hello, or to talk about a story. Or how many times he had invited her to sit in one of the chairs facing his desk to listen, or how many times their conversation had turned toward trying to get a handle on her substance abuse problem and how to get beyond it.

She remembered how stressful the week leading up to April's custody hearing with Esther Church had been, and how he had helped her get through it.

She had gone to an AA meeting without him because the urge, as Wilson had said, had *pounced* on her, and she knew the only way to get beyond it was to attend a meeting. She was sitting in his office when she told him she had gone.

"That's a big step for you, going alone," Wilson had said. "You've come a long way since the night you called me from Tim's Place."

She laughed. It was harsh and unforgiving. "The night I found out the guy I was dating was married and would never screw around with fat women? Yeah, I remember it, too, Wilson. In fact, so well I never want to forget it."

She looked down, unable to give him her eyes, feeling her body heat rise as humiliation engulfed her. "As bad as it was, it's a night I want to remember. How I was at the very outer limits of my desperation. So I can remember how degraded I was at the way you had to see me. Slurring my words; how you had to dial Howard's number because I was too drunk to drive home and I couldn't see the numbers on the phone, how I was stumbling like an idiot and you tried to help me out the door, how—"

"Sam. I remember that night, too." He spoke quietly, evenly. "Let's focus on what's good about that night. Look how far you've come since then."

Sam sniffed. "You can only measure my success in inches. That's how the judge will see it."

"Inches, seconds, minutes, hours, at least it's forward movement and I think the judge will recognize your efforts as genuine."

And, the judge did and April was able to come home.

It was nearly eleven-thirty p.m. and Sam couldn't keep her eyes open any longer. She started to put her cell phone in her bag when a gleaming white truck caught her eye as it entered the parking lot. It was so pristinely polished, it looked as though it had just been driven off the showroom floor.

She tracked the vehicle until it pulled into a spot near the back of the parking lot. She glanced at the spaces near the front of the store; all were empty. The truck sat idle for a few minutes, exhaust billowing from the tailpipe. The tinted windows made it impossible for Sam to see inside.

She sat up taller as the door opened and a man started to climb down from the truck. The moment he set a foot on the ground her eyes widened. Something about his boots captured her attention. The conversation with Sandy flickered in Sam's mind as she grabbed the steering wheel and pulled herself closer to the windshield.

She watched him walk around the bed of the truck and start for the entrance. He looked to be sixtyish, but carried himself well. She noticed he was looking left and right and tugging at his ball cap as he walked toward the automatic double doors. She kept an eye on his combat boots, a coyote brown, they looked sharp and tactical, spotless as though he had just pulled them from the box.

She scrambled for her bag and pulled out a camera. She was able to get several photographs of him before he disappeared inside the store, then she snapped a handful of the shiny truck.

She sat back against the cushioned seat, blinking hard, retracing the man's steps. She grabbed her phone and sifted through her contacts until she found Sandy's number. She dialed it, holding her breath and keeping an eye on the entrances.

"Hi Sam."

"Sandy, hi, I'm sorry for calling this late. I hope I didn't wake you."

"Oh no, I'm grading papers. I'll be at it for at least another hour. *Que Paso?* Is everything alright?"

"Yes, yes, everything's fine. I'm here at the grocery store and I was about to wrap things up when this fancy truck pulled into the parking lot. Didn't you tell me Jenny's companion was wearing a sharp-looking pair of military-style boots?"

Sandy put her pen down and centered the phone in front of her mouth. "Yes, that's right, sort of a tannish brown color. I thought they looked brand new. Why?"

"Well, I don't know, probably could be nothing, but I noticed this man's boots immediately as he was crossing the parking lot. They look a lot like you described."

"Is he by himself?"

"I think so, at least he went in the store alone," Sam said. "The windows on the truck are tinted so it's hard to see if anyone else is inside, at least from this distance."

"Are you going in?"

"I don't think so," Sam said and her voice sounded hollow, her attention distracted as she stared at the double doors. "I'd hate to. What if I go in and lose him and he drives away before I can get back to my car? Besides, if I do and we do happen to see each other, I'd rather not make eye contact."

"Good point," Sandy said.

"I brought a camera the staff photographer let me use, so I've already taken a handful of pictures of him. Thank goodness for the zoom lens."

"Good idea, Sam. What about photos of the truck?"

"Got that, too," Sam said. "And I also got a few photos of the truck with my cell phone."

"It could be him," Sandy said, sounding hopeful. "This is about the time I saw them the night I went. Did you get a good look at his face?"

"Not really. I could tell he was clean shaven, though. The lights in this parking lot aren't the best and besides, tonight he's wearing a ball cap. I could tell it has something written on it when he walked around the back of the truck, but not what it says."

Sam thought, tapping her index finger against her chin. She started the car. "I'll tell you what I am going to do, Sandy. I'm going to be ready to follow that truck."

"Sam, do you think that's a good idea?"

"I don't have very many options," Sam said.

"Please be careful."

The handful of times she and Hunter had followed several vehicles during their investigation came to mind. Her face softened as she

119

remembered his enthusiasm while he navigated their drive, making sure Sam kept a safe distance so they wouldn't become too suspicious.

"Don't worry," she said. "I will."

Twenty-two

Shortly after Sam hung up with Sandy, the man emerged from the store carrying plastic grocery bags in each hand. Sam watched as he retraced his steps back to his truck, looking left then right, just as he had done previously.

She managed to snap several photos of him with the digital camera and her cell phone before he could get back inside his truck, where he would be hidden behind dark windows.

The truck rolled slowly toward the main entrance, signaling a right turn from the parking lot onto the main street. Sam carefully followed the vehicle from the lot and stayed behind him through one intersection and then another. Two blocks later the truck came to a red light and she stopped a safe distance behind.

She did her best to discreetly take photos of the back of the truck. From this distance she was able to see a military medal of honor on the left side of the black and white Texas license plate. She squinted, leaning closer to the windshield, but couldn't make out the type of medal. Three military-type decals in the back window caught her eye, but the light turned green and the truck started to roll through the intersection and she wasn't able to tell which branch of the military he had served.

"Hopefully I got a few decent photos," she said to the car's interior.

They had traveled a few miles from the grocery store and though Sam didn't know the area well, she could see Franklin Elementary School in the distance. The school grounds were dark save for a few security lights inside the building and the surrounding perimeter.

She was thankful there was a generous amount of traffic given the late hour. Her rental car, a nondescript silver four-door sedan, blended in easily. They passed through another major intersection before the truck made a left turn. From the distance, Sam watched it turn into an apartment complex with a large open parking lot. The perimeter of the lot was lined with carports that faced the street. She could see the decorative entrance that led to the office, and two illuminated American flags billowing lightly in the night breeze. Ornate lighting showcased the name of the complex in a large block of colorful stone: Camino Rael Apartments. Below the name were the words, *Apartment Living at its Best*.

She sighed with relief when she saw a gas and convenience store adjacent to the complex. She stopped next to a gas pump that provided a decent view of the parking lot. Seconds later the truck pulled into an empty spot under the carport.

Sam watched him get out and walk the length of the parking lot, carrying his grocery bags. He walked alone. Two three-story apartment buildings with deep blue doors and reddish-brown stucco faced the lot. The man headed toward the one on the right and disappeared inside an arched entryway.

Sam stared at the building, hoping to see a light illuminate one of the darkened windows. Nothing. She waited another ten minutes before she drove from the convenience store into the apartment parking lot.

She drove cautiously in front of the white truck, then, as she passed along the front of the building, she could see that the entrance he had disappeared through extended beyond to what looked like another parking lot. She drove around to the other side of the buildings, looking at every window. Only one was illuminated on the third floor with what looked like lights on in a bedroom and living room.

Sam didn't want to press her luck, so she left the complex and parked again at the convenience store. She glanced at the digital clock on the dashboard, the time lit up in bright blueish-green numbers: twelve forty-five a.m.

She took her phone out of her bag and called Wilson.

He answered on the second ring, raspy with sleep, his baritone voice noticeably deeper. "Sam." He cleared his throat. "Is everything alright? Where are you?"

"Wilson, everything's good and I know I woke you, but I had to call."

"What is it? Were you in an accident?"

Sam smiled at his concern. "No, everything is good, but you're not going to believe what happened after we hung up."

She didn't wait for him to respond. "I'm pretty certain I saw the man Sandy said was with Jenny."

Wilson rolled over and cupped the phone in his hand. "At the grocery store?"

"Yes, about eleven thirty. I was so tired and I was about to drive back to the hotel when this brand-new looking white truck entered the parking lot."

"Did Sandy tell you what kind of vehicle he was driving?"

"No, she didn't, and while the truck did capture my attention, it wasn't until he got out and I saw his boots that I really started to pay attention."

"Yes, I remember you saying Sandy commented on his boots that they looked new."

"Brand new," Sam said.

"Are you still at the grocery store?"

"No. I followed him back to an apartment complex, though I don't know which one is his because he disappeared inside an entrance and I lost him."

"How far did you follow him from the store?"

"Couple miles, I guess. I was so excited to follow him out of the lot, I forgot to check the mileage, so I'm going to backtrack there before going back to the hotel."

"That's some piece of news, Sam, providing it's him. I assume he was by himself?"

"Yes, I couldn't tell at the grocery store because the truck windows are tinted, but I was able to park at a convenience store across the street from the apartments and he was alone when he walked across the lot."

Sam went on. "Oh, and another thing! I was right behind him at a traffic light. He must be or was in the military and is a decorated veteran."

"How do you know?"

"His license plate has some sort of military medal on it, but I didn't want to get any closer so I couldn't tell the type of medal. I did take photos of the back of his truck, so I'll enlarge them when I get back to the hotel to see if that'll help me decipher it."

"Well, at least we know our mystery man was a service member."

"Oh, and what's that thing called on the back of a pickup?"

"The bed?"

"No, no, it's below the bed, the part that's used to hook up to pull something."

"A hitch."

"Yes! A hitch! His has some kind of military emblem on it, too. It's a beautiful truck, Wilson. Obviously, he takes good care of it."

"Interesting," he said. "Also, since he's in or was in the military, it's a pretty good guess it's a customized insignia on the hitch."

"I've never noticed anything like that before, but I'd have to agree. Hopefully I'll have a better look from the photos when I get back to my room."

"You have the license number, Sam, and where he lives. That's excellent."

Hopefulness rose up in her like bubbles, like the moment she saw Jenny's birth certificate pop up on the computer screen at the El Paso County Clerk's office.

"It may end up going nowhere, Wilson," Sam said. "But for now, it's a lead and I'm going to pursue it. Later this morning I'm going to call Chief Page and ask if he'll run the plate."

TWENTY-THREE

S am stayed in the convenience store parking lot another fifteen
minutes, staring at the apartment complex, doing a mental
checklist of what had happened so far in her search for Jenny.

In the quiet moments she allowed herself to feel a sense of
accomplishment, a sense of liberation and hope, no matter the
incremental size. *Am I any closer to finding Jenny?* Only time, if it were
on her side, would tell.

And her stomach was growling. The last of the premade salad she
ate was long gone.

Inside the store a lone male clerk was stocking cigarettes on a shelf
behind the counter. Since she had conveniently been sitting at the gas
pump and using it for surveillance, Sam thought she should at least buy
something. The clerk gave her a friendly, but deadpanned smile as she
entered the store. She bought water, a big bag of pretzels, cashews and
a large hot chocolate from an automatic dispenser. More hot water filled
the cup than milk. Of course, it wouldn't taste like Howard's hot cocoa,

but it would have to do. She bought a small carton of milk, which she would add to the cocoa later to give it a richer taste.

Sam returned to her car while keeping her gaze fixed on the white truck under the carport. Retracing her route back to the grocery store showed nearly a five-mile trip. Traffic on the interstate was nonexistent and she was back downtown and in her hotel room in thirty minutes. She turned on the television as she warmed the milk to doctor her hot chocolate and changed her clothes.

She watched a rerun of the local news, a slow news day with one reporter covering the opening of a local arts and culture center as the lead story. Between the news and weather, she watched a handful of commercials, including one that aired with Amanda Moore. Sam couldn't help smiling and shaking her head as she recalled the incident with Amanda and Mia at *La Dolce Vita*. Sam could still see herself turning to one side and carefully eyeing Amanda's henchman waiting portentously at the door.

The commercial ended with Amanda standing in front of what Sam guessed was the reception area of the law firm. She looked stylish as usual with her carefully coiffed silver hair, a serious lawyer-looking glare, and dressed in a trendy black suit. Her arms were folded in front of her. Her smile more of a steely grin. Behind the front desk Amanda Moore's name was on the wall in large golden script. Beneath her name were the same words Sam saw on the billboard on the interstate. Smart. Aggressive. Compassionate. *Well, at least she's not lying about the aggressive part,* she thought.

It was three a.m. when she finally got into bed. She had set her alarm to call April while Howard took her to school. After they talked, Sam fell immediately back to sleep with the sweet sound of her daughter's voice resonating in her ears. She was still sleeping when her cell phone vibrated and chimed with a text message. She stirred slightly, looking at the time before she clicked on the message, almost ten thirty.

"Sandy," Sam said her name as she clicked on her message.

Morning Sam, how'd it go last night? I almost couldn't fall asleep after your call. I was so excited!

Me, too! I followed his truck to an apartment complex.

Which one?

126

Sam could see the decorative entrance leading into the complex. *Camino Rael.*

Oh, yes! Super nice place and only like five miles from the grocery store.

Yes, but I don't know which apartment was his.

Following him there is a good first step. Sandy had inserted a thumbs up emoji.

It sure is!

Do you think it really is the man Jenny was with?

Sam sat up in bed. *I want to believe it is.*

What are you going to do now?

Sam considered her options looking out her hotel window. The sweeping view of the foothills beyond the tall buildings was cast in a full late-morning sun.

For starters, I'm going to reach out to the police chief in Grandview and ask if he'll run the plate.

Good luck and I'm keeping my fingers crossed!

Me too.

Keep me posted if you don't mind.

Absolutely! If it wasn't for you, Sandy, I'd still be in Denver wondering what to do next.

Sam showered and dressed and within the hour was greeted by the homey atmosphere and scent of fresh coffee at *La Dolce Vita.*

Mia was at the bar making coffee when she saw Sam enter the café. By the time Sam got to the counter, her Americano was waiting for her. Sam paid and raised her cup at Mia in appreciation.

"You missed the fun earlier this morning," Mia said as Sam stopped in front of the bar.

"Was Amanda here?" Sam asked.

Mia giggled and from this distance, Sam could see the soft deep-brown color of her eyes. Instead of answering Sam, Mia looked to the employee at the register. "Hey, Gigi, how was Amanda Moore this morning?"

Gigi, a tall, slender young woman with a milky complexion against a long face, rolled her eyes. She clutched her apron and answered in dramatic fashion, "Oh. My. God. Was she *ever*. She was in rare form today, that's for sure!" She pointed playfully at Mia. "You had to make her drink three times!"

Mia gave Sam a dubious smile as her right eyebrow floated upward.

Sam tilted her head and said in a shameful voice, "Mia, did you do that on purpose?"

Mia continued to give Sam her I'll-never-tell expression.

"Was the henchman with her?"

Mia started steaming milk for another drink. "Oh, yeah. The lug was dutifully at his perch right by the door."

"Yeah, standing there like he always does, his eyes hidden behind those silly aviator glasses, and lookin' like a big dumb oak tree," Gigi added.

"Does she ever get him anything to drink?" Sam asked. "A cup of coffee, water, something?"

Mia and Gigi looked at each other, wide-eyed and answered nearly in unison, "Not since we've been here!"

Sam thanked them both and put a generous tip in the jar.

The table she liked in front of the window was open, and she set her coffee and several notebooks down. She scanned through the photos on her cell phone until she came to the one that showed the back of the white truck.

The make was a GMC, but she had to enlarge the photo to get a better look at the model; a Canyon Denali. A quick internet search told her the Denali was the higher end of three models of the truck. She couldn't see a speck of dirt anywhere on the truck from the expanded view on her phone.

Just like those boots, she thought.

She made the frame slightly larger to examine the decals in the back window. The sticker on driver's side showed the symbol of a military rank, and the words *retired marine* were below the image. Another quick internet search of the rank revealed it was a Master Sergeant.

The image in the center window was too blurry to read and Sam cursed herself for not taking a second picture of the pickup. On the passenger side the third decal had the words *Vietnam* on top and *veteran* below. There was an image between the two words, but it was too blurry to read and Sam cursed herself again for only taking a single photo.

She turned her attention to the license plate. Centered at the top of the black and white plate was the word Texas, with a lone star in the right top corner. To the left of the numbers was an image of a military medal. The plate started with DV and she took an educated guess that it meant disabled veteran.

She checked the time on her phone, nearly one p.m. Sam sifted through her contacts for James Page's number, hoping he would be back from lunch. His administrative assistant answered her call on the first ring. After an exchange of pleasant salutations, Sam learned James was still at lunch and would return shortly. She informed Sam she would give him the message as soon as she saw him.

Sam continued her internet research turning to the insignia on the hitch while she waited for the police chief to return her call. She landed on a website with a host of military paraphernalia, which showed a similarly-looking hitch. The description read it was a custom-made, bronze-colored United States Marine Corps tow hitch cover. It had a hand-sculpted look that created a 3D effect.

She was scribbling notes in her Reporter's Notebook when her cell phone lit up fifteen minutes later with James Page's name and number. She answered before it could ring a second time, allowing herself a satisfied smile knowing not many reporters had his personal cell phone number. "Good afternoon, James. That was fast."

"Sam Church, I know whenever you're calling something's up. Are you back in El Paso?" His voice sounded firm, but pleased to hear from her.

"As a matter of fact, that's exactly where I am."

"Are you having any luck? But wait, before you answer, Sam, let me rephrase that. I suspect the reason for this call is that you may be on to something?"

"You know me well, Chief," she said and laughed into the phone.

Sam filled James in on what had happened to this point and ended by telling him about the white GMC truck in the grocery store parking lot.

"So, you followed him from the grocery store last night back to what could be his apartment and managed to get a photo of his truck?"

"Yes, unfortunately it's not the best photo because like I said the decals in the back window are blurry."

"But you got a good look at it?"

"I did, yes."

"And you'd like me to run that plate?"

"If you can, it'd be helpful."

"Text me the photo."

Sam sent James the photo and waited silently for him to receive it.

"That's an emblem of a Master Sergeant rank in the back window," the police chief said.

"I only knew that because I Google searched military ranks," Sam said and circled the words *Master Sergeant* she had written in her Reporter's Notebook. "But it looks like there's several levels of that rank."

"There are," James said. "My father was a Master Sergeant in the Marines, too. My dad's role, or a Master Sergeant role, is the chief administrative assistant for an Army headquarters. They are important members of staff elements at a battalion level or higher."

"The photo's terrible, but you can see there's some type of medal there on the right."

They were quiet for a moment as James studied the photo. "It's hard to make out."

"But would you be able to tell what type of medal it is?"

"Most likely," James said. "Lemme make a few phone calls and I'll get back to you."

Sam ended their call, feeling a light lift of hope in her heart. She sat staring out the café window, watching traffic and pedestrians pass in front of her. Sandy came to mind and Sam envisioned her standing before her students at the front of the classroom.

She grabbed her phone and sent Sandy a text.

Buenas tardes! I just talked to the police chief and he's going to run the plate. I've decided I'm going to skip the grocery store today and camp out at Camino Rael. Hopefully I'll spot our mystery man coming home at some point. I may sit there all night, but at least it'll be a nice change of scenery.

TWENTY-FOUR

Sam sat up on the bed in her hotel room, dazed with sleep.
She could feel her phone buzzing somewhere near her and
ran her hand along the bedspread searching for it. She had returned to
her room after talking with James at the café and sat down on the bed
to rest for what she thought would be a few minutes. She was surprised
she had fallen into a sleep so deeply the phone was pulling her from a
dream.

She found it sticking out under a pillow. "Sam Church," she said,
trying to sound attentive.

"Sam? Everything okay?"

Sam blinked hard as she checked the caller ID and saw James Page's
number. Her brain was so thick with sleep and she had answered the
phone so fast, she didn't take the time to look to see who was calling.

"Hi James," she said, feeling her face flame with embarrassment.
"Yes, everything's fine. She glanced at the numbers illuminating on
the clock radio on the nightstand. She had been asleep for more than

an hour. Feeling her bearings starting to return, she stood and walked to the window. Low flat clouds made the late afternoon light dull and uninviting and her hotel room so gloomy she had to turn on a light.

"Well, I have some good news for you, Sam," he said.

"The name of the mystery man in the GMC truck?"

"Yes, ma'am."

James had her complete attention. "That's wonderful," she said and scrambled to flip her Reporter's Notebook open to a clean page. "Tell me."

"His name is Houston Meyers," James said.

"Is that two e's and an s in Meyers?" Sam asked.

"You got it."

Sam repeated the name, wrote it down and underlined it twice.

"He was born in Slidell, a relatively small city in Louisiana, sixty-eight years ago and served in Vietnam for two years until the war ended in 1975.

"When Saigon fell."

"Yeah. He was a career military guy," James continued. "He served in the Persian Gulf war and retired as that war ended in '91."

"So, he *is* a veteran," Sam said.

"A decorated veteran at that," James said.

"Were you able to tell the type of medal that's on his license plate?"

"Didn't really need it off the plate, Sam," the police chief said. "He was awarded the commendation medal while serving in the Persian Gulf. That kind of honor comes either from heroism or some kind of meritorious service. Since he's got the disabled veteran letters on his license plate and retired in '91 before serving his full twenty years so he could honorably retire, my guess is he was probably wounded during that war."

"Since your father was also a career military guy, what does the military consider a veteran?" Sam asked.

"A veteran, Sam, is any service member who met the obligations of their contract and was discharged from the service or, as it looks to be in Houston Meyers' case, was separated for medical reasons and unable to complete their or his service."

"So, a veteran is a…" her voice drifted as she tried to reiterate.

James finished for her. "A retired member is any service member who honorably served a minimum of twenty years, or whose injuries sustained in combat were so severe the military chose to retire them for medical reasons. They're also considered veterans."

"What about Camino Rael? Does he live there?"

"Yes, in addition to Slidell, that's his known address in Texas, and apartment 303, since you already know the address," James said. "And he's got a clean record, too, no traffic citations, no arrests, nothing."

"That's good to know."

"So, you're thinking this is the guy Jenny was with?"

Sam underlined his name again. "I want to believe it is, James. I want to find Jenny so badly I want to believe anything's possible. I know this sounds foolish, and I should stop everything and go back to Denver where I belong, but I … I can't, at least, not right now. I want to believe everything is just going to fall into place and I'll be able to tell Jenny about her brother. That's it," she said through a long sigh. "That's all I want to do. Even if she'll never know him, I just want to be able to give her what's rightfully hers and to let her know he was on this earth and what a true, good person he was."

"I know you do, Sam, but please think things through before you decide to go and do something."

"You mean something stupid?" Sam asked, clarifying.

"I mean doing something that could get you hurt, or, and I'll be frank with you, Sam, doing something in an unfamiliar place. I'd hate for anything to happen to you so far from home."

Sam smiled into the phone. "James, I appreciate your concern, but I promise y—"

He cut her off with a commanding voice. "Don't promise me, Sam. You remember what happened the last time you promised you wouldn't move without letting me know."

The space between them dropped to a deafening silence.

Sam cleared her throat softly, shaking her head, remembering the night she and Hunter were eavesdropping at the construction site, and when they were spotted how they tried to run from the truck that had started to chase them. How Sam had told Hunter she wanted to wait for James Page to return her call before they went to the site. How insistent Hunter had been they couldn't wait. How he started for the construction site. How Sam had no choice but to follow.

She could still hear the frustration, the disappointment in James' voice on the phone after he had learned Hunter was in the ICU fighting for his life.

"I wish you would have waited for me to call you back, Sam."

She had swallowed hard and closed her eyes. "Me, too."

"Sam? You there?" James asked.

His voice snapped her back to the present.

"Yes, James, sorry. I'm here. Yes, I won't do anything without calling you first."

"Remember I told you I have a few buddies on the police force down there? I can call them if it comes to that."

"Thank you," Sam said.

"I can, but don't put me in a precarious position where I have to do so on the fly." After another brief silence he added in a softer voice, "I know how you work, Sam Church. I know you'll be careful, so please be, okay?"

"Yes, James, I will. I'll keep you posted."

As soon as they ended their call, her dream rushed back in a way so palpable and hit her with such force it would have knocked her over had she not placed her hands on the window sill to steady herself.

In her dream, she was standing in a row boat in the middle of a large lake surrounded by dense fog. As the fog began to lift its long, curly fingers, she could make out someone standing on the distant shore. The next instant the sky was suddenly open and clear, and Sam saw it was Hunter. He was facing her with his arms folded, his face firmly set, his strong legs spread in a V formation, looking like a super hero. Out of nowhere a diminutive sprite in the shape of a delicate, beautiful, seemingly ageless winged woman appeared. She was dressed in gauzy white clothing and couldn't have been more than three inches tall. She came into the dream as though she was riding the wind. She was to his left, facing him, her long green hair billowing behind her in an invisible breeze, her tiny fragile hand resting on the side of his folded arm.

It only took Sam a moment to recognize her.

"Abby! Hunter! Wait! I'm coming! I'm coming!" she shouted. "Wait for me, please!"

Sam looked desperately from side to side for the oars, the boat was rocking fiercely back and forth. Suddenly the bottom of the boat disintegrated and she felt herself about to sink when her cell phone pulled her from the dream.

She closed her eyes and pressed the tips of her fingers hard against her forehead. If Hunter's dream wasn't torturous enough, now Abby Love appeared alongside him. Sam had been so consumed with Hunter and finding Jenny that she couldn't recall the last time she thought of Abby.

Shame surged through her when she realized she hadn't been to the Denver Diner since last summer. Whenever she went there, she always came filled with hope she might see Abby Love again. The diner was the first place they had met. Sam still couldn't shake the feeling that she was somewhat to blame for Abby's disappearance. It had been more than a year since Abby and Sam had parted ways at the Care Center off West Thirty-Second Avenue and Tejon Street—the same night they had confirmed every grisly thing about Hilltop Gardens Mortuary.

The very same night that Abby vanished.

Sam pictured Hunter standing mightily on the shore as if he was about to protect Abby. She pressed the tips of her fingers against the glass, the cold sending a chill racing up her arm.

"If only you were a super hero, Hunter. You might still be here today," she said and stared out the window for what seemed a long time, thinking of her dream.

Eventually, the buildings across the way came into view.

And reality, too.

And she knew he never would be coming back.

TWENTY-FIVE

When Sam arrived at the Camino Rael Apartments shortly after sunset, the spot under the carport where Houston Meyers' truck had been parked less than twenty-four hours earlier was empty.

When she entered the complex the two American flags were floodlit and resting lifelessly against the tall poles. She parked in front of the office. Save for a security light illuminating the main door, the interior was dark. She had deliberately waited until after hours to arrive at the complex so she wouldn't have to worry about running into someone who may have worked for the apartments.

The homey scent of burning wood filled the air as she got out of the car. She walked under the light of a near-full moon toward a sheltered area containing mailboxes. Inside, the area was dimly lit and a standing chill within the confined space made her shiver. A sturdy corkboard on the wall to her left captured her attention. It was filled with information tacked on by residents about everything from selling exercise equipment to needing dog sitters or housekeepers.

She spotted a flyer on legal-sized paper in the upper right corner and walked toward it.

At the top were the words in bold letters: **HAVE YOU SEEN ME?**

The copy contained mostly grainy photographs of more than a dozen men and women of all ages, ethnicities and race who had been reported missing.

Sam frowned as she studied the snapshots of the missing. She gave only passing glances to the male photographs, but her attention lingered longer on the women's pictures. She shook her head as she scanned the brief bios under their faces, not surprised to read that some of those who had disappeared hadn't been seen in years.

She spied one pretty young Hispanic woman's photo and placed her fingertips lightly against it. The image showed the woman with flowing long dark hair, and Sam imagined that she could resemble Jenny. The missing woman would be nineteen years old now according to her bio and hadn't been seen in more than five years. She had disappeared walking home from school one afternoon. Her backpack had been found at the front gate where she lived and Sam couldn't help wondering if she had been only moments away from entering the yard and stepping inside the sanctuary of home before she went missing.

She stepped away from the paper, looking at each of the black and white photos once more. Unfamiliar images stared back at her. Strangers. Strangers to all except a handful, a few who still held out even the smallest fraction of hope for these lost souls.

She turned her attention to the thin silver mailboxes. Rows of them lined the walls and she scanned those nearest her. No names were on the front of the plates, only apartment numbers. A young couple came in to get their mail. They ignored Sam, but she turned away, pretending to read the corkboard until they left the area.

Sam scanned each of the mailboxes until she reached apartment number 303. She tapped it twice with her index finger.

On the way back to her car, she took note of a tall decorative black metal fence surrounding the pool. She drove slowly in front of the two buildings, looking up at the apartments on the third level. All the windows were dark. She glanced at the time on the car radio, seven-fifteen p.m.

Driving through the parking lot, she hunted for a decent place to park where she could blend in easily with the other vehicles while allowing her to observe the area without drawing any unwanted attention. She backed into an end spot under a hefty Cottonwood tree thick with bare branches. From here she could see the main entrance. She left the car running and with the heater on, she could feel the heat hitting the tops of her tennis shoes. Warmth crawled up her legs and she shivered again.

She lost count of the cars that drove in and out of the parking lot. She had eaten another premade sandwich, which left a sour taste in her mouth that was spreading fast to her stomach. She read the ingredients listed on the empty package, and discarded it in an empty grocery bag, deciding she'd have to find something else, better, to eat in the car. She didn't feel satisfied, so she continued snacking on her pretzels. She had ordered an Americano from *La Dolce Vita*, a drink that Mia, of course, had already prepared for Sam by the time she reached the bar. Sam slid the cover on the mug to the side and a faint scent of fresh coffee floated upward. She closed her eyes with delight and took her first sip.

After she had paid for her coffee, the café was nearly empty so she lingered a few minutes longer and chatted with Mia.

"Do you have family here in El Paso?" Mia asked.

"I'm here on business," Sam had said. She held up her drink in front of Mia. "In fact, I'm working tonight so I'm going to need this."

Mia pointed to her drink. "You're saving this for later?"

"Yes, maybe in an hour or so."

"Wait here, Sam." Mia disappeared behind a set of metal double doors. Within minutes she returned with a shiny gold-colored commuter mug. Mia removed the wrapping and rinsed the mug out. She filled it with steaming hot water.

She returned to Sam. "May I have your drink back?"

Sam handed it to Mia and watched her pour the coffee in the mug, steam rising as she covered it.

She returned it to Sam. "This'll be warm for hours."

Sam's eyes widened then matched the big smile in Mia's eyes.

"How much do I owe you for the mug?"

Mia waved her off. "Consider it my mark out. We get 'em every week."

As Sam enjoyed the warm brew in the car now, she thought first of Mia's kindness, and then of the confrontation she had witnessed between the barista and Amanda Moore.

The clock radio showed a few minutes before nine. April would have already had her bath and would be getting ready for bed. She called home and Howard answered.

"How's my girl?" he asked.

Sam smiled into the phone. "Doin' better now that I've heard your voice, Howard. What's goin' on at the ranch? Did April already have her bath?"

"She's taking it now. She and your grandmother got carried away with a project."

"A school project?" Sam asked.

"No. We were watching television and your grandmother was busy crocheting or knitting, whichever it is because you know I can never tell the difference, and April was sitting on the floor beside her recliner. She became fascinated watching her twist that yarn around those tiny metal sticks. April started asking questions and before you knew it, Frances was coaching her on how to start a pattern. I was impressed. April caught on pretty quickly and she was able to get the rows started without much of a problem."

Sam chuckled. Sports and riding ATVs, yes, but knitting (or crocheting) was the last thing she could see her daughter doing. "What's she making?"

"Well, it's supposed to be a blanket, I think, for Step," Howard said. "But unless it's going to be a small blanket, then she's got a long way to go. She said she wanted to make it with blues and yellows 'because that's Mommie's favorite colors.'"

Sam laughed and pictured April sitting next to her grandmother doing crafts. It made her feel light as air. "Well, Howard, she loves making windmills with you and now crocheting with Nona, it makes me so happy. I can't wait to see her progress once I get home."

"Speaking of home, Samantha, any idea when you'll be heading back this way?"

Sam glanced toward the carport. Houston Meyers' spot was still empty.

She sighed as she rubbed her eyes between the tips of her fingers. "Tomorrow if I could, Howard, because God knows I'm more than ready, but who knows. I do have one small development that has happened over the last few days. Of course, I'm encouraged by it right now, but who knows if it'll go anywhere. If this doesn't, then I'll give it up at least for now and come home. I miss you guys so much."

Sam told Howard about the white GMC truck and ended by saying, "I'm parked under a tree in his apartment complex right now, waiting to see what time he comes home."

"How long have you been following him?" Howard asked.

"Not long. I spotted the truck in the grocery store parking lot last night and I followed him back here."

"What kind of car are you driving?"

She glanced along the dashboard toward the glovebox. "I don't know, some kind of silver sedan. There's a half-dozen other cars in this complex that look pretty similar."

"You say he's a military guy?"

"Yeah. What're you getting at?"

"Nothing really, but I want you to be careful when following this guy. Who knows what kind of military training he's had."

"Humm," Sam said vaguely. "Thanks for pointing that out, that would've never crossed my mind, but, of course, with your military background it makes sense."

"Not that I had much in the way of that type of training, Sam, it was mainly the Merchant Marines," he said. "But I know how you operate and you're so far away from home, so I'm telling you so you can be careful. Keep your eyes open."

Sam spotted a white truck entering the complex and immediately sat taller behind the steering wheel, but it turned toward the right and disappeared around the building. "You know me well, Howard," she said. "I'll make sure to keep my distance."

Sam ended the call home talking to April who told her mother all about the new blanket she was making for Step with her mother's favorite colors.

By ten o'clock the spot under the carport was still empty and Sam was struggling to keep her eyes open. If last night was an indicator, it might be another two hours before Houston may show up.

Sam got out of the car. Several long stretches in the cold evening air revived her. The night was still and the moon had travelled its silent path toward the horizon. Thinking of what Howard had told her about her rental car, she checked the license plate and was relieved to see it was a Texas plate.

Back in the car she waited until nearly eleven p.m. until she picked up her phone and dialed Wilson's number.

"Hi, it's me," she said. "I hope I didn't wake you."

"Hello, Sam, good to hear your voice," Wilson said and she could hear voices emanating from the television in the background until he turned it down. "I've told you, call anytime. Where are you?"

"In the parking lot but not at the grocery store, at Camino Rael," Sam said and she brought him up to date on the new information and what she had learned from her conversation with police chief James Page.

"You've been sitting there all day waiting for this Houston Meyers fella to come home?"

"Yeah, I know, Wilson, it's probably a waste of time, but it's better than me sitting in my hotel room staring at the television. Besides, I've only been here since about seven. I needed to clear my head a little, so I got out this afternoon for some exercise. I didn't do anything but walk all over downtown and in and out of the shops near the border. And…" her voice faded as she shifted slightly to a more comfortable position. "I can't tell you how stiff I am from sitting in this car all the time. I feel like my bottom is about to become permanently attached to this car seat. But I can tell you one thing."

"What's that?"

"Sitting in a parked car in a parking lot for hours does give a person a lot of quiet time to think and stare."

"How did you leave it with James?" Wilson asked.

"The same way I left it with Howard, they both told me to be careful."

"You know I echo their sentiment, Sam."

"Yes, I know you do," she said and the conversation with April the night she was packing for her first trip to El Paso tiptoed in. Until her dream this afternoon with Hunter and Abby, that evening with April was nearly all she thought about.

"You and Hunter did it for hours," Wilson said.

Sadness stabbed at her heart and she spoke softly. "He made that seem so easy. Time passed so effortlessly when we had our vigils sitting in the car. Now that I'm sitting here alone, time seems to move like a glacier." She hesitated and then added, "I had a dream about Hunter and Abby. They were both standing on a distant shore and I was in a row boat about to sink. Hunter looked like a super hero and Abby was a fairy."

"Is that what you think about when you're sitting alone in the car?"

"A lot runs through my mind," Sam answered. "Tonight, especially I've thought a lot about the last night I saw Abby alive and I can still see myself screaming at Hunter to slow down and wait for me."

"Sam, you're not responsible for Hunter's death or Abby's disappearance." His calm, deep voice was firm, defined around the edges.

"I try and tell myself that too, Wilson." She felt her throat beginning to close and her eyes starting to sting. "Would you answer a question for me?"

Wilson knew from the tone in her voice it could have something to do with his sobriety.

"Maybe it's because of Hunter and wanting, really, nothing more than to find his sister that I haven't found myself wanting to drink. The urge just hasn't been there. Does that happen to you?"

"It happens to all alcoholics from time to time. It's as if you've lived a care-free life and you've never had the problem to begin with. One moment we don't think we'll make it through another minute unless we take that drink. Other times we feel so invincible we wonder why we ever thought we had the problem in the first place."

Wilson went on. "But I can tell you, Sam, each and every moment, regardless of how you're feeling or I'm feeling, comes down to one thing - choice. No matter how long it's been, ten days, ten weeks, ten years, for every single one of our choices, day in and day out, you and I are only one mistake away from having to start this journey all over again."

Sam cleared her throat softly, but said nothing. Everything he said was true.

"How much longer do you think you're going to stay there?" Wilson asked.

"I don't know. Maybe another week? I told Howard if this development doesn't pan out, I'll give it up at least for now and come home. I hope I'll still have my job…" her voice faded with expectation.

"Sam, I was talking about now, this evening. How much longer are you going to camp out at Camino Rael?"

"Oh!" she said and her laughter was filled with relief. "I thought you meant in general."

"More than anything of course I want you to come home safely, Sam, but I know how much he did for this newspaper, and how important finding Jenny was to Hunter and how much it means to you. Last thing you have to worry about from my end at least, is your job. It'll be waiting for you when you return."

They talked another ten minutes and Sam ended their phone call, staring at the empty space under the carport, alone with her thoughts.

The eleventh hour rolled into midnight, then one a.m. Long after their phone call had ended, remnants of Wilson's words, and the safe, reassuring sound of his resonant voice, kept her company in the cold car.

Sam woke with a start.

Her head was resting against the car window and she could feel a little dribble tickling the corner of her mouth.

She sat straight up and wiped away the saliva. After a moment for the fogginess to clear, she realized she had fallen asleep after her phone call with Wilson. Her feet and legs were so cold she almost couldn't feel them. Her phone had fallen on the seat between her legs. She fumbled for it and checked the time.

Three a.m.

She looked toward the carport.

Still empty.

TWENTY-SIX

S am's hand was so stiff from the cold when she tried to start the car, she had to use both hands to put the key in the ignition.

Her bladder was uncomfortably full and she knew she'd never make it back downtown to her hotel room. She left Camino Rael and was relieved to see the convenience store across the street was still open. She bought a bottle of water so she could use the bathroom.

Once on the interstate, she passed the Amanda Moore billboards until she reached her exit to the city center. In the pre-dawn hour, the amber lights along the avenues glowed in golden light, and as she reached the corner of Oregon and Mills streets, the alligator fiberglass sculpture in the center of San Jacinto Plaza was bathed in purple light so deep it gave off a blueish hue. Sam waved at the hotel attendant as she headed into the lobby. She started a hot bath as soon as she got in her room and her cell phone was down to its final bar, so she plugged it in to charge. She didn't turn on the television, preferring the quiet.

Houston Meyers apparently didn't come home. Sam couldn't help the frustration she felt when she woke in the car and saw the still-empty spot under the carport, a frustration that had continued to build during the drive back to the hotel. But by the time she warmed up in the bath her irritation had eased. When she got in bed at close to five a.m., the view beyond her hotel window showed a distant skyline still hidden in winter darkness.

Sam had her phone alarm set so she could call April, as she always did, on the way to school. April answered on the first ring and Sam listened to her chatter on about her classes and basketball practice after school with her eyes closed letting the sound of her young innocent voice fall all over her like soft summer rain. Sam fell back to sleep almost immediately after she told her daughter to be good and she'd call her tonight.

Four hours later her phone was ringing again, dragging her from a dreamless sleep. The hotel window was bathed in light, the distant foothills so bright with sunlight and shadow Sam could see crevices in the gentle rise and fall of the slopes.

She looked at the caller ID and cleared her throat before she answered.

"Wilson, hi, how are you?" she said trying to sound alert and awake.

"Good, Sam. Are you okay? It almost sounds like I woke you."

"You did, but that's okay. I got back to my room pretty late."

"How late is late?"

"About four a.m."

"That's why I was calling, to see what happened after we talked last night."

"You're going to think I'm crazy, but I fell asleep in the car."

"What time did you finally wake up?"

"Around three. I was so cold; I think that's what woke me."

"And still no Houston?"

She felt a prickle of irritation. "No, he hadn't come by the time I left."

"Interesting," Wilson said.

"What do you think that means?"

"Could mean a lot of things, Sam. Maybe he has a night job, or maybe…" Wilson's voice dropped off. "We could speculate about a lot of things, but the fact is he hadn't returned to the apartments by the time you left. What're you going to do now?"

Sam sat up in bed and pulled the sheet under her chin. "Camp out there until he comes home, I guess. It's not like I have many options."

"And then what?"

Sam gave an uncertain shrug. "Then, hopefully, I can follow him and see where he goes, what he does and if he ever does hook up with Jenny. But I keep thinking about what Sandy Petersen told me about the first night she saw them together."

"You thought Jenny had been kidnapped."

"Right, I did, but Sandy said it didn't seem like that to her because of how close Jenny was next to Houston, assuming, of course, that this Houston guy was the one with Jenny that night. For that matter, Wilson, I know Sandy said the rendering of Jenny was spot on, but who knows if it really was her? It could have easily been someone who happened to look a lot like her."

"Could've been, but what's your theory?"

Sam drew a deep long breath, letting her thoughts take over. "I wish I had a theory really, but I don't know, maybe she's caught up in something like, I don't know, human trafficking, but that seems far-fetched."

"Why do you say that?"

"Because I don't think Jenny would be so willing to stand that close to him and why would they be in the store while he was buying her junk food, which I'm guessing was for her, and give her the chance to get away or ask for help?"

"Traffickers have a lot of power over their victims. You know that, Sam."

"Yes, I know and I can only imagine," she said in a gritty voice.

"Until you ever talk to him, assuming you can, you're not going to know. As far as staking out his apartment, sounds like the most logical next step, but please don't stay so late next time. I'm not sure how safe that could be. I'd hate for a security guard or someone to tap on your window and you'd have to explain yourself."

"I agree, it's pretty foolish," Sam said and covered her mouth as she gave an embarrassed laugh. "This bed here is a lot more comfortable than that cold car."

"And if and when the situation ever presents itself, try to make sure this meeting takes place in a public area please, and preferably in the daytime."

"You know how I operate, Wilson."

"Yes, I know, that's why I'm telling you. Call me later and let me know how your day is going."

"I will. I'm going to a coffee shop I stumbled onto near the hotel, a cute little place with great coffee. When I take my first sip, I always feel like my grandmother is there with me. It's the perfect place to plan my day. Oh, by the way, how's Nick doing? Is he back to work?"

"He just came back yesterday, looking pretty haggard, too. He felt so weak, he had to leave early," Wilson said. "That flu really took a lot out of him."

After their call, Sam dressed in a clean pair of sweats and primped slightly in the bathroom mirror before she headed out to *La Dolce Vita*. She was about to enter the café when she spotted Amanda Moore's lug, as the baristas lovingly referred to him, waiting near the door. He looked even bigger than she remembered him.

She gave the giant a casual glance as she passed him and headed toward the counter. Amanda Moore was waiting for her coffee at the bar, looking sharp and sophisticated with her fine silver hair perfectly in place, and wrapped in a long dark cashmere coat that was tied tightly enough to accentuate her willowy frame. Her perfume, Coco Chanel, if Sam had to guess, was competing with the fresh coffee aroma. Amanda was wearing large round fashionable sunglasses that concealed most of her upper face. Her rose-colored lips were pursed tersely to one side, her arms folded and her hands covered with black leather gloves.

Mia was at the bar and Jeff was handling the register. They were making drinks and taking orders with their chins almost touching their chests. Mia looked up to put a drink on the bar. She spotted Sam and immediately broke into a wide grin. When she waved slightly at Sam,

Amanda looked in Sam's direction. She pulled her glasses down and the women made eye contact. Amanda set her gaze on Sam with polar-blue eyes, her right eyebrow cast in a deep arch. Sam returned the stare with an even look, emanating nothing, neither hostility or warmth.

The women kept their stance until Mia set Amanda's drink on the counter. "Here you go, Amanda, two pumps of classic syrup and steamed just the way you want, at one hundred and twenty degrees."

Amanda slipped her glasses back in place and took the coffee without offering the slightest gratitude and ignoring the tip jar. Sam and Mia watched as Amanda's henchman opened the door and followed her outside.

When Sam reached Mia she said, "I know I don't know that woman, and I shouldn't judge, but my goodness, does she have to be so hateful and rude?"

Mia shrugged. "You shouldn't worry about her. Our manager always tells us, don't be surprised at what Amanda usually does when she comes in here, only be shocked if she should give you a friendly hello or some small gesture of gratitude. *Then* be worried."

"Good words to live by," Sam said and she saluted Jeff and Mia with her coffee. "Is her office close by?"

"Just around the corner," Mia said, pointing in the general direction.

"Yeah, supposedly she has some big swanky corner office on the top floor with a great view," Jeff said from his place at the register. "One of my buddies is a delivery driver and I guess he's seen her digs."

"I have to say she's quite an attractive woman," Sam said and then did a quick inventory of her own attire. At least her sweats were clean and her shoes, casual slip-ons, new. "Looks like I don't quite measure up to her looks. I worked a little late last night and threw this on so at least I could be somewhat presentable."

Mia scoffed and dismissed Sam with a firm wave of her hand. "Oh, Sam, I remember the first day you came in here you looked so nice in that poncho you were wearing. You're so pretty."

Sam nodded graciously. "Thank you. My grandmother made that for me."

"Amanda may be beautiful on the outside and may be all about her appearance and puff her chest at all her success, but she sure as heck isn't a beautiful person on the inside," Jeff said.

Sam thanked them both and pointed to her favorite table near the window. "That's my office over there, so I'd better get to work," she said and started toward it.

Once Sam got comfortable, she opened the Reporter's Notebook she'd brought with her and promptly started to stare at it. Save for her scant notes from Margaret Sheffield and Sandy Petersen, all the remaining pages, and there were many, were blank. She wrote Houston Meyers' name at the top of a new page.

Below his name she drew an arrow facing the page and wrote: *Veteran. New truck. New boots… Wealthy, perhaps?*

Next to another arrow she wrote: *Where do you go?*

And another arrow: *What do you do?*

Sam stared at the words, her shaking her head then she wrote, *what am I missing here?*

She tried to allow herself not to feel discouraged at how little she had to go on. Hunter worked his way into her mind, and her culpability started to rise within her filling up like a well. Her emotions started to churn, but before her thoughts had the time to build, Mia came to her table with a broad smile and holding a plate. She set a toasted egg sandwich in front of Sam.

"Here, Sam, Jeff and I thought you might be getting hungry since you said you had worked late last night. I always toast them open-faced, that way the bacon and cheese cook better." She set several packets of siracha sauce down on the table. "These sandwiches can be a little bland, too, so eat it with these. It really spices it up."

Sam touched Mia lightly on the arm. "That's very sweet of you both, thank you. Looks delicious. In fact, I was starting to wonder where I should go to eat. How much do I owe you?"

"On us," Mia said and waved Sam off as she walked away from the table.

After finishing her sandwich and staring out the window for almost an hour, Sam checked her watch. The staff meeting would be starting in twenty minutes. She pulled her phone out of her bag and called Wilson.

"Hi, it's me," she said when he answered.

"Everything okay?"

It always seemed to be the first thing he asked her and she smiled at his constant concern. "Yes, everything's fine. I know you're getting ready for the staff meeting, but I wanted to run an idea by you for tonight, well, more like tomorrow morning, to see what you think."

"What're you thinking?"

"Well, I'm going back to Camino Rael, but not until around five-thirty tomorrow morning."

Wilson offered his guess. "You think if his truck is there, you'll get there in time to follow him if he leaves early to go to work."

"Precisely."

"Given that you don't have much else to go on, it's worth a try," he said. "Hopefully you'll get lucky. Keep me posted and be—"

"Careful," Sam said. "Yes, I know, Wilson, I will be."

Sam made it a point to get in bed as soon as her call home ended that evening. She left the television on through the early newscast and weather. An Amanda Moore commercial aired right after the weather forecast, a client testimonial about how Amanda got the client a settlement of nearly a quarter million dollars. "I was in my minivan with my children and waiting at a stoplight when the car behind me didn't stop," said a motherly-looking young woman. "My insurance company only offered me $50,000, but I called Amanda Moore and she made them pay. She got me almost $250,000!"

Sam grabbed the remote and turned off the TV just as the commercial finished. Though she was still awake at midnight, she must have managed to fall asleep because her phone alarm was ringing at fifteen minutes past four a.m. She showered, dressed in a dark hooded sweat top and denim, and managed to get to Camino Rael Apartments exactly one hour later.

She was relieved to see the white GMC truck was backed in under the carport. She glanced at the apartment buildings. Several lights were on in the apartments on the first and second floors, but only one apartment, the end unit on the third floor, was illuminated. Lights looked as though they were coming from a bedroom and living room.

She parked under the same Cottonwood tree, one row over.

At five thirty-five a.m. the third-floor apartment went dark. Sam sat up behind the steering wheel, her gaze fixed on the arched entryway.

A few moments later a man emerged. It was too dark to see his face or the kind of shoes he was wearing, but she was certain it was a pair of work-type boots.

He was heading toward the GMC under the carport, carrying a white hard hat under his arm and a rugged stainless steel compact lunchbox and colorful neon green vest with the other hand.

Twenty-seven

S am waited and watched as the GMC idled in place under the carport, exhaust fumes collecting around the back end.

It was hard to make out Houston's facial features behind the wheel, but she could tell he had put on a ball cap once he got in the cab.

She pulled the hood up on her sweat top to keep her blonde hair hidden and scooted as far down as she could behind the steering wheel. After five minutes, the GMC rolled slowly away from the carport. Sam waited to start the engine until the truck had reached the complex's main entrance with its left turn signal active. When Sam reached the entrance, she waited briefly before following.

That it was early was a blessing and a curse. The cover of darkness, of course, would help keep her presence to a minimum. The light pre-dawn traffic, however, would make her sedan easier to spot. Once she started to follow him, she couldn't risk getting too close to be noticed in the mirrors, yet she couldn't take the chance of falling too far behind and losing him.

Houston was less than a quarter mile in front of her and came to a stop at the intersection. She slowed her sedan to a crawl, hoping the light would change before she got much closer.

The light turned green and the GMC proceeded through the intersection and she followed a few moments later. Sam was getting to know the area well enough that she knew the interstate was about three miles ahead and guessed that's where Houston was headed. She hung back behind a delivery truck, hoping she was right. She continued to follow him at a safe distance blending in with the other early-morning traffic until Houston did signal and merge onto the interstate heading east, away from downtown. Sam had never driven this direction and she gripped the steering wheel a little tighter, feeling a lump of uncertainty in the back of her throat.

She eased onto the highway and followed him roughly two miles until he took an exit ramp. He made a left turn to head north on a two-lane road. She pulled off the interstate and coasted to the stop sign, hesitant to continue. The roadway was deserted and she did not want to bring attention to the only other set of headlights in the area. The night sky was beginning to lighten and the flat, open landscape allowed her an expansive view of the area. Off to the right she could see a housing development under construction.

Houston's GMC appeared to be heading in that general vicinity. She checked her mirrors. No one was behind her, so she was content to wait a little longer at the stop sign. As Houston signaled and turned into the construction site, Sam glanced at the time on the car radio, two minutes before six a.m.

"Well, if he's starting at six, he's right on time," she said to herself.

She made the turn and drove slowly. As she neared the site's main entrance, a tall narrow lighted sign to a small retail center loomed to her left. She continued toward the strip mall, relieved the businesses would open soon so her car wouldn't be the only vehicle in the lot. A handful of businesses were listed on the sign, a tire store and an automotive parts store served as anchors. A smoke shop and an empty storefront occupied the center of the strip.

Sam pulled into the lot and stopped along the wall by the tire store, parking as far back as she could. From here she could see the wooden ribs of homes under construction. The GMC and two other trucks were parked in front of a portable trailer that had to be the office for the project. The digital camera was on the seat next to her, with the zoom lens still attached, and she snapped a few photographs of Houston's truck and the others in front of the building. Despite using the zoom lens, she was still too far away to get useable photos of the license plates.

The construction area was fully fenced. A Zia sun symbol was centered in the middle of a large bright yellow tarp, which covered a portion of the fence nearest the entrance. In the center of the Zia's circle was the name of the company, Zia Construction. Two large No Trespassing signs were posted on the opposite side of the main gate and another sizeable sign positioned directly below threatened trespassers with arrest and prosecution.

Sam snapped a handful of photos of the entrance. In her Reporter's Notebook she wrote the name of the construction company, thinking of Hunter. If he were sitting here with her, he would have used his natural artistic talent to draw the Zia symbol. No doubt he would have captured the circle perfectly, with its four groups of varying lines extending from top to bottom, left to right, lines which represented the four cardinal directions, the four seasons, the four periods of the day and the four seasons of life.

Sam settled in to wait. By seven a.m. the tire store was open and already bustling with business and vehicles continued to arrive at the construction site. An hour later, the auto parts store had opened and the entire area in front of the portable building was filled with cars.

It was a few minutes after nine when Sam thought to send Sandy a text.

Sandy, I had a little luck. I was able to follow Houston to work!

Sandy responded immediately. *That's wonderful, Sam! Where?*

He drove to a construction site east of downtown.

Oh yeah, Zia Construction. It's a New Mexico-based company (obviously!) They've had a pretty strong presence in ELP for the last few years.

I'm guessing he's a foreman or something.

Maybe. What's your plan?

Sam sent a text with a half-dozen question marks followed by *I wish I knew!*

Making it up as you go, was Sandy's reply.

Yeah. From the seat of my pants and hoping for the best.

But look how far you've come since that night in the grocery store!

Thanks to you. With that and knowing more about this guy, I'm feeling more encouraged. I'll keep you posted.

Call or text anytime.

Sam responded with a thumbs-up emoji.

By nine a.m. the sun had fully risen above the Franklin Mountains and was reflecting so brightly off the roofs of the vehicles and the portable building Sam had to put on her sunglasses. Without having to check the time on her cell phone she knew it was past time for coffee. She remembered seeing a trailblazing sign on the interstate with the logo of a popular coffee company. She was sure the coffee wouldn't be as good or as comforting as *La Dolce Vita's*, but it would have to do.

Construction activity was teeming and she remembered seeing Houston carrying a lunch box. Certain he wouldn't be leaving before she returned, she decided it was safe to venture out for coffee.

Within the hour, Sam was back near the construction site and parked in a different spot. She had settled again and was sipping coffee, looking at Zia Construction's website, when her phone lit up with Wilson's phone number.

"Morning," she said and felt herself smiling.

"Sam, how are you?"

"Better now that I'm here having coffee."

"Where's here?"

"At the construction site where it looks like Houston works."

"I take it you were able to follow him from Camino Rael this morning?"

"This gamble paid off," Sam said and brought Wilson up to date on her early-morning venture.

"Where are you parked?"

"There's a retail strip center across the road from the main entrance." Sam watched an employee from the tire shop changing a tire in front of

155

one of the garages. "Thankfully, there's a tire shop and an auto parts store in here because cars have come and gone already all morning."

"That's good, that way you won't be so noticeable. What else is in the area?"

Sam looked south. The arid landscape was open and empty, stretching toward the Rio Grande and the Mexican border. She glanced toward the north. "Nothing to the south of here. The mountains are to the north and the road continues in that direction. I see another, smaller housing development a few miles from here. I'll take a drive up there later."

"Keep me posted," Wilson said and they ended the call in their usual way, with Wilson telling her to be careful.

It was nearing five p.m., and save for a quick drive through the other housing development and using the bathroom in the tire shop, Sam hadn't left the retail center all day.

Most of the construction workers had left the site by four thirty. Only the three original trucks from the morning remained in front of the building. At fifteen minutes past the hour, one man emerged from the building. Sam was too far away to see his face, but she knew it wasn't Houston. She grabbed the camera and took photos of him in rapid succession.

A half-hour later, Houston emerged from the building and removed his ball cap as he headed for his vehicle. Sam leaned slightly to her right to hide from view as his truck reached the gate and waited for traffic to pass. He headed for the interstate and she followed moments later behind a row of cars. She spotted the GMC getting on the highway and two miles later, he took the same exit. Sam followed him back to Camino Rael. He backed in under the carport as she pulled into the convenience store. She watched him cross the parking lot carrying his lunchbox and vest. His hard hat tucked under his arm.

She waited until he disappeared under the entryway before she entered the complex. Her spot under the Cottonwood tree was vacant and she backed in. She was about to settle in for another wait but by six-thirty, her backside was aching and she kept rolling her head from side to side trying to relieve the stiffness. And she was starving. "I'm sorry, Hunter," she said, attempting to stretch behind the steering wheel. "But

I just can't do this another minute."

Sam was back downtown and in her hotel room thirty minutes later.

The following day was a carbon copy of day one. Sam arrived at Camino Rael by five-thirty a.m. and Houston left for work ten minutes later. She got coffee after nine a.m. and used the bathroom again in the tire shop. While getting coffee, she also bought a protein box filled with fruit, cheese and nuts and that kept her satisfied through the early afternoon. Houston didn't emerge from the portable office building the entire day. She was relieved the winter weather was pleasant and no one from the stores in the retail center questioned her about being parked in the area.

By five-fifteen, the orb of the sun hovered just above the horizon.

Houston emerged from the building and walked toward his truck as he had done the day before. He was back at Camino Rael and parked under the carport and Sam back under the Cottonwood tree before six p.m. She decided to wait at least until seven and tried to make good use of her time sifting through work emails, but she was too hungry to concentrate. She put her phone in her bag and started the car and was about to leave when she happened to look toward the curved entryway.

To her surprise, Houston emerged.

She forgot her hunger and sat up taller behind the wheel. "Well, what have we here?"

Houston had changed from his construction clothes to a gray long sleeve shirt that opened at the collar and dark slacks. There was a large red logo on the side of his sleeve. He was carrying his lunchbox again.

Sam squinted. "Looks like a security guard's uniform."

He got in the GMC, and at the apartment's entrance, turned in the same direction he had for work. Sam guessed he would be heading toward the interstate again and waited a moment before starting to follow him. Houston did take the same exit onto the interstate, but this time headed west toward downtown. Sam had to speed up to reach the exit. Traffic heading toward the city center was heavy and she was thankful to be able to blend in easily.

Houston took the same downtown exit Sam would take to get to the hotel. He turned on the street before her hotel. She managed to get close enough to see him pull into an underground garage. She passed in front of it, but his truck had already traveled down an incline and disappeared deeper inside. She noted the name of the office building and pulled to the side of the street and wrote it in her Reporter's Notebook.

She drove to her hotel and waved at the attendant as she entered the lobby. She placed her things on the desk in her room and went to the bathroom. "Why do you need two jobs, Houston?" she asked, looking at herself in the mirror. She brushed her teeth and took a few moments to primp, then grabbed her bag and left her room.

A rush of cold evening air hit Sam as she left the hotel and headed back toward the office building. It was dark now and activity downtown had subsided. She deliberately stayed on the opposite side of the street as she reached the office building. Through the expansive windows she could see an information desk in the lobby situated in front of the main entrance. Houston was standing at the far corner of the desk, talking to another security guard who was sitting behind it. He had set his lunchbox on the counter. Moments later the two men changed positions and the other man waved at Houston as he headed toward the elevators.

Sam shrugged. *A night watchman.*

Her cell phone showed ten minutes after seven and she speculated he was settling in for an eight-hour shift. Sam was back in her room twenty minutes later and had ordered room service. After she called home, she returned to the lobby and ventured back to the office building. Houston was still sitting at the information desk. When she got back in her room, she turned on the television for the local news and called Wilson.

"Hi Sam, I was just going to call you," Wilson said when he answered. "Anything new?"

"In fact, there may be," she said and relayed the events of the day and ended by saying, "I walked over there again about thirty minutes ago and he's still sitting at the desk."

"An eight-hour shift puts him at about four a.m. A long day," Wilson said.

"Right, so I'm guessing he's either off from the construction job tomorrow or he's got another long day ahead of him."

"One or the other, but keep me posted," Wilson said.

Before Sam got in bed at midnight, she returned to the office building for another, final look. Houston was still perched behind the desk, looking as though he hadn't moved since her last visit.

At four-fifteen a.m. Sam's alarm sounded. She opened her eyes halfway and stared at the window, feeling the fatigue that seemed to have settled deep in her bones. She did not want to get up, but Hunter's cheerful, relaxed face the night in front of the bonfire at the ranch, the day before his life—and hers—would drastically change, flashed before her. She threw the bedspread aside and headed for the shower.

By five-thirty a.m. she was back at Camino Rael and Houston had backed his GMC under the carport, just as Wilson and Sam had surmised.

Ten minutes later he emerged from the vaulted entryway and headed for his truck, carrying his lunchbox, hard hat and neon green vest.

TWENTY-EIGHT

The third day passed in a mirror image of the previous ones.

At five-fifteen p.m. Sam watched Houston emerge from the portable office building, wearing his ball cap and vest and carrying his hard hat and lunchbox. She fastened her seatbelt, ready for the journey back toward Camino Rael, wondering how long she would have to sit under the Cottonwood tree tonight.

Houston pulled to a stop at the main entrance and waited for traffic to clear. Once it did, however, he didn't move and the truck's turn signal wasn't flashing.

More vehicles passed north and south.

Sam frowned. Considered. Frowned again.

Another round of vehicles passed in front of the main gate. The third time there was a break in traffic, the GMC started to move. And then, to her surprise, instead of turning toward the interstate he crossed the road and entered the strip mall.

Houston pulled up right in front of Sam's sedan with such speed, she didn't have time to react.

She was still sitting there with her hands on the steering wheel when he jumped down out of his truck and charged to the driver's side window.

He glared at her, his face an angry, contorted mess. His dark eyes nearly bulging out of his head. "Why the hell are you following me?!"

Sam felt so paralyzed with fear, she couldn't move.

TWENTY-NINE

Sam kept her hands on top of the steering wheel and looked up at Houston.

Sandy Peterson was right the night she told Sam he had the jowls of a bulldog. She remembered what Sandy had said about his hair, but he was still wearing his ball cap, so it was difficult to tell how thin it was or how it was combed, but at this distance Sam could see every crevasse in his craggy face.

She held her breath as she tilted her head toward the passenger seat. "I have something in my bag, photos, I want to show you." She was trying to think as quickly and clearly as she could while speaking with a confidence that eluded her. "But I don't want to move my hands unless you're comfortable with me doing so."

Houston took a step back from the car door, his hands clenched against his side. He was medium height, though he didn't appear threatening, his frame was wiry and gritty and seemingly packed with strength.

Sam took a hard swallow, trying to control her breathing and hoped he wasn't carrying a weapon. "How did you know I was following you?"

Houston's chin jutted out toward the businesses in the strip mall. "I've got buddies here who gave me a heads up that your sedan's been in the parking lot all day for the last three days. When I'd leave, you'd leave. I saw your car yesterday when I was leaving, so you know where I live."

Sam nodded trying to keep her poise. "Camino Rael."

He didn't react and didn't mention her following him to the office building downtown last night, so neither did she.

Sam was churning inside with fear, yet was surprised her trepidation didn't seem to be getting the better of her. Hunter's image in front of the fire at the ranch flashed before her again just as it did this morning when her alarm sounded.

She was afraid of what Houston could do to her now, she knew he was certainly angry enough to hurt her. She was, however, more afraid of letting this moment, this finite opportunity, slip by because her fear was too great not to take the next step.

Sam attempted to keep her voice calm and even. "Obviously then you already know I've been over here."

He jabbed an angry finger toward her face. "Lady, if I were you, I'd start talking and then get lost or you're not gonna like the consequences."

"I happen to know your name is Houston Meyers and I know you're a decorated veteran." She pointed toward his GMC. "Your license plate notwithstanding."

His eyes narrowed and his mouth dropped open slightly. Though his body language was tense and uninviting, Sam felt almost immediately there was something else about him that ran deeper, like still waters perhaps, an underlying sense of calmness and self-assurance that couldn't be rattled and seemed to emanate from the core of him.

"How do you know me?" he asked, his voice slightly less hostile.

"I don't," Sam replied calmly, matter-of-factly. "I don't know you at all, but yes, since you know now, I've been following you because I have to talk to you. I've come all the way from Denver to talk to you because you're the only one who can help me."

"From Denver?"

"Yes."

"What're you doing here in El Paso?"

She would answer his query with time. "I'm, well, looking for someone."

He looked at her sideways.

"Is there a place we can go, a public place where we can talk?" Sam asked. "If you can't help me, I promise you, I'll leave and go back to Denver, but I can't do that until at least I've had the chance to talk to you."

She stared across the roadway. The last truck at the construction site was stopped at the main gate and a man was pulling it closed. She went on. "Right now, you're the only hope I have, the only person who can help me." She removed her hands from the steering wheel and let them fall in her lap. "I'm not a threat. I mean, look at me. At least hear what I have to say. Please."

His face went flat as he considered her request. "Follow me," he said finally and stepped away from her car.

Sam watched Houston return to his pickup, taking note of his boots. He climbed back in his truck and Sam followed him from the parking lot toward the interstate. He took the exit ramp, heading toward downtown.

Sam called Wilson after she got on the highway. He answered on the second ring, his deep voice spilling out through the speaker and filling the interior of the car like a reservoir.

"Did I catch you at a good time?" she asked, glancing quickly at the time on the car radio.

"Just heading to a meeting, Sam, is everything okay?"

"I think so. First, I have to tell you I didn't do such a hot job of keeping myself hidden, but I hope everything's okay. Wilson, you're not going to believe what happened."

He listened intently as Sam told him about Houston approaching her car.

"He came up to the window just like that?" he said when she finished telling him.

"Yes, at first I thought I was going to throw up, I was so scared. But

I was still in the parking lot, thank goodness, and there was still plenty of activity going on around us."

"Where're you going now?"

Sam kept her eyes on Houston's truck as it passed by the exit to the city center she normally took. "I don't know. We just passed the exit to my hotel."

"Sam, is this such a good idea? You have no idea where you're going."

"No, I don't, but if it's not a public place that doesn't seem safe, I won't get out of the car. I'll just keep driving."

Wilson's dissatisfaction, his fear for her came through in his voice. "Sam, I don't think this is a good idea. You should turn around now and go back to the hotel."

"And do what, Wilson, stare at the wall? This is the only lead I have right now, and probably ever will have. Returning to the hotel is not an option."

She passed by Concordia Cemetery. She could see some of the makeshift crosses sticking up from the ground.

She took one hand off the wheel and pressed it firmly against her chest. "I can only live with myself knowing that I tried to find Jenny and coming all this way to go back to the hotel room is not an option."

"What makes you think he'll talk to you?"

"I don't know if he will, but I have to try," she said, irritation climbing in her voice. "At least he seemed open to this much."

Wilson sighed with resignation, knowing when her mind was made up, there was nothing he could do to change it. "Okay, just make sure he knows you've told someone else you're with him, and that you have told this person everything about him right down to his license plate and shoe size."

"You have my word," she said.

"Keep me posted, Sam, and please be careful."

"I'll call you as soon as I'm back in my room."

Houston took the next exit and waited by the side of the road for Sam to catch up. At the light he turned right and she followed him another half mile. He made another left on what turned out to be a residential street and Sam felt a bubble of apprehension start to climb in her chest. She slowed down taking in her surroundings, modest Spanish-style houses dotted with ornamental iron work and terracotta roofs on both sides of the street.

They stopped at a stop sign at the corner of Mobile Avenue and Piedras Street. Across the street, Sam saw the name of a pub, Nite Owl, a battered-looking tan stucco building with brown and crimson trim and black ornate bars against the windows that occupied the entire left corner of the street. As she followed the GMC into a parking lot behind the restaurant, her fear eased slightly at seeing a half-dozen other vehicles, trucks mostly, parked around the tavern.

Houston parked and Sam pulled in next to him. He was already standing at her car door, waiting for her. Stiff with inactivity Sam was slow to get out. She put her tote over her shoulder and grabbed the bag with Jenny and Hunter's photos inside. Houston pointed toward the entrance and stepped aside, allowing her to go first.

When the door opened, a handful of burly-looking men bent over the bar turned toward it. They eyed Sam suspiciously until they saw Houston enter behind her. Their rugged faces relaxed and they turned back toward the bar.

Houston pointed to a booth near a saloon-style door that led into the kitchen and they headed toward it. Brass sconces hung on dark-paneled walls, and the interior looked as weather-beaten as the exterior.

Sam took the side facing the main entrance. A moment after Houston was seated the waitress was standing at their table, smiling and looking clearly as though she knew him. She was tall and skinny with fashionable, light pink hair pulled back in a ponytail. She wore a simple and stylish diamond nose stud near her right nostril that accentuated her pretty, soft skin. She wore white fashionable sneakers without laces and the tattoos on both arms went beyond the cap sleeves of her T-shirt, which had an owl on a perch over the pocket. Sam didn't notice a nametag.

"Hey, big guy, how was your day?" The waitress was pulling a small white pad and pen from her apron pocket.

"Can't complain," Houston said.

"Your usual?"

He nodded and pointed at Sam. "You wanna beer?"

She looked at the waitress and said, "A club soda, please."

"You got it, be back in a few." She stuck the pad back in her apron pocket without writing down the order. When she turned toward the bar, Sam noticed the same image of the owl on the back of her T-shirt.

Houston was giving her a searing look when she finally turned toward him.

"Who are you?" he asked.

"My name is Samantha Church. I'm a newspaper reporter from Denver, Colorado."

That was the easy part.

THIRTY

"Start talking," Houston said, giving Sam a flinty, cynical look. "How'd you know my name and where I live?"

"A friend at the Grandview police department back home ran your license plate."

Houston's right eyebrow flickered upward.

"I know you were born sixty-eight years ago in Slidell, Louisiana, and Meyers is spelled with two e's and an s. Reporters have a thing with getting names spelled correctly," Sam said lightly, hoping to ease the tension between them. "I had already followed you to your apartment, but I was given your address, too."

He gave her a sideways glare. "You'd already been following me?"

She nodded and swallowed hard. "I followed you home from the grocery store."

"The one a few miles from my apartment?"

Again, she nodded.

"You had followed me to the grocery store?"

Sam shook her head. "I had been staking out the grocery store for about three days. And, to be honest, I was about to give up you'd show up at all. When you got out of the truck and I saw your boots, that's what got my attention."

"My boots?" Houston stuck his foot out from under the table and they both looked at it. The cameo-colored boot looked clean and rugged. He turned it slightly and Sam noticed a military emblem intricately carved into the side of the heel, just as Sandy said she had noticed when he and Jenny were standing in the checkout line.

"Yes, military-style boots," Sam said.

"Why was that important?" he asked.

"It's not really," Sam said. "It's just that the person who saw you that first night commented on how sharp your boots looked. I had to believe you were the person my friend saw, so I followed you back to Camino Rael."

"How'd you know I shopped there?"

"Well, that's what I want to talk to you about."

"Then get to the point," Houston snapped. "You've stalled enough already with all this crap about grocery stores and military boots."

Sam pulled a thin white napkin from the dispenser and started to fidget with it, not knowing where or how to begin to tell him what had brought her all this way. She wished she were back home and back at *The Grandview Perspective*. She wished Hunter was still alive and sitting across the desk from her, calling her *Blondie* and talking about his mother's home cooking, and she didn't have to do this.

Finally, Sam said, "Does the name Hunter John Hollingsworth mean anything to you?"

Houston's rough face remained blank.

She sighed, of course it wouldn't.

"You say you're from Denver and work for a newspaper up there?"

"That's right," Sam said.

"How do I know you're telling me the truth?"

She pulled her phone from her bag and brought the newspaper's website up and showed him her name in the masthead. Several stories with her byline appeared on the main page and she showed them to Houston. Then she went to the *About Us* page and showed him her headshot and the bio below it.

"So, you're here to cover a story about someone named Hunter Hollings-something or other."

"Hollingsworth." Sam grimaced. "And I'm not here to cover a story about him. In fact, I'm not here covering any kind of story."

The waitress came to the table carrying a brown tray at her side. She set Sam's club soda in front of her and a long-neck bottle of beer before Houston. She placed a small dish of nuts and snack crackers in the center of the table.

"You guys enjoy," she said and tapped Houston on the shoulder. "Holler at me, big guy, if you need anything."

Houston removed his ball cap and set it on the bench beside him and then took a long swallow of beer, his Adam's apple bobbing. Sam remembered how Sandy had described his hair. Though his gray hair didn't appear greasy or dirty, as she had said, only sparse and he had combed it straight back from his high forehead.

"Will you at least hear me out before you say anything?" Sam asked. "Please."

His stony silence gave her permission to continue, and knowing she had nothing to lose, spent the next thirty minutes telling Hunter's story. How he had started as a cub reporter at the *Perspective*. About the anonymous letter for help written in Spanish that came addressed to her at the newspaper and how Hunter, because he was fluent in Spanish, was pulled in to help Sam work on the story. She explained everything to Houston, the places they had gone together to cover the story, how many nights they sat in the station wagon watching the activity at the cell phone store and, finally, what had led to his death.

"Hunter and I spent a lot of time in the car together last summer, talking about everything," Sam went on. "How his parents were killed, how he became an orphan, what brought him to Denver and what had happened to his sister, Jenny, after the car accident."

Sam paused, ready for a visible reaction from Houston.

She had deliberately waited until the end of her story before she said

Hunter had a sister named Jenny. Houston remained just as he had when she started her story, indifferent with his hands folded on the table in front of him.

Sam tried not to feel deflated at his lack of reaction. "Does the name Jenny Hollingsworth mean anything to you?"

Houston shook his head slowly and grabbed his beer bottle with two fingers.

"I want to show you something," Sam said and reached for her bag. She pulled out the rendering Elsa Greer had done of Jenny. She placed it on the table and slid it toward Houston, holding it up at the corner with the tips of her fingers.

Houston tried to keep his face impartial, but before it could turn flinty again Sam saw in it the slightest hesitation, a softening around his eyes and a slight upward curve at the corners of his mouth. His forehead, heavy with lines so deep it looked like a washboard, softened; his shoulders eased and he leaned closer to the table. He stared at the rendering a moment longer before he pulled a pair of reading glasses from his shirt pocket and put them on. He slid the rendering out of Sam's grasp and pulled it close to him with such care and tenderness it was as though he had picked up a wounded baby chick.

Sam's heartbeat quickened as she watched Houston study the photo. Blinking slowly, his eyes moved methodically over her image as though he was committing the sight of her to memory. He continued to hold the photograph softly between his fingers.

"Who is this?" he asked.

"I think you know."

When he didn't respond, Sam said, "Her name is Jenny Hollingsworth. She was Hunter's sister and only months old when the accident happened. She was in her car seat and wasn't hurt in the crash. Hunter was badly injured and their cousin, who was in the car, too, also died."

"When did this happen?"

"September," Sam said and told him the year. She added, "Hunter was in the hospital for almost a month after the accident. Marked his birthday while in the ICU. When he got out, he and Jenny went to live with their aunt, their mother's sister, in *Juárez* for a year or so. That's how he became fluent in Spanish. The aunt didn't know English."

Sam told Houston why Hunter had returned to the United States and why Jenny had stayed with their aunt.

"The aunt was their mother's sister?"

Sam nodded.

"And their parents were from Mexico?"

"Only Rita. John was born here in El Paso."

The waitress returned to the table with a glass of water and set it in front of Houston. He touched her lightly on the forearm as a gesture of gratitude and the waitress nodded.

"Another club soda?" she asked, looking at Sam.

"No thank you. I'm fine."

"Where did the aunt live in Mexico?" Houston asked as the waitress retreated from the table.

Sam shrugged. "I don't remember the name of the town. I'm sorry, but I'm not good enough with Spanish names like that without looking at a map. It was somewhere deep in Mexico, though, from what Hunter told me."

Houston let the photo of Jenny fall on the table in front of him and he folded his hands over the top of it, as if he had no intention of returning it to Sam.

Sam reached in her bag and pulled out the photo of Hunter by the fire. She slid it in front of him. He looked at it but didn't reach for it.

"That's Hunter," Sam said, pointing at it. "My daughter took this photo of him last September at the ranch where I live. The next day was the beginning of the end for him." She stopped and took a sip of her club soda, struggling not to become emotional. The bubbles cooled the back of her throat, refreshing her.

"I came here to El Paso, Houston, because Hunter wanted nothing more than to find his sister, and this was the only place he knew to start. I've used this photo of him and these…" her voice faded as she reached in her bag for the last three photos. She placed them in front of Houston.

"This one," Sam was pointing to Hunter and Jenny as children sitting on the couch, "Was taken just months before the accident, and this one," she pointed to the photo of John and Rita in the hospital room, "was taken when Hunter was born, and this one here was also taken weeks, maybe a month or so before the accident."

It showed his mother holding Jenny and Hunter sitting in the bed of an old pickup, an image Hunter's father had captured somewhere in the Franklin Mountains.

"I gave all these to a forensic artist with the police department in Grandview and from those she drew this rendering of Jenny."

"That still doesn't explain how you think I'm involved or how I could possibly help you," Houston said.

"When I came to El Paso for the first time in January, I talked to a professor at UTEP where Hunter's father taught. Through him I hooked up with another teacher who had Hunter in her kindergarten and first grade class. I gave her a copy of this rendering and she's the one who saw you that night in the grocery store..." Sam paused for a moment, running the tips of her fingers over the rim of her glass. "With Jenny."

For the first time Sam became aware of music playing in the background. The familiar country song, *What if,* captured her attention. She thought of listening to it through her headphones off the playlist April had created for her, the first night she rode her exercise bike.

What if. What if this were only a bad dream and I'll wake up soon, get ready for work and Hunter will already be there when I walk in the newsroom. What if. If only. What if.

Houston continued to stare numbly at the photos.

Sam added, "She said Jenny was standing so close to you in the checkout line and that you paid for the items, mostly junk food, with cash. She said it looked like Jenny was wearing a man's winter jacket."

Sam stopped and let the song finish before she continued. "Was that your jacket, Houston?"

For a long time neither spoke. Houston regarded Sam; his flat expression unchanged. She stared at him, her lips thin, her nostrils flared.

He removed his reading glasses, returned them to his pocket and sat against the tall back of the booth. His hands still covering the rendering. When he spoke, finally, it was a low murmur. "I can't believe how much this looks like her."

Sam couldn't help the gasp that escaped her mouth. The conversation she had with Sandy the first night she saw them forced its way in.

"That rendering was spot on, but it sure didn't do her justice."

"What do you mean?"

"It captured her image, but it didn't capture how beautiful she is."

"It is Jenny then," Sam said, and it wasn't a question.

Houston nodded with conviction. "It's her, exactly the way she looks." He touched the right side of his face, near the corner of his mouth. "She has a little beauty mark here. Sometimes it gets lost in a small dimple that forms when she laughs or smiles."

Sam was thankful to be sitting down, otherwise she was certain her knees would have buckled beneath her. His words, his confirmation of Jenny made Sam feel so giddy with excitement her head started to spin. She placed her hands firmly on the seat and took a deep breath to calm herself.

"Jenny doesn't know any of this," Houston said.

She nodded. "How could she? If she was told something different by someone else? She was a baby the last time Hunter saw her, and from what he guessed she may never have learned any of this from her aunt."

Houston's demeanor turned icy again and he sneered at Sam. "How do I know any of this, this story, this Hunter guy, you're telling me is true? Yeah, I know the person in the picture is her, but how do I know your story about her is real and this isn't some elaborate con?"

"Because it isn't, Houston," Sam said simply and she gestured toward Jenny's rendering. "I saw your reaction when I first set that in front of you. Even if you never told me a thing, the way you reacted, I knew it was her the moment I put it in front of you. And this picture here," her voice faded as she sifted through the renderings until she found the one of Hunter and Jenny on the couch. She pointed to the little stuffed elephant next to Jenny. "That was in a box of Hunter's personal items I took from his apartment. It's in my bedroom at home."

Houston took the rendering of Jenny, folded it carefully and Sam watched him slip it gently inside his shirt pocket. They had been in the tavern for over an hour. His face was weary, the lines on his brow thicker, deeper now, his brown eyes rimmed with red. He had to be exhausted, working all day, then the night as a security guard and returning to work another full day with so little sleep.

Sam wanted to know more about that, about everything and she wanted Houston to take her to Jenny this very moment, but she couldn't push anymore tonight.

"What I'm telling you is true, Houston. Hunter only wanted to find his sister, to find the only connection to his family he had left."

She waited a time before she continued, hoping her words would find a place deep within him and settle like an anchor. "Now that he's gone, it's all the more urgent I find her." She placed an open hand against her chest. "At least it is to me. This is the last thing I can do for him. If you can help me, help me do that for Hunter, that's all I'm asking."

"She doesn't have much, nothing really, and she's so thin that when we're out like that and it's cold," Houston started by saying, "I make sure I have something warm in the truck she can wear."

Sam realized he was referring to the jacket. It was his jacket that kept Jenny warm and a deep sorrow bracketed her eyes.

"But I can't talk about this anymore tonight," Houston said without apologizing. "I've had a few long days with work and I gotta get some sleep."

"Will you meet me somewhere tomorrow, Houston? Please. There's still more I need to tell you."

"Where?" he asked and he placed his hand lightly against his shirt pocket over the rendering of Jenny.

Sam couldn't help wondering if he realized what he was doing.

"Where?" Sam shrugged. "I don't know much about El Paso."

Then she remembered passing the cemetery on the way to the pub.

"Can you meet me at Concordia Cemetery in the morning? There you can see for yourself."

Houston reached for his ball cap, considering her request. "What time?"

"Ten?"

He centered his cap over his brow and signaled for the waitress.

"Heading out, big guy?" she asked when she got to the table.

Sam reached for her bag to pay the tab, but he waved her off. He nodded at the waitress and Sam watched him take two twenties from his wallet and hand it to her.

"Change?" she asked, but Sam could tell she already knew the answer.

Her smile was gracious. "See ya soon," she said and left the table.

Houston got to his feet, but Sam stayed in the booth, looking up at him.

"Which entrance?" he asked.

"I'll look for your truck."

Houston headed for the door. Sam watched and waited until he went outside and the door closed behind him. She collected the other photos and returned them to her bag. By the time she got outside, the GMC was gone and the air had grown considerably colder. The wind had picked up with enough force that it caught Sam off guard, slightly pushing her backward.

She lowered her head and started for her sedan, her arms folded while a harsh wind gnawed at her heels.

THIRTY-ONE

Wilson was trying to stay focused on the evening news, but he couldn't keep his mind off Sam.

It was ten minutes past ten and she still hadn't called. He had wanted to call her, but each time he talked himself out of dialing her number.

He knew she could take care of herself, but he couldn't take it any longer. He grabbed his cell phone off the coffee table and dialed her number, uneasiness churning in his gut like a winter storm. He held his breath, counting the number of rings when Sam finally answered on the fifth one.

"Sam, where are you? Is everything okay?"

"Hi Wilson, I was just about to call, everything's fine."

As her voice spilled out evenly from the speaker, his worry for her lifted like fog and he couldn't help smiling.

"I'm pulling into the garage at the hotel right now," she said. "Can I call you back in a few minutes once I get upstairs?"

"Yes, yes, I'll be here," he said and ended the call.

Wilson sat on the couch and put his phone back on the coffee table. Ten minutes later Sam's face and phone number lit up his screen. He answered before the first ring could finish. "I was getting a little worried," he said. "How did it go?"

"We went to a tavern of all places," Sam started by saying. "But it could've been a coffee shop or whatever because it didn't seem to bother me. Thank goodness. But then I had other things on my mind."

"Yes, you do," Wilson agreed.

"Wilson, it's her. It's Jenny. When I showed Houston the rendering, his reaction at seeing her picture was unmistakable."

"That's good to hear, Sam, hopefully another step closer," Wilson said.

"At first, he was pretty hostile toward me. He didn't believe what I told him about Hunter, but the longer he looked at Jenny's photo, the more it seemed like he was coming around."

She gave Wilson the highlights of her conversation with Houston and ended by saying, "We're meeting tomorrow at Concordia Cemetery."

"What time?"

She told him. "I still have so much more to tell him, but I deliberately kept some things close to my chest. We'll see how tomorrow goes before I say anything else."

"Sounds promising," Wilson said.

"I hope so. I was thinking of Hunter on the way back here and I'll be honest, I cried because I know this is all he wanted and I can only imagine given the way I feel, the excitement, the anticipation at seeing someone you love and haven't seen in years…" her voice fell away and she felt herself on the verge of more tears, so she changed the subject.

"How's work?"

"Good. Of course, it's not the same without you," Wilson said and gave a small laugh. "I think even Nick misses you a little."

Sam laughed, too, but hers was more cutting. "I doubt that."

"He stopped by my office this afternoon on his way out and actually asked if I had heard from you. I gave him the Reader's Digest version of what you had uncovered so far. And, Sam, I have to be honest, he did seem impressed, though I also think he was trying not to show it."

"Did he ask when I was coming back?"

"He did, but I said at least at this moment, there's no time frame. I reminded him of what Hunter had done for this newspaper. He knows why it is so important."

"Thank you, Wilson," Sam said. "Thank you for being so understanding with this because I know you don't have to be. Most employers would never do what you've done."

"I'm not most employers."

Sam laughed with relief and gratitude. "Yes, I know that and I know I don't have to tell you, but your support has made being here so much easier."

They talked another few minutes and Wilson told her goodnight and to sleep well.

When their call ended and her photo faded from view on his cell phone, Wilson went to his contacts and brought up her information again, simply to look at her photo.

He had taken it of her when he was at the ranch in September for his sixtieth birthday.

Sam was walking toward him in the emerging mellow darkness with April at her side. She had taken April's hand and had bent down to listen to something her daughter was saying. Wilson had managed to capture the look of a mother's love on her face as she listened.

He stared at it for what seemed a long time, rubbing his thumb over her image, happily feeling the corners of his mouth inch upward.

THIRTY-TWO

When Sam woke the next morning, the view from her hotel window revealed cold, iron skies, and she thought of the bitter wind that had pushed her toward her car the night before.

Perhaps not the best weather for a trip to the cemetery, but cold or not, she would be there and could only hope Houston wouldn't let her down.

After she talked to April on her way to school, Sam got ready. Getting dressed in front of the bathroom mirror, she thought of her daughter wearing her basketball jersey with the number ten emblazoned on the back and over the left front pocket. She was wearing black sweatpants and the new tennis shoes she got with the gift card Wilson had given her for her birthday. April was always happy when she could wear something to school besides her uniform. Sam stood gazing out the window listening to her daughter chatter away as Howard drove her to school, telling her mother about the double-header basketball game in the school gymnasium tomorrow morning.

"Another game on Saturday?" Sam had asked.

"Mom, whenever we play our doubleheaders, it's always on Saturday."

Sam was on speaker phone, so Howard chimed in, "Don't worry, Samantha, I'll make sure the games are recorded."

"Thank you, Howard, of course I'd rather be there in person to watch you, Baby, but I can't wait to see a replay of all your games when I get home."

"When are you comin' home, Mommie?"

April's words wounded Sam and she closed her eyes so she couldn't see herself now in the mirror. She had stopped counting the days she had been in El Paso and away from home. One day, two days, three days were more than she wanted to be away from her daughter.

"Baby, I'm still looking, but I have some good news. I…"

Before Sam could finish her sentence, April said, "I know, Mommie! You have a new lead!"

Sam felt her heart leap with delight. "Yes, Baby, a lead! That's why it was too late for me to call you last night."

Sam had called Howard after her conversation with Wilson last night and told him what had happened with Houston Meyers at the Nite Owl.

"That's encouraging," Howard had told her. "Sounds like he's a regular there with the way everyone seemed to know him."

Sam agreed and said, "It put me at ease almost immediately." Then she added, "I want to believe I am one step closer to finding Jenny now, Howard."

He had pointed out something during their conversation that hadn't occurred to Sam until they had talked. When Sam said she was one step closer to finding Jenny, Howard had said, "Samantha, I think it's safe to say you've already found her. You know she's apparently in El Paso, now it's just a matter of this Houston fella taking you to meet her, assuming he will."

"You're absolutely right," Sam had said. "I hadn't thought of it that way."

"But please do one thing for me, Samantha," Howard said, his voice deep with concern. "Before you go anywhere else with him, make sure Wilson and I know. I think I can speak for Wilson, too, when I say I'm sure, like me, he'll feel better knowing."

That conversation with Howard had kept her wide awake until after midnight.

Sam took one final look at herself in the bathroom mirror, then slipped her poncho over her head, grabbed her bag and left the room. She walked to *La Dolce Vita* against a biting wind and under a blanket of grubby dishwasher skies. She could see Mia at the register waiting on a customer, but it wasn't until Sam entered the café and reached the counter that she realized who it was.

Amanda Moore's henchman. He was just as tall and massive from behind as he was when Sam would see him standing guard at the entrance to *La Dolce Vita*.

Sam was only in line for a few moments before she realized why he was there—Amanda must not have liked her drink, so she sent it back for a remake. Having never heard him utter a word, he was surprisingly soft-spoken for his size and more cordial than Sam had ever witnessed Amanda being with the baristas.

The man moved to the end of the bar as Jeff remade Amanda's drink. Sam also noticed Mia and Jeff didn't seem as nervous around the henchman as they normally appeared to be when Amanda was standing at the counter growling at them. He apparently lacked manners, too, however. When Jeff set the remade drink on the counter, he took it and left the café without a word of thanks or adding to the tip jar.

Sam waited at the register until he was out the door. She greeted Mia warmly and said, "A remake, I guess?"

"Morning, Sam," Mia said. "Yep, for sure. She claims it wasn't hot enough when she got back to her office and started to drink it."

"Couldn't have been that bad. It was half gone," Jeff said.

"Well," Sam said with a smile. "Maybe you made it so good, Jeff, she just had to have another."

Sam got her drink and placed a dollar in the tip jar. She sat at her favorite table by the window and checked the time, nine-fifteen. Sam sent a text to Sandy about the meeting with Houston at the Nite Owl and they exchanged a flurry of communication before Sam left the café a few minutes after nine thirty and started for Concordia Cemetery.

When she arrived shortly before ten a.m., she didn't see Houston's truck.

"Please, please don't do this to me, Houston," she said as she arrived at the stone entrance near Hunter's and his parents' graves. At five minutes after ten her anxiety turned to relief as she saw the GMC approaching her rental car, the headlights illuminating the way. Houston parked across the street from her and she met him at the back of his pickup.

"Morning," she said with a reserved smile. "I am so glad you came."

Houston nodded and pulled the tip of his ball cap at her; the same one he was wearing last night and the first morning she saw him walk toward his truck. "When I say I'm gonna be somewhere, I keep my word."

Sam pointed to the entrance and they walked toward it, side by side. In the flat winter light, El Paso stood before them wan and featureless, stifled between a fallow landscape and dull skies.

She pointed to the tall twin yucca plants in the distance and said, "They're over there."

They traversed along the rocky ground in silence, making their own path. Sam observed Houston wasn't much taller than her five-foot-six-inch frame, and that he walked with a slight limp with his right leg. When they reached the markers, Houston removed his cap and held it in front of him with both hands. He took the time to study each marker, starting with Hunter's mother, before moving to his father's grave and then finally Hunter's.

"They died so young," he said finally.

"Yes," Sam said softly. "All of them. Jenny was lucky she was in her car seat."

For a moment the wind whispered and moaned between them, forcing Sam to pull her poncho close to her neck.

"She doesn't know anything about having a brother or this John and Rita as her parents," Houston said finally.

Sam took a step closer to the graves. "They're right here."

"She's never said anything to me and besides," he held his hands out over the graves, his ball cap limp in his right hand. "This could be anyone."

"Maybe not to you, Houston, and even though she may have never known them, that doesn't mean they weren't her family."

"Jenny has told me often that her mother raised her after her father got cancer and died. She was an only child."

"Yes, that part is true, her aunt did raise Jenny as her own, but as I told you last night that was Rita's sister, Jenny and Hunter's mother, and the man who died of cancer was her uncle."

Houston nodded but Sam could tell he was unconvinced.

Different parents? An only child? Then a thought came to Sam, slowly, the way ice melts.

"Houston, does Jenny know she was born here in El Paso, in the same hospital as her brother?"

Houston hesitated a fleeting moment before he started to shake his head slowly.

"She thinks she was born in Mexico," Sam said. It was more of a confirmation.

This time Houston nodded. "In a place called *San Ciro de Acosta,* near *San Luis Potosí* in Central Mexico."

Sam gave a short laugh of disbelief. She spoke trying to keep any inflection from her voice. "Of course, it makes sense, after having Jenny and raising her for a year, her aunt couldn't bear to part with her. Yes, I heard Hunter mention *San Luis Potosí* many times, but I told you last night I couldn't remember the name of the town Jenny was taken to unless I was looking at a map."

Houston shook his head.

Sam pointed toward the buildings downtown as if that would help put things in better perspective. "I have Jenny's birth certificate back in my hotel room. At least let me show you."

Houston remained silent, keeping his attention on the graves, which stood before him like mute, laden sentinels.

"What brought Jenny back here to El Paso?" Sam asked. She was trying to ignore the desperate feeling that this meeting was going nowhere.

Houston ignored her question by starting to move away from the markers, the limp more pronounced now after standing still.

"It's too cold to stay here any longer," he said, motioning for Sam to follow.

She had no choice and felt her shoulders start to soften as they headed for their vehicles.

They didn't speak again until they were standing behind the GMC. Sam took notice of the veteran's license plate and was certain that was the reason for his limp.

"Houston, there's still things I need to tell you," she said. "Is there some place else we could go to talk? Please. All I'm asking is for you to hear me out."

He started for the driver-side door. He opened it and grabbed his cell phone off the seat. "What's your number?"

Sam told him.

"I'm going to send you the name of a place where we can eat lunch." Houston glanced at his watch, a big-face military tactical black watch with a thick rubber band strapped on his wrist. She could see the strength in his wiry forearm.

"Meet me there at noon."

THIRTY-THREE

S am stayed in her car, watching Houston drive away.

She took her cell phone out of her bag and clicked on his message. He gave her the name of a pizzeria and included the address. A map quest showed the restaurant was on the other side of town. She saved Houston's name to her contacts and glanced at her watch, ten-forty-five.

She called Wilson. "Hi, it's me," she said when he answered.

"How'd it go?" he asked outright.

"I'll answer in Spanish as I think Hunter might have if I had asked him the same thing, *mas o menos*. So, so, I guess, but I don't think he believes me."

"I think I know where this is going," Wilson said. "I'm guessing the aunt told Jenny she was her mother and never bothered to tell her what happened to her real parents and Hunter?"

"And not only that," Sam went on. "Jenny evidently has no idea she was born in the United States, right here in El Paso."

"That wasn't a very long meeting," Wilson said.

Sam could feel the cold pressing against the car window, where beyond flat, lifeless clouds collected on the horizon. "It's freezing here today, that's one reason. I can tell you, standing out there between the graves, the wind was unforgiving and I was starting to lose hope this was going anywhere."

"How'd you guys leave it?"

"He sent me a place to meet for lunch, some pizza place, I'm guessing, it's about twenty minutes from here and I am going to bring Jenny's birth certificate with me."

"Keep me posted," Wilson said and they ended the call.

When Sam arrived at the pizzeria a few minutes before noon, Houston's white truck was already in the parking lot. He had the window down and his arm resting casually over the door.

The restaurant took up one corner of a small nondescript retail mall. The word PIZZA in big red letters was positioned in the brick wall above the entrance.

She waved to Houston as she pulled in next to him and they walked together toward the main entrance, a single glass door. He wore demin work pants over his military boots and kept his hands inside his black winter jacket.

They were greeted by the homey smell of tomato sauce, a mixture of basil, parsley and oregano. Sam couldn't help inhaling; she wanted to linger at the door and take in the rich scent. The fresh spices immediately brought her back to the ranch and the many times she stood at the stove with her grandmother making sauce together. It made her long to return home.

Booths lined the two walls and sets of plain tables and chairs filled in the middle and the place was nearly full. Houston pointed to the menu, which was situated on the wall behind a long glass counter. Inside the glass case was an inviting display, an assortment of olives, salads and cold cuts. Sam could see the name *Anthony's* within the menu written in script in the green, white and red colors of the Italian flag.

A stocky man with a wide neck that spread out into his thick shoulders was standing at the register and gave Houston a familiar nod.

His curly gray hair was sticking out the sides of his chef's beanie and his white apron, dappled in red sauce, covered a white T-shirt. Sam guessed he was about Houston's age.

Houston held up to two fingers to acknowledge him.

"Get what you want," he told Sam. "But the pizza's the best in town."

The man heard Houston's comment and his bushy eyebrows drifted upward happily at Sam, clearly appreciating his recommendation.

They ordered, got their drinks from the fountain and went to the only empty table near the main door. Before Houston sat down, he removed his ball cap and jacket and placed them over the chair next to him.

They sat in silence for a time, watching customers come and go from the counter before Sam gave Houston her earnest attention. She noticed he had shaved, the gray that had collected evenly along the sides of his chin now gone. Though his face looked scratchy and dry, his eyes were clear and he looked rested.

"Would you mind if I asked how you were injured in the Army?"

"I was in the Marines, not the Army."

"I'm sorry," Sam said and she wanted to crawl under the table as she remembered the decals in the back window of his truck. "I should've said the military."

Houston shrugged her off as if to say *happens all the time.* "I enlisted in the Marines as soon as I turned eighteen and served the final two years in Vietnam as the war was coming to an end."

"Is that where you were injured?"

He shook his head. "In the Persian Gulf war. I was ridin' in a High Mobility Multipurpose Wheeled Vehicle, or better known by civilians as a Humvee, when we hit an IED, an Improvised—"

Sam finished the sentence for him, "Explosive Device."

"Yeah, that's right. The tibia and fibula in my right leg shattered in the blast."

Sam couldn't help wincing. "Did the bone protrude?"

"No, I was lucky in that way, I guess. But I had to have a rod inserted in my leg for a year to help strengthen the bones."

They called their order from the counter and Sam watched Houston move toward it, the limp in his gait only slightly noticeable. He set the tray in the middle of their table and Sam removed her slice of pepperoni pizza and salad. Houston took his two slices of pepperoni pizza and salad off the tray and returned it to the counter.

Sam sprinkled red chili flakes heavily over her pizza. "My daughter, April, loves pepperoni pizza," she said. "As our treat together, sometimes I'll pick her up after school and we'll go for pizza. We know a place like this in Denver, too. Same wonderful and welcoming smell as soon as you walk in."

"Are you married?" Houston asked.

"Divorced. And you're right," she said. "This is delicious."

Houston nodded, his mouth full.

After a few minutes Sam said, "How did you earn your medal? If you don't mind me asking. A Commendation Medal, right?"

Houston nodded and said what he always said to people who asked, as little as possible. "After the bomb detonated the Humvee rolled once and then again before landing on its side. The other guys were injured pretty badly, but I managed to be near the top and started pulling my guys out and dragging them to cover as safely and as fast as I could."

"With a badly broken leg?"

Houston shrugged and finished his salad, picking around the cherry tomatoes. "Bullets were flying all over the place, but I got 'em all to safety. No one else was injured any worse. They said I was a hero, but any of my guys would've done the same for me."

"Thanks to you, it sounds like. I am grateful for your service."

Houston shrugged; his face stony as he struggled to accept Sam's praise.

"What happened after the surgery?" she asked, continuing to probe. "Were you medically retired due to your injury?"

"I was two years shy of twenty years, but yeah, that's what happened, but I was ready," he said. "I wanted to get back to my place in Slidell, so I could clear my head and start over."

"That's where home is?" Sam said, sensing it was time to change the subject.

"Born and raised there. It's my place on earth."

"I live on a ranch, too," she said with a composed, purposeful smile that well related to Houston's connection. "It's my grandmother's, and a place I've come and gone from all my life."

She thought about the ranch nestled at the foot of the twin peaks, tall and majestic, stretching across open fields full with oak brush and deep valleys steeped in Evergreens. *This place has helped me to survive. It's the only reason I've made it this far. It is the bouquet of my childhood, of all my life.*

Sam took a sip of her soda, the dark liquid climbing up the straw. "What brought you to El Paso?"

"You followed me there."

"To the housing development?"

Houston nodded. "I'd done some consulting work with Zia Construction and they wanted someone to lead their field office in the southwest. I accepted only with the thought of doing it for a year. Thought a little change of scenery would be nice. Nothing makes home a better place than being gone from it for a while."

"How long ago was that?"

"Going on four years."

Sam's eyebrows drifted and disappeared beneath her bangs. "What's kept you here?"

Houston finished the last of his pizza and set the plate to the side. He folded his hands in front of his face and stared at Sam over the top of them. She could tell he was struggling with what to say and perhaps, she guessed, how to say it.

His voice was muted when he said, "Jenny."

Sam stiffened against the back of the chair and absently brought a hand to her mouth. "Jenny?"

Houston nodded, his jaw firmly set. He looked beyond her toward the main door, where a young family of four still holding their fountain drinks, was leaving. "The first time I met her, she was watching cartoons."

"Cartoons?"

"Tom and Jerry."

"How old was she?"

Houston thought for a moment, doing the math in his head. "She had just turned fifteen."

"By my calculations she's about to be eighteen," Sam said, her eyes flicking briefly to his graying hair.

He nodded. "May sixth."

"Yes, yes, that's right," Sam said breathlessly. "Where was that? Where did you meet Jenny?"

Houston ignored her query. "She was sitting on the bed and the first thing she said to me was, 'I'm hungry.' Then, a commercial came on for one of those pizza chains and she pointed at the screen and said, 'can I have that?' I looked at the television set and said, 'you want pizza?' She nodded and then she said, 'what're those little round things?'

"I said, 'pepperoni?' She nodded and said, 'they look good.' I said, 'haven't you ever had pizza before?' She shook her head."

After a long moment he said with a soft sigh, "She didn't even know what pepperoni was." Houston's weathered face seem to fold into a gathering softness, the lines disappearing, becoming smaller across his forehead and Sam could tell the memory came from within, from a deep, hallowed place reserved, perhaps, for remembrance.

"If she came from Mexico, did she know English?"

"Very little when she first came, but she picked it up just like that," Houston said and snapped his fingers.

"Do you know Spanish?"

He held his thumb and index finger close together. "*Poquito*. Enough to get by."

Sam pressed her hand against her chest. "*Yo también,* but nothing to brag about. Hunter was fluent as I told you, so he taught me some simple words and phrases, which I've managed to remember."

"Jenny learned a lot of English watching cartoons and soap operas all day. She soaked it up as I always say like water to thirsty ground."

"All day? Wasn't she in school?"

He didn't answer.

"How did you meet her, Houston?"

He shifted uneasily in his chair and wouldn't give Sam his attention.

"Houston, please."

His eyes slid coolly in her direction, they were narrow and dark. He took a deep breath, and realizing he had come to a watermark moment, started talking. "You can say I was a perv because it's true. I went there that night with every intention of doing it."

Sam failed to immediately grasp what Houston was getting at and naively said, "Doing what?"

"What the hell do you think? Have sex."

She felt herself recoil abruptly, but attempted to keep her gaze that was still fixed on Houston, impartial. "But, but she's a…" She struggled to find the words and process her thoughts, which were jumbled together like a jigsaw puzzle. "Just a little girl."

"Yeah, and I was a deviant, miserable bastard, too. I mean look at me." Houston held his hands up in front of his face. "I mean look at this mug. I'm so frickin' ugly I scare people."

"You're not." Sam shook her head, her gaze cold, her lips pressed together in a thin, tight line.

Houston was not oblivious to the poorly concealed disgust in her voice. "Don't patronize me. I know what I see when I look in the mirror. You wanna have sex with someone? When you look like me, you gotta pay for it. My uncle helped my mother raise me and my seven brothers after my father died in a farming accident on the property, and he used to remind me how ugly I was. All the time. He thought he was so funny, so witty with his stupid remarks. He'd say to me in that thick Deep South drawl that came out of his mouth longer than a yardstick, 'boy, you so ugly, you gotta sneak up on a glass of water,' or sometimes he'd be sitting at the table watching me eat, shaking that bald head of his, 'cause I know he didn't like me, not the way he liked my brothers. Then I'd wait for it and he'd say, 'boy, you so ugly, you gotta brace yourself when you look in the mirror.' Then he'd laugh so loud and slam his hand down so hard on the table, it seemed like the whole house would shake.

"And these here," Houston pointed to his two upper incisors. "My older brothers, too, they'd say 'hey, squirrel, the water's backin' up in the creek, get out there and gnaw at some of that dead wood before we have ourselves a flood.'"

Sam shook her head in a pathetic way. "Squirrel? That was your nickname?"

Houston nodded and then he chuckled. "Squirrel. I've never minded that for some reason, I guess because it came from my brothers and we've always been close. Still are, two of 'em are gone, but I'm still close with the others. They still call me Squirrel, too, when we get together."

"Is that why you brought me here?"

Houston glanced around the restaurant, hesitating a moment on the word *Anthony's* in the menu.

"If she was going to have pizza for the first time, then goddammit I wanted to make sure it came from a good place." He nodded firmly. "I told her 'you gotta wait here. I'll get us some, but it's on the other side of town. So, it'll take time for me to get it and get back.' It was almost an hour before I got back and she ate every bit of it, everything but two slices. She looked at me at one point," he stopped and brushed the side of his face lightly with the tips of his fingers. "With crumbs here on the side of her mouth where her beauty mark and dimple are, and gave me the most beautiful smile I've ever seen. When she looked at me like that, I was done. I felt something hit me inside like a bolt of lightning. It just ripped me apart."

Houston grabbed his dirty napkin, but stopped short of bringing it to his eyes. "When I realized what I was about to do with her, with all the women, the tramps, the whores I've been with, I've never loathed myself as much as I did that night."

Sam looked at him, her face mellow, yet veiled in pain.

"I've never had a family, Sam, but if I had a daughter like Jenny and she was in a motel room with a man like me, I'd kill him." He raised his clenched fists in front of her face. "I swear to you, I'd kill 'em. ... You can think of me or judge me any way you want, Sam, because it's true, it is the reason I went in that motel room in the first place, but I swear to you and on my mother's grave," Houston jabbed forcefully at his chest. "I'd never been with an underage girl before and I swear, I've never,

ever laid a hand on her. Not that night, not in every one since. And I want to kill every man, and one in particular, every loser like me who has gone in that room with that intention…" his voice fell away as his head dropped heavily.

When he could make himself look at her again, he said, "Men like me, we're only one step out of the jungle." He kept her gaze, as if hoping for some form of absolution.

Sam pointed at the black jacket over the chair with a nod of her head. "That's the jacket Jenny was wearing that night in the grocery store, isn't it?"

"I told you she's so thin and cold all the time that I make sure I have something in the truck she can put on. When she jumps in that's the first thing she does, puts it on."

"What happened that night, the night you met Jenny for the first time?"

"We were in a cheap motel room and there was nothing, no robe or anything, for her to put on. I kept thinking what if this were my daughter. I was wearing a sweat top that zipped up. I took it off and handed it to her and said 'here, Jenny, put this on.' And that was it. I got the pizza. She ate and stayed on the bed and I sat in a chair and we watched television 'til midnight when they came knocking at the door. She took off my top, got dressed as fast as she could in this faded cheap dress with holes under the arms, and disappeared out the door. She was so scared, she didn't even look back.

"For a long, long time, Sam, I stayed where I was and stared at the door, thinking of the fear in her face, as though she was seeing hell for the first time. I looked down at my hands and I remember making them into tight fists." He put his fists up in front of Sam again and shook them vigorously. "I just wanted to find them and with one good twist, break their necks with my bare hands for every evil, vile thing they've done to her."

Sam felt sick to her stomach. She closed her eyes, trying to quell the nausea that was building and about to burst forth like an inferno.

Houston went on. "Last night, I thought about meeting you at the cemetery this morning and decided I wasn't going to."

"What changed your mind?"

"I dunno, maybe it's something in your demeanor. Something about you tells me you are here in earnest. Leaving your family, your daughter, your job and everything to come to El Paso because you really want nothing more than to do what Hunter couldn't and find his sister. After enough years in the service, I think I can read people pretty good, you know."

Tears welled helplessly in Sam's eyes.

"I woke up thinking this morning, thinking how much I've tried to help get Jenny away from all this, this nightmare, but she won't budge. And I know the statistics, Sam. Every single one of them. Because in every free minute I had when I first learned all about this shit going on, I know she doesn't have much time left. I can see it, her decline, already starting to happen. I know it and Jenny knows it, too, but she's too afraid. Truth be told, Sam, I don't blame her. I know she is so afraid, but there's nothing else I can do." He pushed his drink to the side and stared at it when he spoke again. "Sometimes I've thought of just grabbing her and hauling her off, but I guess, deep down I know it's gotta be her choice. I can't force her to leave them, I can't change her or erase her fear of leaving and getting out of this situation."

He held up his hands hopelessly in front of her. "That's why I decided to come today."

"Why, Houston? What's the real reason you think I'd be able to do something you haven't been able to?"

He answered without hesitation. "Maybe you're the one who can get through to her."

THIRTY-FOUR

S am sat in a daze as the harsh reality of Houston's revelation set in.

Her hands were folded on the table in front of her and she was squeezing them. Her thoughts were a maelstrom, spinning out of control, as though they were trapped in an eddy, about to circle down, down, down into darkness.

Houston was staring numbly at her, as if his admission about Jenny had drained the life from him.

Sam managed to focus on pizza crumbs that were scattered on the table before she swept everything into the palm of her hand and dropped them onto their dirty dishes. She became aware she was facing a television set in the upper corner of the restaurant. An Amanda Moore commercial was airing, showing her standing in front of her name and her slogan in the elegant lobby of her office. Sam had seen that same one air almost every night when she'd watch the late local news.

When the commercial ended, she said, "The night my friend saw you and Jenny in the grocery store, she said Jenny seemed frightened and was standing very close to you."

"She gets scared when we go out like that."

"Of what?"

"Of what could happen if she were caught," Houston said. "That's the first time we'd gone anywhere like that in months, so your friend was lucky she saw us there when she did."

"Lucky, perhaps," Sam said and nodded. "She told me she only looked in your direction because she heard you say Jenny's name."

Sam did not want to give words to what she was thinking, unwilling to breathe life to the dark thoughts that had been swirling around in her head, but the words tumbled from her mouth as if they had minds of their own.

"How old was she when they took her?" Her voice was stiff and forced, angry.

Houston shrugged, looking out the tall windows.

"What kind of lie, Houston, did they tell her to bring her here from Mexico?" Sam leaned into the table and lowered her voice. "Or was it a lie? You say the rendering captured the way Jenny looks and if she's as pretty as you say and as my friend who saw you in the grocery store says, then perhaps they didn't have to lie, maybe they just saw her and snatched her off the street and brought her here."

"Will you come with me?" Houston asked abruptly, meeting her eyes. "I want to show you something."

Sam's eyes narrowed with distrust and she pushed back against the chair. "Where?"

"My telling you won't help. Better for you to see for yourself."

"Will I be able to see Jenny?"

Houston put on his ball cap and firmly centered it, then slowly shook his head.

Sam hesitated considering her options, remembering what Howard had told her. "I'll follow you."

"No, that won't work. It has to be in my truck." His voice was absolute. "I can tell you more as we go. You'll be safe, Sam, I promise."

"Fine," she said, agreeing reluctantly. "But I won't go with you unless I tell some trusted people exactly who I am going with." She gave him a hard stare.

"Fine," he said, ending the impasse after a few minutes. "I'll wait for you in my truck."

Sam called Howard and Wilson in her rental car. Before she ended the call with Howard, she told him to tell April she had a new lead and would tell her more tonight.

When Wilson answered Sam's call, she said without preamble, "It's sex trafficking."

He couldn't immediately answer her as a sinking feeling expanded in his gut. Like Sam, the more they discussed Jenny, the more they learned about her, he had been fearing the worst, and now it was confirmed, all roads did indeed lead in that shadowy, ominous direction.

"Where are you now?" he asked.

"They kidnap or trick these pretty young girls, take them across the border and rape and abuse them for however many years until the old perverts who pay for them lose interest, then new younger girls just replace them. Then these girls die because you know the life expectancy for them drops to practically nothing once they've been caught up in this, or they end up on the streets alone with nowhere to go."

"Where are you now?" Wilson asked again

She angrily brushed aside a tear. "Still outside the pizzeria."

"Are you heading back to the hotel?"

"That's why I'm calling. I'm going with Houston. He's going to take me to see Jenny."

His voice sounded guarded. "You're going to meet her?"

"Not exactly. I think it's where she lives, but I won't be able to meet her. At least not yet."

"You're following him, right?" Wilson asked.

"No," Sam said. "I'm going in his truck."

She could hear Wilson take a deep breath in concern, just as Howard had done when she told him the same news.

"It's not like you have much choice," he offered. "But if you don't check in with me within one hour, I'm calling Page."

She smiled, thinking of what Houston had told her about leaving her family, her friends, her work, her daughter, everything, to try and find Jenny.

"I'm counting on it, Wilson, Howard felt the same way when I told him, but don't worry. I can't tell you why, but I believe Houston. I believe everything he has told me and I believe he wants to help Jenny. He wants to try and save her before it's too late."

"Save her?"

"I'll explain everything when we talk later."

"Be safe, Sam. Remember, one hour," Wilson said and they ended the call.

Sam could feel the trepidation working its way up her spine as she got out of her sedan and climbed in the GMC. The cab's interior did little against the afternoon chill and she couldn't help shivering.

"I'll keep the heater on," Houston said and they drove from the parking lot.

"Where are we going?"

"It's not far from here," he said, navigating the streets.

"Is this the motel where you meet Jenny?"

Houston shook his head. "This shithole—and I'm sorry, Sam, I hate to use that kinda language in front of a lady, but I can't think of any other way to describe it—Jenny is housed in an absolute shithole."

They were silent as Houston navigated another maze of right-hand and left-hand streets before he turned right down a two-way street and slowed the truck to a crawl. He found a spot and parallel parked with ease. He left the truck running and pointed across the street as though he was looking down a gun barrel.

"She's in there."

Sam followed Houston's aim toward a ramshackle row of sandstone-colored brick buildings that extended the length of the block. The names of two businesses garnered Sam's attention, Green Spa and Aromatherapy Spa. The windows in both businesses had blacked-out glass. The blinds were shuttered and industrial-looking black bars against the windows appeared so old rust was streaming down the sides. Some portions of the window screens behind the bars were held together with duct tape.

All Sam could see with clarity was an ATM between the front entrances.

"Get a look at that," Houston said and his chin protruded toward a crooked LED sign situated between both businesses. It read: OPEN 24/7.

"Is that where you go to meet Jenny?"

Houston shook his head and pointed to a row of windows above the businesses. "That one on the end there." Sam looked with him. "That's where Jenny lives with as many as four, five, six other girls just like her in the same room."

Sam leaned closer to the front windshield and put her hand on the dash. The pulse in her neck quickened. She wanted to get out of the truck, run across the street and shatter the front door. Jenny was so close. Yet. She might as well still have been in Mexico.

"If you don't meet her here, then where?"

"They drive the girls to a motel six blocks from here."

"That's where you meet her?"

"Yeah."

"How long has this been going on, Houston?"

"I met Jenny not even a month after I came."

"Four years ago?"

"Yes," he said. "Ever since."

"How often do you see here?"

"As much as I can, but always twice a week." He clenched his jaw as his eyes narrowed. "It just kills me to know that other guys, and a lot of 'em, are violating her. Once I couldn't see her for almost two weeks."

"Why?"

"I dunno, but I could still see the shiner under her eye when I finally saw her again. She just said she'd made a mistake, but that's all she'd say. I wanted to find that bastard and bash his fu—." Houston stopped himself. "Face in, but Jenny wouldn't tell me. Who knows what else they've done to her or she's had to do that she won't tell me."

Sam felt herself starting to do a slow burn. She couldn't take her eyes off the end window.

"And when I do see her, it's for the entire evening," Houston went on. "It's the reason I still work, so I can pay for anything, so I can know that at least two nights a week, eight times a month, I can get her out of there. Buy her whatever she wants to eat because I told you they feed them practically nothing. At least on those nights she doesn't have to … you know…"

Sam nodded, but he didn't bring up the night security job, so she didn't mention it.

She removed the digital camera from her bag and began snapping photos of the buildings and the perimeter, the whirl of the camera taking the place of conversation. She attached a zoom lens to the camera and trained it on Jenny's window. The enlarged frame allowed her to see that a blanket covered it.

"That doesn't look like drapes or blinds across her window," Sam said and considered each one. "Or any of them for that matter."

"Not that it matters if there's curtains or whatever, the windows are blacked out, anyway. Jenny told me the first week she came, they stuck her in that room and she didn't see the sun that entire time. They were kept in there with the blinds drawn and the doors locked."

She took more pictures of the building with the zoom lens and another handful with her cell phone.

"Are they apartments?"

"If you can call them that. There's only two bathrooms and a single kitchen. The rest are just cramped rooms where a bunch of girls live together."

"All underage?"

"Most, but not all. I don't know honestly."

"Have you ever been inside?"

Houston answered simply. "No."

Sam felt her nausea starting to return. "I've seen enough. Since we've come this far, can you at least take me to the motel where you meet with her?"

Houston started the truck and they drove away in silence, Sam keeping her eye on Jenny's window as long as she could until the truck moved out of sight.

They reached the motel. The split-leveled, darkly painted building, as rundown as the building that housed the spas and apartments, was as Sam guessed, part of a cheap national chain for lodging. She wouldn't let herself think of what the mattresses would look like. He drove beyond it and parked on a side street that still allowed them a decent view of the motel. A collection of vehicles nearly filled the parking lot.

"Do you know how Jenny came to the US?"

Houston nodded but remained silent.

"Houston?"

He placed his hands over the steering wheel. "They spotted her one afternoon in the city coming out of a *taqueria* with some friends. A woman approached her to tell her how pretty she was. She told Jenny if she wanted to come to the United States, she could arrange it. She said she knew how poor Jenny and her family were and she could help change that."

"She didn't really know, did she," Sam said.

"She didn't have to, Sam. There's not a family in that God-forsaken place that isn't poor and on the edge."

"Then what happened?"

"She asked Jenny if she'd ever heard of modelling. Jenny shook her head; she was just a little girl growing up in a town with dirt roads and houses without heat. She told me once that as the woman explained it to her, she showed her pictures of runway models. Jenny said the woman told her she was every bit as beautiful as those women walking the runway. She was barely a teenager, for Christ's sake."

Houston gripped the steering wheel tighter, his weathered knuckles turning red, then white. "That's when Jenny said the woman told her to 'come with me.' At first, Jenny said she resisted, but the woman persisted and promised they would take good care of her and train her to be a model, and she would be able to send money home to her family."

"Did she leave with them right then?"

Houston was clenching his jaw so tightly, the muscles on the side of his face were protruding into thick round balls.

Sam asked the question though certain she already knew the response. "That was four years ago and she hasn't been able to contact anyone from her hometown since."

Houston spoke so low Sam could hardly hear him. "Yes."

For a long time neither spoke, both trapped in dark thoughts.

"In the beginning," Houston went on. "She'd talk so much about her family and how they would start receiving the money she was making."

"Of course, it never happened."

"Jenny was devastated and pleaded to go home. When they wouldn't let her, she tried to run away. She didn't even get to the end of the block before they grabbed her and dragged her back literally by her hair. She was punished with a beating so severe I couldn't see her for two weeks.

"But that wasn't even the worst of it. One week later, Jenny said they showed her a picture. They said it was her mother with a black eye and a broken nose. Whether it was really was her mother, I don't know, but they told Jenny the next time she tries to run they wouldn't just beat her mother. They'd kill her. That was the last time she tried to escape."

"So, it's been twice you've been unable to see her because of what they've done to her," Sam said.

Houston's hands dropped into his lap. "I've tried to convince her to come with me, told her I can protect her, but she won't listen. That's why she's so afraid when we go to a store that someone will see her. She's terrified of being punished and what they'll do to her mother."

Sam was sitting with her arms folded tightly over her midsection, trying to calm her nausea. "She's an American citizen."

"She doesn't know that, but you don't know how relieved I was when you told me at the Nite Owl," Houston said and the tension in his face eased some. "After I left, I was dog-tired, but I came and stared at Jenny's window for more than an hour. I was so glad I didn't have a weapon on me last night, Sam, otherwise I would've burst in there and shot those bastards in the head and then shot my way upstairs until I found Jenny."

He looked at her over the center console, slightly nodding, his eyes beaming, holding a confident look. "I've thought about that a lot, you know. I could manage it. Bursting in there and shooting every one of 'em right in the middle of the forehead even before they knew what hit 'em."

"Yeah, with your military background you'd probably come out of there without a scratch," Sam said. "And then what, Houston? You'd be arrested for murder; they'd take Jenny, and who knows where she'd end up."

Houston laughed with regret and embarrassment. "Ever since you told me Jenny was born here, I've envisioned us running away from there like in the movies, me grabbing her hand and pulling her along, telling her, 'run, Jenny, run. It's okay! You're an American citizen. You don't have to go back to Mexico! You can bring your mom here.'"

They sat in a long silence, watching cars, people, come and go from the motel parking lot.

Sam said finally, "She will, Houston, but not like that."

"What're you getting at?"

"Jenny and Hunter's parents had a life insurance policy," she said. "Hunter had used some of his money from the trust to go to college. The rest he was saving for the future and for his sister. It's all Jenny's now, more than enough money for her to care for her mother, her family and herself." Sam thought about giving him a rough figure–250,000 dollars, more than enough to change her life, but decided against it. As much as she was beginning to trust him, that alone was Jenny's business.

Their eyes met again over the console.

"We have to find a way to get her out of there, Houston."

He responded with a solemn nod.

"My daughter's going to be a teenager next year," Sam went on. "She wants to be an attorney and a journalist, and I am going to do everything I can to make that happen. Jenny should be afforded the same opportunity."

They continued to stare at each other.

"When are you going to see her again?"

"Tomorrow night."

"Will I be able to meet her then?"

He was silent, frowning to himself, staring owlishly away into space, his face pale.

Moments later he nodded with conviction. "I'll send you a text with instructions, time and place tomorrow afternoon. Do exactly as I tell you."

THIRTY-FIVE

It was nearly two-thirty when Houston brought Sam back to her rental car.

"I'll be in touch tomorrow," he said and she watched his GMC leave the parking lot.

As soon as his truck disappeared, she called Wilson.

"I was going to give you five more minutes," Wilson said as he answered.

"Sorry, took a little longer than I thought," Sam said and cradled the phone as she told him about the spas and the motel.

"What're you going to do now?"

"I want to find a computer somewhere. A bigger screen makes it easier to do research."

"Keep me posted," Wilson said.

As Sam ended the call, Sandy popped in her mind. She sent her a text.

Hi. Lots to tell! Any chance there's a computer at the school I can use for research, maybe an hour or so?

Sam got in the car and waited for Sandy's reply. Ten minutes later, it came.

Sam! Happy to hear from you! Did you finally meet Jenny?

Not yet. Fingers crossed for tomorrow night. Time is going to inch by between now and then, but every time I think about it, it almost drives me crazy. I get excited and nervous.

I know what you mean! I would, too, absolutely! Yes, come to Franklin. I can set you up in the library. You can give me the highlights.

Thirty minutes later Sam was in the school library staring at a computer screen with the rising sun over the Franklin Mountains as the screen saver. She had a Reporter's Notebook open on the table beside her.

She typed in the name of the first spa, Green Spa, and the business' website loaded on the screen before her. She clicked on the image, which showed the front of the spa just as it looked in the photos she had taken with her cameras.

The website showed a seemingly legitimate business offering spa and full-body massage treatments. It caught her attention that services were offered twenty-four hours a day. The spa had been open for five years and of the nearly one hundred and fifty reviews and ratings, most were positive. The majority of the reviews indicated it was "full service." Another review hinted that 'anything you want' was on the service list.

Sam opened another window and typed in the second business, Aromatherapy Spa. The website was nearly identical to the Green Spa, including the same type of reviews, years in business and services offered.

She sat back against the chair listening to the quiet that being in libraries usually brought and tried to remember seeing similar businesses in Denver. Nothing immediately came to mind, though she wasn't surprised, it wasn't something for which she ever had the need to look. She thought of the darkened windows in both locations and wondered why the secrecy if the businesses were lawful. She scribbled the information from both places in her notebook and wrote James Page's name next to it. She jotted down the words "full service" to make sure she'd remember to ask James.

She opened a third window and typed in the date and place of the deadly accident that had claimed the lives of Hunter and Jenny's parents, hoping to find dated newspaper articles that would give more details of the accident.

Her search netted articles written in newspapers in New Mexico and in Hunter's hometown of El Paso. She clicked on an article written in the *El Paso Times*. It was one of the initial stories of the accident and was positioned at the top of page three, the second front. The layout showed a single picture of the accident spread across three columns. The enlarged photo showed both cars a mangled mess and personal items scattered throughout the wreckage site. The article also showed a headshot of Hunter's father that Sam guessed came from the university. She stared at the image, marveling at how much Hunter looked like him, the same tilt of the head, wavy chestnut-colored hair, same crooked, relaxed smile.

The bold headline across the top of page read:

POPULAR UTEP TEACHER, WIFE KILLED BY DRUNK DRIVER

The story under the reporter's byline read:

> A well-liked UTEP professor and his wife were killed by a drunk driver in a head-on collision on Interstate 25 Sunday afternoon, just south of Santa Fe, New Mexico.
>
> John Hunter Hollingsworth, 31, and his wife, Rita, 29, were returning home to El Paso when the accident occurred. The driver, who was also killed, was travelling the wrong way on the interstate, heading north in the southbound lanes, when the cars collided. John Hollingsworth died at the scene. Rita Hollingsworth died at the hospital, a short time later. The driver died on the way to the hospital. New Mexico State Police reported the drunk driver's blood alcohol content was more than twice the legal limit.
>
> John Hollingsworth was a professor at the University of Texas at El Paso, where his teaching concentration was the US/Mexico border region and the American West.

The couple's children, Hunter and Jennifer Hollingsworth, were also in the car. Hunter Hollingsworth, age seven, remains in serious condition at an Albuquerque hospital. Jennifer Hollingsworth, four months old, was in a car seat and was not injured in the accident. An eight-year-old cousin travelling with the family was also killed.

Sam found several stories written by the staff at the UTEP school newspaper, *The Prospector*, including one in Spanish. Satisfied she had found enough, she asked to make several copies of the stories, including the article in Spanish, hoping she would be able to show them to Jenny tomorrow night, or whenever she'd get the chance.

Sandy was teaching in front of her class when Sam passed by her door. Sam pointed to the exit door next to her room and Sandy gave a quick wave of acknowledgement. She left the building, happy to see that the stubborn cloud cover had finally lifted. A warm sun touched her face as she walked to her car.

She waited until she was back downtown and in her hotel room before she called the police chief. Though she had James' personal cell phone number, she didn't take advantage of the easy access when it wasn't necessary.

James' secretary greeted Sam pleasantly when she answered the call and then said, "Hang on a moment, Sam, he's got someone in his office. Don't hang up, I'll put you through shortly."

Two minutes later James Page answered her call. "Sam Church, I was beginning to wonder what happened to you. Are you digging up a storm down there?" As always, his voice was pleasant but firm.

Sam laughed and shook her head. "James, things certainly seem to have unfolded quite a bit over these last few days. Do you have a few minutes?"

"You have my undivided attention," he said.

Sam brought James up to date on the events of the last several days, including her meetings with Houston Meyers. She ended by telling him about the spa's darkened windows and twenty-four-hour access.

"Doesn't surprise me," he said when she finished. "They're all over.

Sex and human trafficking are big, big business, Sam, and from what it sounds like, Hunter's sister, unfortunately, appears to be caught up in it."

"With these places offering services twenty-four hours a day they're doing more than just cutting hair," Sam said.

"A lot more," James said. "And my guess is if you would have tried the doors they likely would've been locked. In many big cities, like, say New York, for instance, a lot of the illicit massage businesses are open late, but you can't just enter the place as if you were going to a salon, let's say. You have to get buzzed in."

"In other words, full service."

"Exactly. Places like that won't just let anyone in; they're constantly screening for whether it's a customer or law enforcement. And my guess, Sam," James went on, "Is on that very same street or one close by is a legitimate salon business that gives traditional salon services."

"Haircuts and perms as well as waxing and eyelash extensions."

"Yes, the works, and aromatherapy massage, too, because it's also a perfectly legitimate business."

"About these two places here in El Paso," Sam said. "How can I tell if they're on the up and up? You said you knew a few people on the police force here. I know it's asking a lot, James, but any chance you could get me in to talk with one of them?"

Sam had been pacing back and forth in front of her hotel window. She stopped and stared at the sun's glow reflecting off the building across the street. "James, you know I'd never ask you something like this if I didn't feel there was an absolute reason."

"You don't have to tell me, Sam."

"From what Houston has told me, Jenny's already declining. He sees it and she does, too. The life expectancy for girls who end up in sex trafficking is five, six years at the most, they either burn out or worse, you know that. Sounds like Jenny is on the verge of giving up, and if we don't get her out soon, I don't know if she will ever fully recover; it may be too late already. I can't imagine what she's been through, but every extra day in that place, with those men, doing…" her voice faded as she fought to control the tears she felt welling at the back of her throat. "We only may not have much time, but I'm worried about what Houston may decide to do."

"Go Rambo on us."

"Exactly," Sam said. "He's already at a point of desperation."

"Sounds like the guy has good intentions because he cares so much for the girl, but that could turn quickly and I'd hate to see that happen," James said. "He certainly has good cause to go over the top."

"A noble cause, but getting arrested for murder isn't going to help either of them."

The line was quiet for a brief moment before Sam heard James draw a deep breath. "I wouldn't do this for just any reporter."

"I know that."

"Let me make a few phone calls," he said. "I'll get back to you as soon as I can."

THIRTY-SIX

"I've never been a big fan of the press."

Mark McDaniel was a man of immense size, nearly six-feet, five-inches, with massive shoulders and a neck as thick as a tree trunk. Sam imagined he could give Amanda Moore's lackey a good match in the body building department. Despite his size, McDaniel looked fashionable in a sharp three-piece navy suit and polka-dot tie. A lieutenant with the El Paso Police Department's major crime division, who oversaw crimes against children, was clean shaven with grizzled close-cropped hair. Sam smiled to herself, visualizing him moonlighting as a masked vigilante who spent his time beating sex traffickers to a bloody pulp with his bare fists.

He had come around his desk and was sitting on the corner, giving Sam a hard stare and a dark smile, almost as if he was aware of his size and how he could intimidate simply by his presence. "That's why we have a public information officer, several PIOs in fact, where reporters are supposed to go for information."

Sam spoke with respect. "I understand how the process works, Lieutenant McDaniel."

"The only reason you're sitting here is because James Page happens to be a good friend of mine and we go way back."

Sam nodded carefully. "Yes, he mentioned you went through the police academy in Denver together." She tried to speak in a brave voice, but she could already tell this lieutenant wasn't going to make her job easy.

McDaniel gave her a doubtful look. "James tells me I can't go wrong trusting you, even though you're a reporter."

"I don't know what your experiences have been with reporters previously, Lieutenant McDaniel, but I've always made sure the relationships I build with credible sources are only ones of trust. If I screw things up from my end, say, publish something in a story you told me in confidence was off the record, then I know I won't get too many more chances to start over with you to make things right."

"Uh huh."

"Did James mention some of the work we've done together?"

"He mentioned it, yes. Sounds to me that you like to stick your nose in and don't know when to stop."

Sam fidgeted in her chair, wishing she could stand to face him, instead of having to look up at him to meet his eyes. She answered as firmly as she could, "When I have a lead, I like to pursue it, as most reporters do, which is why I'm here today."

McDaniel kept his hands folded casually in front of him. Sam noticed a gold band on his left ring finger. "So, you're investigating a human trafficking ring? Got anything concrete, or are you just hunting for a headline?"

Sam tried not to frown with irritation. She knew from having been married to a cop that he was only trying to frazzle her. She also knew James Page had said nothing of the kind to him, only her real reason for coming to El Paso.

"I'm not here for that, lieutenant. Unfortunately—"

"So that would be a no?"

Sam took a long breath while letting his comment pass. "Unfortunately, though that seems to be what I've stumbled onto. I worked with a young man, Hunter Hollingsworth, at my newspaper in Denver for a short time last year. We covered a story together on undocumented workers, which of course, involved James. Years ago, Hunter had lost his parents in a car accident and eventually his sister, Jenny, when he went into foster care in the United States and she moved with their aunt to Mexico. She was just a baby the last time Hunter saw her and it was his wish to find her and reconnect with her again. Unfortunately, that didn't happen."

Sam took the article of the accident out of her bag and handed it to him. She pointed at it as she spoke. "This is what started it all."

McDaniel's face smoothed evenly into recognition as he scanned the article. "Yeah, I remember this. I had just started on the force." He handed the copy back to Sam without finishing it. "It was a big deal back then."

"That's why I'm here," Sam said and she told Mark McDaniel the same story she had told numerous times since she'd come to El Paso. She ended by saying, "I came here because if Hunter were still alive, this is the place, the only place he knew to start. I had no idea Jenny would be here, let alone involved in human trafficking."

"Do you have a picture of her?"

Sam reached in her bag for the rendering of Jenny and handed it to him.

"Do you know Elsa Greer, by chance?"

McDaniel nodded as he studied the photo. "Sure. She's with James' department. I was one of the first ones he called when she finally agreed to come work for him. She's one of the best."

"I've been told that photo, which she did," Sam said, continuing to point at it. "Is spot on."

"How do you know that?"

"One of my sources spotted Jenny in a grocery store with another, older man in late January. Essentially, that's what started all this."

While still keeping his perch at the desk corner, he reached for a tablet and pen. "What about the guy at the grocery store she was with?"

"What about him?" Sam eyed his pen cautiously.

"You've seen him, right? Talked to him?"

Sam nodded but was instantly sorry she did. She had no choice but to answer. "I have."

"So, you got info on the guy, right? Name? What he looks like? Age maybe?"

"Lieutenant, he's one of my sources, as is the woman who saw them in the supermarket." Sam spoke tightly. "You know reporters don't reveal their sources' names or anything about them."

McDaniel snorted. "Is that why you're here today?" Instead of handing Jenny's rendering back to Sam, he let it fall on his desk, where it landed softly over a collection of Manilla folders.

"Honestly, Lieutenant McDaniel, if the world were a perfect place, I'd rather be home in Denver, taking my daughter to school, watching her basketball games and writing feature stories for my newspaper. I would rather Hunter and his parents still be alive and Jenny a happy high school student about to graduate. But I'm here because it's the least I can do for my friend. He was a good, decent man who just wanted to find his sister and share what he had with her."

Sam realized she was rambling; she sat back against the chair and willed herself to be calm. "I appreciate that you're willing to meet with me today because I know you don't have to, despite knowing James. I just wanted to ask you about two spa businesses that could, perhaps, be questionable in the types of services they provide."

"They are?"

"Green Spa and Aromatherapy Spa."

McDaniel rattled off the name of the street where they were located.

"Yes, those are the ones," Sam confirmed.

He thought for a moment, squeezing his chin between two fingers, then shook his head. "We've never had any incidents at either one. They're not off the radar, but as far as we know they're legit."

"Even though some of the reviews suggest that sex is on the service list and the windows are blacked out?"

"It's not a crime to have blacked out windows."

Sam cleared her throat softly. "Sir, I understand that, it's just that a number of reviews between the two establishments raise, it seems, a lot of red flags about questionable services."

"You think Jenny's involved with one of those spas?"

Sam shook her head. She had decided before meeting McDaniel she wouldn't reveal that Jenny lived in the rooms above the spas. She had to wait until at least tomorrow night and having the chance to meet Jenny before she could or would say anything regarding her whereabouts.

"But you know she's involved in human trafficking?"

Sam nodded.

"Is that from your source?" McDaniel asked.

Again, she nodded.

"You tell me you're a reporter, Miss Church, so I'm sure it's not lost on you that it is a crime to withhold information about somebody who you are aware is engaging in illicit activities with a minor."

"I can assure you, Lieutenant McDaniel, my source is engaged in no such activities."

"Uh huh."

"Is trafficking a big problem in El Paso, Lieutenant?"

"A border city? Really?" He raised his eyebrows and frowned at her in a sarcastic way. "I think you know the answer to that. I'm not going to bore you with a bunch of stats, but lemme just say that crimes for the FBI related to sex and labor trafficking have increased significantly in the past several years."

McDaniel left the corner of his desk and returned to his chair, dropping the pen and tablet over the top as he sat down. "As of November last year, there were more than fifteen-hundred pending trafficking investigations, including those involving minors exploited through commercial sex trafficking. In the last fiscal year, the FBI initiated more than six hundred and fifty human trafficking investigations nationwide."

"Were any arrests made?"

"More than four hundred seventy traffickers were arrested."

"So many," Sam said and her voice was weary.

"That's just the tip of the proverbial iceberg," the lieutenant said.

McDaniel eyed Sam carefully for a full minute and she could feel the heat and heaviness of his stare. She wanted to look away, but forced herself to keep eye contact.

"So, can I trust you?" he asked evenly.

Sam felt herself sit up internally with a jolt. "I think James assured you, Lieutenant, that you can."

He pointed a thick finger over the desk at her and spoke in a gritty voice. "If this gets out of this office, I'll make sure James never trusts you again."

Sam held up her hands and clasped them lightly in front of her. "You have my word, Lieutenant."

He pointed to a white board on a wall behind her and she had to turn to face it. At the top of the board written with a blue marker were the words:

OPERATION WINTER HOPE

Below the words were columns containing numbers and jurisdictions that meant nothing to Sam.

"Law enforcement agencies across Texas and New Mexico have been cooperating in an investigation that started in January," he said. "We're hoping to get similar results to an operation conducted in the upper Midwest last fall that led to one hundred and eighty arrests and the recovery of forty-eight missing children. During that operation one hundred and ten human trafficking victims were rescued and referred to social services."

"That's impressive," Sam said.

"More than fifty agencies participated in that operation," McDaniel continued and he was emphatic. "Which also included the arrest of a man and the recovery of two children in Michigan. What's more, nearly seventy missing and exploited children's cases were cleared. In fact, there are a host of similar operations like ours happening right now across the nation."

"Looks like that operation highlighted the vast number of potential victims," Sam said.

"That's right, and it also allowed authorities the opportunity to make contact and link those children with the proper services. There's a lot more out there, and each one of these stings does take a few perps off the street and free children to get the help they need."

"Is your investigation focusing on anyone, traffickers, here in this region?"

He sat back against his chair, his upper body covering it completely. "Specifically? No. But we've cast a wide net, so there's a pretty high chance we'll snare some of 'em. Who knows? Maybe even Jenny will be among the victims."

Sam took another moment to study the white board, scrutinizing the businesses on the list. They were listed alphabetically and she couldn't help gasping when she saw Aromatherapy Spa.

She turned to find McDaniel staring at her, trying to keep a stoic face.

"It's already on the list," she said.

"Look down a little further," the lieutenant said, not taking his eyes off her.

Sam glanced at the list until she got to Green Spa. "It's there, too," she said without turning back to him.

"Look at both businesses and then to that last column on the right."

"What am I looking for?" she asked.

He gave her a minute to study the board. "See a green dot next to either of those two?"

Sam shook her head. When she turned to face him, he said, "We have every known name of those types of facilities in the El Paso area on that board right there. If it doesn't have a green mark next to it, it means supposedly they're on the up and up. Not necessarily off the hook, but there are no red flags at the moment. Like I said they're on our radar."

"So, it's a working document that changes constantly," Sam said.

"Yes, ma'am."

"Maybe you'll change it now, Lieutenant."

Sam left McDaniel's office ten minutes later, eager to get in her car and check her phone. She had it on silent, but she felt it vibrate with at least one text message while she was in the lieutenant's office.

She pulled her phone from her bag and closed her eyes with relief after she read Houston's message.

Come to the motel tomorrow night at ten p.m. Ask the clerk at the front desk for room 210.

THIRTY-SEVEN

Tendrils of light were spreading across the morning sky when Sam opened her eyes.

Each morning since coming to El Paso, she woke to the weight of being away from home, the search for Jenny bearing down on her shoulders.

This morning she woke feeling light with hope.

Sam had talked to April on the phone before bed last night, eagerly waiting for her to ask about Jenny. When she did, Sam spoke like a child waking up on Christmas morning, thrilled to tell her daughter about the new lead she had followed, what had happened with Houston, and her chance to meet Jenny.

April shared her mother's enthusiasm. "Mommie, are you going to bring Jenny home to the ranch?!"

"Baby, I don't know what's going to happen. We'll have to wait and see how things go tomorrow night."

Until April had said *home to the ranch*, the thought of bringing Jenny to Colorado had been a distant one. Sam deliberately wouldn't think about it; the last thing she wanted was to build false hope for herself. She almost couldn't bear the thought of traveling to Texas, coming up empty-handed and, worse, letting Hunter down.

She rolled over in bed in no hurry to get up. Her thoughts worked in unison with the sun as it began to lighten the distant hills, bringing them into view.

What will I do after I finally have the chance to talk to Jenny?

Am I really the one who could get her to leave?

Why does Houston think she'll listen to me?

She grabbed her cell phone off the nightstand. Twenty minutes before she would call April on her way to school. She got up and primped in the bathroom mirror so she could walk to *La Dolce Vita* after they spoke. While there, she'd let Wilson and Howard know the developments and plan for tonight, though she wasn't sure what that plan was.

The day passed at a glacier's pace, and Sam was ready to leave her hotel room at nine p.m. Her bag was full with the items she wanted and hoped she'd have the chance to show Jenny—her rendering, the photos of her with her brother and mother, and the newspaper articles she found online yesterday at Franklin Elementary about the accident that had made them orphans.

And, perhaps, most importantly, Sam made sure to include Jenny's birth certificate.

By nine-thirty, she was parked down the street from the motel where she and Houston had been the day before. From this distance, she couldn't immediately tell if his GMC was in the parking lot.

At ten minutes to ten she drove into the parking lot, feeling fidgety and a tightness in her chest. Her tension eased slightly when she spotted Houston's truck in the last parking place in the row in front of the motel, spotless as usual, glistening under the towering outdoor lights in the parking lot. She selected a spot closer to the entrance and headed toward an oval-shaped blue and red sign that flashed *OPEN* intermittently.

The sliding glass door slid to the side as Sam approached. As she entered her senses were assaulted by stale cigarette smoke and cheap cleaning disinfectant. The lobby was sparse and a solitary Black male was standing behind the front desk, looking down at the computer. Two tatty faded-blue armchairs were facing each other between a small dated wooden coffee table near the main window in the lobby. There was an empty Styrofoam cup sitting on a napkin on the coffee table. Down the hallway Sam could see a vending and soda machine.

She approached the counter and smiled when the man looked up from his computer. He offered a subtle nod in return. He was tall and lean and his long face was plain, making him look younger than he probably was.

When she tried to talk, her mouth was so dry she couldn't form the words. She held her hand against her chest and cleared her throat several times, realizing she didn't know what she was supposed to say. Finally, she said, "Yes, I'm checking in for the night. I believe you have me in room 210."

The man nodded as he briefly studied the computer. After a moment he placed a key, an old-fashioned kind, not an activation card, on top the counter. It was attached to a plastic holder that displayed the name of the motel. He pointed toward the elevators and said, "Or the stairs are by the vending machines."

Sam took the key, wondering why he didn't ask for her information or payment, but was relieved he didn't. She got to the elevator. The stainless-steel panel between the double doors was filthy and discolored with something Sam could not identify. She used her room key to press the up arrow.

She left the elevator and was met with the same sour smells of stale smoke and bleach. She stood in front of a sign on the wall before her that listed room numbers. She followed the arrow to the right, walking on wafer-thin, heavily stained carpet. She could hear the muted sounds of television sets behind closed doors as she passed by, outside sirens from emergency vehicles wailed down the street. Room 210 was near the last room on the right, the second one before an exit door that led to the stairway.

Sam inserted the key holding her breath, half expecting the room to be well lit and perhaps Houston standing near the window and Jenny sitting on the bed, waiting for her. To her surprise the room was dark, save for a dim light falling from the bathroom on the floor in front of the door. She could feel the chill of the air conditioner running and wondered who would need cooler air this time of year.

She stuck her head in, unwilling, unsure, if she should go any further.

"Hello? Houston? Anyone here?" The tightness in her chest had been replaced with a hard knocking, her heart thundering so loud, she wondered if anyone else could hear it.

Her eyes shifted back and forth, adjusting to dimmer light. She stepped over the threshold. "Houston?"

She walked deeper into the room. Dropping her bag on the bed, she turned on the lamp on a small night table between the beds. Light fell on top of a phone with a long, twisted cord that dangled over the side. Two queen beds were facing a single dresser and a mirror attached on the wall above. Save for a large generic landscape picture on the wall next to the bed, the room was barren.

Sam went to the window, turned off the air conditioner and pulled the drapes to one side, light from the outdoor lamps fell on the window ledge. She saw Houston's truck parked directly beneath her window and put a hand over her chest with relief, feeling her heartbeat starting to slow. *Well, he's somewhere close.*

Sam had just set her phone on the night table when it vibrated and chimed with a text message. The room was so quiet, the sound seemed to magnify off the walls and she couldn't help jumping.

She saw the time, ten-fifteen, then read Houston's message.

You're in the room, I heard you come in.

Sam replied immediately. *Yes, I'm here. Where are you?*

We're in the room next to you. Go to the door that connects them. I'll let you in.

Those doors were such common parts of guest rooms that Sam had paid no attention to it when she entered. She grabbed her bag and started toward it, her eyes on the knob, walking as though she were on shards of glass, her phone still in her hand, her heart clamoring in her chest.

THIRTY-EIGHT

Jenny was sitting on the bed, looking toward the door as Sam stepped over the threshold into their room. For a sweeping moment, their eyes locked and Sam softened so deeply from within, she felt as though she had dropped to her knees.

Jenny was wearing a long teal-colored robe tied at her waist and sitting with one leg dangling off the edge of the bed. Her other leg was tucked under her and sticking out from beneath her robe. Her feet were bare. One of her hands was resting on the bedspread beside her, the other was in her lap. The robe looked new and Sam couldn't help wondering if Houston had purchased it specifically for this occasion. Despite the robe's plush, thick look, however, it couldn't conceal Jenny's rail-thin frame.

The robe's deep color deepened the brown in her long, fine hair, which was partially draped over her left shoulder, coming to rest over her breast. Sam remembered what Sandy Petersen had told her about the time Rita was a chaperon on one of Hunter's school field trips. Her hair was pulled back in a ponytail instead of the way she usually wore it, captured in a colorful clip neatly away from her face. Sandy had said, *"I remember Rita had the most beautiful natural-looking brown hair I had ever seen."*

Houston was standing next to the window and the drapes were drawn.

He motioned to Sam. "Come in and close the door."

Sam stepped to the side as she closed it, but remained near it, holding onto the door knob. She felt the depths of her emotions swell and catch the back of her throat with such intensity, she couldn't speak. She did not want to move, not trusting her legs. She had to force herself to breathe, and took a moment to scan the room to gather her emotions.

Both beds were made, the bedspreads, muted colors in shades of autumn, were well worn and reedy. Every light was on and the television set was muted; characters in a cop drama were silently moving across the screen with their weapons drawn. Unlike Sam's room, chilled by the air conditioner, Houston's room was cozy with warmth. A pizza box and discarded napkins were on the bed opposite Jenny's, the lid was open and Sam recognized the *Anthony's* logo in the center of the box. There were three bottles of Mexican Coke on the dresser, two were empty.

The room smelled of dinner, pizza dough and pepperoni. And something else, but it took Sam a moment before she recognized the aroma as men's cologne, a fresh, out-of-the shower scent.

Houston looked as he did the few times Sam now had been with him, wearing a black short-sleeve T-shirt tucked inside dark Demin cargo pants, a black canvas belt and metal buckle, and, of course, his camel-colored combat boots. His winter jacket, the black one he'd let Jenny wear when it was cold, was on the corner of the bed. Sam noticed a skimpy dress with a dark floral print next to the jacket. Well-worn black flats were on the floor beneath the dress.

Houston's arms were crossed over his chest, the big black tactical watch prominent on his left wrist. The dark outfit revealed his slender, wiry frame. His thinning hair was combed neatly in place away from his craggy face, and Sam could tell he was freshly shaven.

Though she did not know him well, despite looking as though he was standing guard and ready to enter mortal combat any moment, she had to believe the forgiving, easy look on his lined face and the softness of his demeanor was only because he was in the room with Jenny.

Houston looked from Jenny and nodded toward Sam. "Jenny, this is the woman I was telling you about, Sam Church." He spoke in a voice laced with love. "She's from Denver and she worked with your brother at a newspaper there."

Houston's words made Sam draw a deep, involuntary breath. She tightened her jaw, squared her shoulders and swallowed hard, willing her emotions to stay at bay.

"I didn't know I had a brother, 'til Houston told me," Jenny said, looking from Houston to Sam.

Sam felt too moved to speak, so she only offered a small smile. Her legs had steadied, so she grabbed the straps of her bag and walked to the bed. Standing so close to Jenny now, Sam could easily see the small beauty mark near the corner of her mouth Houston had told her about. She had the same hazel eyes as Hunter and the light from the lamp on the nightstand revealed flecks of brown within them.

Sam wanted nothing more than at this moment to gobble Jenny up in her arms, wishing she could change what had happened so many years ago. Instead, she started to pull the photos of her family from her bag. Houston came and stood beside them.

The first one Sam placed on the bed beside Jenny was of John and Rita in the hospital room after giving birth to Hunter. She waited, allowing Jenny a moment to study the photo.

Sam pointed to it. "That's your mother and father. They're holding your brother."

"Hunter?" Jenny asked, her head tilted toward the photo.

Sam looked at Houston, her eyebrows high, her eyes bright, grateful he'd been able to prepare Jenny somewhat before they finally had the chance to meet.

Next, Sam placed the photo of Hunter and his mother sitting on the bed of their truck, she was holding Jenny in her arms. She watched Jenny scan the photos, her eyes shifting back and forth between them. Then, Sam placed the photo of Hunter and Jenny sitting on the couch next to each other, mere weeks before the fatal accident.

She pointed to Hunter and their mother sitting on the truck. "That's you in your mother's arms."

"Me?" Jenny's voice was fragile. She placed a hand against her robe and Sam saw that her fingernails had been bitten to the nubs, some so close to the cuticles they were caked with bits of dried blood.

"Yes, you. He was born here in El Paso. You both were," Sam said. Her tears were so close, she could taste the salt in her mouth. She swallowed hard, forcing them back. "Your brother used to tell me that your father often took his family on camping trips over the weekend to the Franklin Mountains."

"The ones here?" Jenny asked.

Sam had to laugh. "Yes, the ones you see nearly everywhere you go in El Paso."

"We were there?"

"Yes, and this one here," Sam pointed to them sitting on the couch. "Was taken in your living room, not long, maybe a month before the accident."

"Accident?" Jenny grabbed the corner of the photo of them on the couch and pulled it closer.

Houston stepped closer to Jenny and placed his hand gently over her arm. His light touch brought her eyes to his. "Jenny, remember I told you Sam would have a lot more to tell you about that accident and what happened to you and your brother after that."

When she nodded Houston removed his hand and stepped back, allowing Sam to continue.

Without another word, Sam reached inside her tote and retrieved the articles she had copied of the accident. First, she placed the article in English down on the bed, the other in Spanish she placed beside it.

Jenny read the headline:

Popular UTEP Teacher, Wife Killed by Drunk Driver

"What's UTEP?" Jenny asked, as she started to read the article.

Houston answered. "It's the university here. Your father was a professor there when he died."

"But my mother said my father died of cancer. I never knew him because he died when I was just a baby."

Sam moved closer to the bed and placed her hand over the articles. "Sweetheart, your mother and father were killed in this accident by a drunk driver going the wrong way on the interstate. You and your brother were in the car, and so was a cousin. Your cousin also died. You were in a car seat and weren't hurt, but Hunter was seriously injured."

Sam went on, choosing her words carefully, "Yes, the woman who raised you, raised you as her own daughter and yes, she loves you very much, just as any mother would, but it was your mother's sister, your aunt, who took you to Mexico and raised you as her own. It was her husband who died of cancer, not your father."

The room fell silent until the distant wail of sirens broke the quiet.

"My mom kept a picture on the window sill over our kitchen sink," Jenny started by saying. "I remember one day when I was six, I came into the kitchen and my mom was holding the photo. She was looking at it and crying like she always did. I saw it so many times when I was in the kitchen." She shrugged deeply. "But I didn't know who it was. That day I asked my mom. She wiped the tears away and said it was my aunt and I said the one who went to the United States and she said yes. And I said the one who died in the car accident with her husband and she said yes. She told me they were my aunt and uncle. I knew I had a cousin, but my mom always told me he was adopted because she said she thought she couldn't have kids until she had me, but she never told me I had a brother."

"Jenny, honestly I don't know much about your cousin, which was your aunt's son, but it was your mother and father who died in the car accident," Sam said.

"Why would my mother lie?" Jenny asked, looking from Sam to Houston, his arms were crossed tightly over his chest. He swallowed hard, his Adam's apple dipping.

Sam answered. "Sweetheart, I don't know why she didn't tell you the truth. Maybe she was afraid. Perhaps she thought you both had been given a second chance, her a second chance at being a mother, and you another chance to be a daughter. Maybe she thought it would be better the way she told you. I don't know. Or she may have been waiting until you were old enough to understand."

"But you say my brother, Hunter, is gone, too."

Sam felt her heart crumbled as though it were a piece of paper as she pulled the photo of Hunter from her bag and set it on the bed. He was sitting in front of the bonfire at the ranch. After a moment, Sam said, "My daughter took this photo of Hunter at our ranch last September. He was twenty-four and the next day he was injured badly in an accident during the story we were covering for the newspaper. He died a few days later."

Jenny collected the photo in her hands. "How'd he die?"

Sam told her the story and Jenny listened intently, not taking her eyes off Hunter's photo.

She finished by saying, "He passed away in September, just a few months ago. I can't tell you how many times he told me how much he wanted to find you again.

"So, you and your brother did live with your aunt in *Juárez* for about a year, but when your uncle got cancer, she brought Hunter back to the United States and then took you to her hometown because she said she couldn't afford to take care of both of you."

"*San Ciro de Acosta,*" Jenny said, the words flowed fluently in Spanish.

"Yes," Sam said.

"That's where my mother said I was born." She turned to Houston with a startled look, her mouth a perfect oval. "That's why I can't go home. They took my passport, everything. I have nothing, no money, no identification, no way to get home. No one knows where I am."

Houston said to Jenny, "Tell Sam what happened to your passport." To Sam he said, "It was one of those manufactured ones."

Sam nodded, her lips a tight line.

"We were in a van and they brought us somewhere, but I don't know where 'cause the van didn't have windows, then we got out in this garage and they made everyone stand in a line."

"Other girls just like you?" Sam asked.

Jenny nodded. "They told us to get our passports out and we had

227

them in our hands when this really big man walked in front of each one of us and grabbed them out of our hands. I jumped out of line and said, 'you can't have that, that's mine!' When I tried to grab it back, he shoved me back in line and pointed his finger at me and said, 'shut up, you little bitch.'"

Houston stepped forward and said to Sam in a gritty voice, "That's the man I was telling you about at *Anthony's*, some man, a monster, a mother fu—" Houston couldn't finish the word and Sam could see fury burning in his eyes.

"If I ever come face to face with him, I'll shove my fist so far up his ass it'll make him gag." Houston lowered his head. "I am sorry to talk like that in front of both of you, but I can hardly stand to think of what he's done to Jenny and the others." He clenched his fists in front of Sam, the way he had done at *Anthony's*. "I swear to you if I ever see this guy, I'll kill 'em. I swear, I will kill him."

"Has he ever hurt you, Jenny?" Sam asked.

Jenny's frame seemed to shrink as she brought her hand to her mouth. "Every time he comes here for me, I lie there waiting for it to be over. I stare at the ceiling and think of my mother. I never got to say goodbye to her. They took me away. They said I would make money that I could send home to her so her life would be better, but that's never happened. I know she doesn't know what's happened to me. She must think I'm dead. That hurts more than anything. I just don't want them to hurt her. She doesn't deserve that because of what I've done. I just want to be able tell her I'm okay and I'm sorry for doing what I did and leaving her the way I did."

Jenny's tears came in a surge and Sam had to look away or hers would soon follow.

"I miss her so much," Jenny went on. "I miss my home, but I can't go back. I'll never be able to go back."

"Sweetheart." Sam felt a fierce wave of anger wash over her. She was so angry when she reached into her bag, her hands were shaking. In all her years, all the wrongs and injustices she had seen, she'd never felt such raw primal anger. *Oh, Hunter, I will do anything to get her out.*

Sam pulled Jenny's birth certificate out and placed it in her lap.

"Sweetheart. You were born in the United States." Sam tapped the top of the paper where it said *Certificate of Live Birth.* "Here in this country. In El Paso. In the very same hospital as your brother. They can't send you back."

At the revelation, Jenny's tears began to slow. "How'd you find me here?"

"Someone I know spotted you one night in a grocery store. You were with Houston."

"But how'd you know it was me?"

Sam pulled the final image from her bag, the police rendering of Jenny. She placed it lightly on the bed. "This is how."

With the likeness of Jenny staring up at each of them the resemblance was striking. "And this is," Sam spread her hands over the dingy room. "Where we are now."

The clock radio on the nightstand was approaching eleven-thirty, and Houston stepped between Sam and Jenny. "Sam, it's almost midnight. You have to go. They'll be coming for her soon."

"You know who comes to get her?" Sam's eyes were wide like dinner plates.

Houston shook his head. "It's someone different every time, usually a couple of punks wearing sunglasses and bandanas, and I could take both of them out before they even knew what was happening, but I am not going to get in the way of the Glock they have."

Sam put her hand lightly on Jenny's lap. "Sweetheart, you don't have to stay here. We can go to the police. You can leave, right now, with Houston, he'll take care of you, he'll bring you back home to your mother."

Jenny was biting the nails on her right hand, shaking her head. "Other girls have done it, tried to run, and they find them and bring them back. Every time they find them and bring them back. I've seen the beatings they've gotten. The pictures they've showed them of dead bodies, telling the girls that's punishment for trying to leave. I can't do that. I just can't. I can't do that to my mom. If I stay, she'll be okay. I've already hurt her enough."

"Sam." Houston looked solemnly between them. "You have to go now."

Sam wanted to cup Jenny's face in her hands. Instead, she felt Houston take her by the wrist and pull her toward the adjoining doors.

Sam took one long last look at Jenny before they crossed the threshold back to the other room. When Houston closed the door, they stood together in front of it staring at each other. Sam crossed her arms against her chest and held herself tightly, her anger continuing to burn. Her stomach felt like it was ablaze in a wildfire. They spoke in whispers.

"Houston, we've got to get her out of this situation. I don't know how, but we've got to find a way. Let's go to the police."

"By now you know, don't you, why that's not possible?" His voice was sharp. "She's afraid, Sam. She says some of the girls ended up in police custody after a raid last year, and they were never heard from again. Jenny and the rest of the girls were told they were killed by authorities as punishment for trying to run away."

"That's a lie. Just like those photos they've shown the girls who've tried to escape, claiming it's one of their family members." Sam growled in a low tone. "That's just a threat. They just want them to believe that so they'll stay frightened for their lives."

"Well, either way it's working. Mainly, Jenny's afraid for her mother. She's afraid of what could happen to her if she were to run."

"We've got to do something."

Houston stuffed his hands deep in his pockets and nodded, his eyes fixed on his combat boots. "I know, Sam, I know, but now you have to go. I always get the room we're in next to the exit and the stairwell. Take the stairs and go back to your hotel. We'll talk tomorrow."

As Houston closed the door behind him, Sam grabbed her jacket off the bed and put it on as she left her room. In the hallway, she let the door close softly and she slipped silently down the stairs. She hurried to her rental car and locked the door once she got inside.

She was about to leave the parking lot when she stopped suddenly, captured in thought, looking at Houston's truck and up to the second story window where she knew Jenny and Houston were. She could see a light on in the room through a small slit in the curtains.

She decided to wait, hoping to witness who might come for Jenny. But by one-thirty a.m. nothing had happened. She saw no one enter or leave the area. Houston's truck was still there, and the light in Jenny's room remained on.

Sam started the car and headed for the interstate and back to her hotel. The tears that had been at bay all evening came rushing forth in a torrent.

THIRTY-NINE

As a one-time promising heavyweight contender Fredrick Lawrence 'Larry' Henderson had never envisioned he'd end up as bodyguard and errand boy for a personal injury attorney with a silver spoon up her rear end.

He scowled as he thought back to the drunk driver who he liked to say had ended his pro boxing career (at least that's what he told those who asked) and also in a roundabout way brought him and Sun City's or *El Chuco's* most famous attorney together.

Stepping off the elevator and heading toward Amanda Moore's office, Larry started down the long office corridor toward the frosted glass doors.

The attorney's name was stenciled in elegant lean black lettering, making it stand out against the opaque glass. Her first name was traced on one door, her last name directly across on the other. He remembered how Amanda threw a fit when they had initially engraved her name on the doors because her first and last names weren't evenly aligned.

Those two hapless characters, as Amanda had called them, had to redo that main door a half-dozen times before she finally felt the names looked even.

He checked his watch and slowed his gait, not wishing to arrive too early. It was after hours and he knew the office would be locked, so he fished his keys from his pocket as he neared it. He unlocked one of the doors and let himself inside the reception area.

The room was quiet, save for the faint whir from the computer. He looked at Amanda Moore's name on the wall behind the receptionist's desk and her slogan directly beneath it:

Smart. Aggressive. Compassionate.

He snorted. *What a joke,* he thought.

Smart. *Not very. Dumb as a bag of hair.*

Aggressive. *She didn't give a shit about her clients and what tragic, life-changing events had happened to them, she only cared about the insurance money.*

Compassionate. He snorted again. *A heart like a stone.*

Whenever he was home watching television and one of her commercials would air, he couldn't change the channel fast enough. He hated her and had since the beginning, but she had made him rich and gave him the pick of the new crop every time, so he couldn't complain. Not really.

It was five minutes before nine p.m. and he already knew she was going to be in a foul mood because the van was late—two hours late— and Amanda Moore didn't like it when things didn't stay on schedule. She didn't like having her evening routine changed—any routine changed for that matter.

Too bad, bitch. Like it or not, that's how it is tonight.

He passed through the reception area, headed down the hall, passing in front of the outer offices. They were dark and computer monitors glowed eerily, reflecting in the black office windows. He kept his pace slow until he reached the corner office. He only knocked twice, any more and she would be furious. He could hear her behind the closed door, telling him in her usual short, clipped tone to come in.

He knew that didn't mean to enter her office in a literal sense, only to open the door far enough to stick his head inside. And he did.

"Amanda."

She didn't look up from her computer.

"They're here."

She closed her laptop and rose from her desk. "'Bout goddamn time."

She met him at the door and he stepped aside as she entered the hallway. "What the hell was the hold up?" she asked. "I've got a commercial to shoot in the morning and I need to get some sleep. I can't go there looking like I'm shitfaced."

He shrugged. "I'm not exactly sure, Amanda. When the driver called, he said there was a hold up at the border."

She gave him a steely stare and her upper lip was curled in a rancid way. "They should've been here two weeks ago." She held up two fingers. "What kind of holdup happened these last two weeks? You told me these guys were supposed to be the best?"

Larry shrugged again and followed her without answering.

"Are they downstairs finally?"

He nodded. "They're waiting for you."

"Then let's see what they've brought us this time."

They took the elevator to the bottom parking garage. He let Amanda leave the elevator first and he followed two steps behind her as he always did—thinking as he always did, *she acts like she's frickin' royalty.* They headed toward a plain brown, windowless van. It was still idling; exhaust vapors dripped from the tailpipe.

The driver, a portly man with thick, dark hair, took up the entire seat behind the wheel. He saw them approach, left the van and met them at the back. They huddled together, waiting for Amanda to give the cue. Larry towered over both of them.

She gave a quick nod with her chin toward the van doors. "Get 'em out."

The driver opened the door and shouted in Spanish and then English for the girls to get out. Larry watched as a dozen girls started to file out, climbing down slowly one after the other, with fear on their faces, their eyes round as the moon, dearly holding onto the only personal

234

possession they had left—their passport.

They lined up in a single-file line and Amanda walked in front of each one like a drill sergeant, her arms folded and a vile, sharp look on her face. Larry followed behind her, demanding each one of their passports. They handed them over with trembling hands.

Of course, they all looked different, a motley crew with diverse hair color, skin tone, body shape and size, but they shared a common bond— they were theirs now, their lives all but over.

Amanda stopped at the girl at the end of the line and gave the driver an incredulous look. "What the hell is this? This bitch looks like she's fifty. You took two weeks longer for this piece of shit?"

Larry worked to keep the foul, disgusted look off his face. *She's maybe twenty, hardly something to get worked up about. She always has to find something wrong with one of them.*

Amanda gave the girl another look and sniffed. "Put her to work doing the cooking, I guess. Hopefully she can boil water. The rest of them will do."

Her henchman nodded, turned to the driver and held out his hand. The driver dropped the keys in his palm. Amanda returned to the elevator, her stilettos echoing sharply on the shiny cement.

Larry waited until the girls were back in the van and then he started the vehicle. He drove from the garage to the city street, heading toward the rooms above the Green and Aromatherapy spas, thinking about his reward, what Amanda always said he could have, his pick of the new girls.

An initiation to a new and unforgiving life.

But he wanted none of them, only one, the same one each and every time.

Jenny. Jenny. Jenny.

She was the prettiest. The only one who had stood up to him, jumping out of line and demanding her passport back when he had taken it from her the first time. He remembered the wrath in her eyes as he shoved her back in line, telling her to shut her mouth.

She had been so young and innocent the first time he set eyes on her, and had his way with her. Not anymore. After nearly four years, her purity and innocence gone, her defiance shattered by the world she now lived in.

But her beauty. It remained.

Saturday night. A few more days before he could get his hands on her again. And he could hardly wait.

FORTY

The alarm on Sam's cell phone was set as it usually was to call April on her way to school. Though she hadn't gotten to bed until after two a.m., she had been up long before it was set to ring.

She had turned the armchair in her room toward the window to watch and wait for the dawn, her bare feet resting on the window sill. The sky was an inky black when she first sat down, now the edges along the horizon were faint with the first signs of morning light.

Wrapped in the scratchy terrycloth hotel robe, she couldn't help thinking not only of her own soft worn robe at home and of the new robe Jenny was wearing, but also how thin the girl's small frame was. Sam could still see the empty pizza box and soda bottles on the dresser, certain it was the first full meal she'd eaten all day. Sam shook her head at Jenny's scant clothing, a flimsy dress and flats meant for a hot summer day. Since she didn't remember seeing a jacket or coat in the room that belonged to Jenny, she had to guess Jenny had nothing to wear going from the motel to the van, or however she was taken back to the rooms above the spas.

The moment Sam had opened her eyes, the evening with Jenny returned and played like a chorus in her mind. The last image she saw of Jenny was a plain-faced, despondent girl with defeated hazel eyes and a flat appearance that made her look like a cardboard cutout. Sam became consumed with that image as she stared out the window, trying to envision Jenny's features from all angles.

Sam found that despite the stark look on Jenny's face and her demeanor, she imagined she saw something else seemingly hovering just beneath her surface. Jenny had an iridescence about her that was illuminating, warm and bright. Sam wondered if, beside her beauty, it's what Houston, too, had found attractive and captivating about Jenny. So alluring about her. When Jenny spoke of her home and the woman she called her mother, she came to life, animated with a luminescence about her like sunlight streaming through stained glass.

April's innocence and naiveté at the cruelty, selfishness and unfairness the world often held, entered her mind. If April were ever in that situation, Sam wouldn't hesitate, she'd shatter every door down until she found her. She was certain the first thing April would ask this morning would be about Jenny. How would she, how *could* she explain the events of last evening to her daughter?

Sam thought of Jenny growing up in Mexico, the only place she knew as home. She may have been born in the United States, but of course why wouldn't she want to return to the only place she really knew, the only place where she knew happiness. El Paso, Texas meant nothing to her before she was forced to come. Now if Jenny ever had the chance to leave and go back to Mexico, this sprawling border city along the Rio Grande would be the last place she'd ever want to return to.

Her alarm sounded. Moments later she was dialing April's number.

"Mommie, did you finally meet Jenny last night?" April asked first thing.

"Yes, I did, Baby. She's such a pretty young girl, just like you." She was forcing herself to talk with a spry voice.

"That was a good lead to follow then, right Mommie?"

Sam laughed into the phone. "Yes, it was, and you know how happy that makes your mother."

"I do!" April's voice was bright and cheery, the way Sam hoped hers sounded coming through the car speaker. "Does that mean you'll be home for my basketball game on Saturday?"

Two days away. February was about to draw to a close, and Sam still had no idea what the next few days, weeks would bring.

"If Jenny comes home with you, Mommie," April chattered on, "She can share my room with me and she can come with us and watch my game, too. Does she like spaghetti? Nona keeps looking at the calendar in the kitchen and saying to me and Howard every night when we're eating dinner, 'Samantha will be home soon and we'll have a big dinner to celebrate.' Nona said she'll even make your favorite lemon cake!"

April's words pierced Sam, a scythe slashing through her heart, making her feel as though the distance between them went beyond the moon. She ached to be home and everything it meant. "Baby, that sounds wonderful. I miss you and being home with everyone so, so much, but I don't think Jenny will be coming back to Denver with me, at least not this time."

Sam deliberately steered the conversation away from Jenny and last night, talking instead about April's upcoming basketball game before they hung up a few minutes later. She put her phone in her lap and was still staring out the window when it began ringing less than ten minutes later.

"Hi Howard," Sam answered in a gloomy voice.

"I could tell the way you sounded, Samantha, things didn't go so well last night."

"As far as meeting Jenny it was good, Howard, she is a beautiful young woman. I can see Hunter in her eyes, but her circumstances, truly a dire situation."

"What are you going to do?"

Sam might as well have been sitting on her hands. "I simply have no idea, Howard. I could go back to Mark McDaniel's office, but I don't know how that would play out, and besides, what if that backfired? I don't know how many contacts these people could have. The last thing we need is for them to get wind the cops are about to raid them.

239

They could disappear overnight, taking Jenny and all the other girls somewhere else. We could lose her forever. At least now I know where she is." After a brief silence she said, "She talked so much about her mother. I can't even imagine what that woman has gone through these last four years, wondering what's ever happened to her."

"Let's think like you're going to find a way to get Jenny to safety. Hopefully you and Houston can find a way to work together."

"Honestly, Howard, he's my only hope."

"Sounds like he might know you're his only hope, too."

"Maybe."

"Keep me posted, Samantha," Howard said. "There's not much I can do from here, but you know I'll do what I can."

Sam thanked him graciously and they ended the call.

It was after seven and Sam knew Houston would already be at work. She sent him a text. *What happened after I left? I waited in the parking lot for over an hour and I never saw you or Jenny leave.*

Ten minutes later, Houston replied.

They finally came, but not til after one.

Why so late?

Don't know. Something obviously was up, they're never that late.

Is that unusual?

It is in that it's pretty much by the book. By one, I'm almost back to my apartment.

Sam didn't respond right away and Houston sent another text.

You probably just missed me leaving.

I guess so, Sam replied.

But you wouldn't have seen Jenny leave. They take her, all the girls, out thru the service entry of the motel.

Sam shook her head as she read Houston's text. That had not occurred to her.

I need to see you today. We need to talk. Please.

I'm busy all day at the construction site, got a few meetings. Tonite at the Nite Owl @ 7. I'll come straight from work. See you there.

She responded simply, *Okay.*

The first hint of sunlight appeared on the distant hills as Sam tried to plan her day until it was time to meet Houston. She decided to spend as much of it as she could observing activity at the motel and spas where Jenny was locked away.

She wasn't expecting her efforts to produce much, if anything, but she'd be as close to Jenny as she could and it was better than staring at the walls in her hotel room.

FORTY-ONE

S am was sitting in her sedan in the parking lot at the Nite Owl.
It was six-thirty-two p.m.

Her hands were on top the steering wheel and she was looking expectantly down the street for Houston's truck. She was hoping he would have finished work early and would already be here when she arrived. The hope and expectation of seeing his truck had faded like a winter storm when she got to the stop sign at Piedras Street and didn't see his GMC.

As she waited, she thought back over her day. When Sam entered *La Dolce Vita*, Mia had given her a warm, enthusiastic wave and Sam responded in kind at seeing her and Jeff. She listened to them replay the scene with Amanda an hour earlier.

"Was she complaining about her coffee again?" Sam had asked.

"Oh no, it's *way* better than that. We've been laughing about it now, but it wasn't very funny this morning," Mia said. "We actually had customers waiting in line who walked out because of the way she was behaving on the phone. It was so embarrassing. I really wish she'd find another place to get her coffee."

Mia looked at Jeff as though giving him the cue to explain what happened.

Jeff mimicked Amanda by dramatically fluffing his hair and pushing an imaginary pair of sunglasses up on his nose. He shaped his hand into a phone and pretended to talk, doing his best to mock the sound of Amanda's crabby, shrill voice. "They're having you call me? You're kidding, right? Who are you, anyway? You sound like you're fifteen. Get me someone who knows what they're doing. I'm not talking to you about my client."

Jeff changed his voice to imitate the male voice on the call. "I'm sorry, Amanda, but they've asked me to talk to you initially about your client's case."

Jeff returned to mocking Amanda, his voice a low growl. "A flunky? Do you know who I am? I've been doing this since you were in diapers. They're stalling, that's what they're trying to do. Get me someone else to talk to."

"I'm so sorry, Amanda," Jeff said talking now as the male caller. "So, if you could please just answer a few questions, we could get started."

Mia jumped in. "They must've gone back and forth like that for five minutes. The poor guy apologizing and Amanda berating him. She was talking so loudly I'm sure people passing on the street could hear her."

"Tell Sam about the couple standing behind Amanda," Jeff said to Mia.

Mia's eyes grew wide and she brought her hands to her mouth. "Oh my god. They're such a nice, older couple, so polite, they come in all the time, and we love waiting on them. He caught my eye and shook his head. He pointed at the door and they walked out. I wanted to run out and apologize, but we were so busy, I couldn't leave the counter. I hope Amanda hasn't scared them away."

"What was the henchman doing?" Sam asked.

"Nothing," Jeff and Mia answered in unison.

"Just standing there with his arms folded, looking like the lug he is with those dumb sunglasses he wears," Mia added.

"Yeah, I guess he figured Amanda could handle being her usual insufferable self," Jeff said.

"How did it end?" Sam asked.

"Amanda was still gabbing on the phone, but we finally got her to order and move away from the bar. She planted herself at that table over there." Sam looked to where Mia pointed. "She was on the phone maybe another fifteen minutes, and then when she was finally through, she had the nerve to complain that her coffee wasn't hot enough."

"What's wrong with you people?" Jeff said, impersonating Amanda again. "One of these days I am going to complain to the manager. How could he hire such inept, useless employees?"

"I told her 'It's a she, Amanda,'" Mia said.

"Amanda pulled her sunglasses down and glared at Mia, looking really confused. She said, 'what?'" Jeff said.

"I took a business card from a card holder by the bar and handed it to her," Mia went on. "I told her 'Our manager's a woman, Amanda. Her name is Judy and she'd love to hear from you.'"

"What did Amanda do then?" Sam asked.

"Oh, she scoffed and ignored the business card in Mia's hand," Jeff said nonchalantly. "I remade her drink, she took it and stormed toward the door."

"Her henchman was holding it open for her," Mia added.

Sam told Mia and Jeff she was glad she had missed it. "That's not the way I'd want to start my day."

Sam then spent six hours waiting and watching the rooms above the spas and activity at the motel. Customers, men mostly, came and went from both places and Sam was pretty certain they weren't going to the respective spas for facials. She drove behind the motel several times to observe the service entry, but each time the area was shuttered and deserted.

She talked to Wilson, a conversation that nearly mirrored the one she had with Howard. He had asked about going to the police with the knowledge she had.

"What about that lieutenant, that Mark McDaniel at the local police department?" Wilson had asked.

"I'd rather talk to James first," Sam had said. "He could be a buffer to Mark. I think Mark would take the information I have better coming from him, not me."

"Are you planning to call him today?"

"I'm going to wait and see where my meeting with Houston goes this evening before I call James."

Wilson's solemn voice filtered out from the car speaker. "Sam, I know I don't need to remind you what happened when Hunter didn't want to wait for you to call James when you both were at the construction site."

"I know, Wilson. I don't need to be reminded. I think about that evening every day. That night is one of the reasons I'm here in El Paso, away from April, home and everything. I'd love to get the police involved, but Jenny's afraid and I won't do anything to make the situation worse than it already is."

Sam had been in the motel parking lot when she was on the phone with Wilson, her attention drifting between the main entrance and the doors on the sides of the building. She closed her eyes and rested her forehead against the steering wheel and spoke barely above a whisper, "I just hope it doesn't result in another fatal decision."

At ten minutes to seven, Sam felt relief mixed with a wave of eagerness rush through her when she saw Houston's GMC arrive at the stop sign, the headlights cutting through the darkness. He gave her a two-finger salute as he parked. Sam was at his car door as he got out and they walked toward the tavern together in silence.

They headed to the same booth near the saloon-style doors that led to the kitchen, country music was blaring overhead and the place smelled of freshly made popcorn. They sat down; this close to the kitchen the air was saturated with grease, probably from a deep fryer, Sam guessed and she couldn't help thinking what a great, pathetic combination of booze and fried food made and how much of both she had consumed.

The same young server came to the table and greeted them.

"Hey, big guy," she said, tapping his shoulder. "Your usual?"

When Houston nodded, she looked at Sam. "Club soda?"

"Yes, please."

"Be right back," she said.

"I'm not sure I slept at all after last night," Sam said after the server left the table.

"That's how it is almost every time I go. Sometimes I don't even bother going to bed," Houston said. He removed his ball cap and placed it on the seat beside him. He looked weary, heavy lines ran the length of his forehead, crow's feet were etched deeply near his eyes. A full day's beard growth revealed more gray than black along the corners of his chin. "I've been with Jenny now two, three times a week for nearly the last four years and, especially these last four, five months, I see more and more the toll it's taken on her. Those girls with no hope, no place to go, burn out so fast."

"How long have you been trying to get her to leave?"

"Seriously for the last year at least, but she won't budge. She's afraid for her life. You heard her last night. Jenny thinks she has no way out. No money, no true way to identify herself and no way to get home. If she runs, then what?" He looked at Sam as if expecting her to answer. When she offered nothing, he continued. "She's afraid of the police. She knows no one on the outside she could trust, only me. Where would she go? What would she do?"

The waitress placed their drinks and snacks between them.

Houston gave her a quick nod of acknowledgement and went on. "Jenny's been trapped in those rooms above that spa and in this situation for so long now, I'm not sure she'd know what to do on her own."

Sam pushed her soda to the side and leaned into the table. "But she's not alone, Houston. She has us. I can call the police chief in Grandview tomorrow morning—right now if I have to—who can quickly connect us with the El Paso police." For now, Sam elected not to tell Houston about her conversation with Mark McDaniel. "When are you going to see her again?"

"Not 'til Saturday night," he said, his voice filled with resignation.

Sam leaned back and sighed in frustration. She watched their server for a moment, her fluid movements coming and going from the bar as she waited on other customers. She was standing at the bar now, waiting on a drink order when she picked up a white towel and started drying shot glasses. "Might as well say it'll be an eternity until then," Sam said finally.

"That's how it feels most of the time between our visits. I stay as busy as I can to help time pass and, honestly, to keep my mind off her."

"Including holding a second job as a night security guard."

Houston was taking a swallow of beer when he stopped and looked at her over the top of his bottle.

She answered before he could ask. "One of the days I had followed you back to your apartment after work, I was still in the parking lot when I saw you again heading back to your truck dressed like a security guard."

"You followed me downtown?"

"I did. The building, as a matter of fact, is just a block from my hotel, right off the plaza, so I returned a few times that night and you were at the front desk in the lobby. Must make for a very long day when you're working both jobs."

Houston kept a stoic look to Sam's revelation. "I had to take a second job so I could spend as much time and money with Jenny as I could," he said matter-of-factly. "To keep her out of that hellhole for a few hours here and there."

Sam nodded, recalling the conversation she'd had in Mark McDaniel's office when they were studying the Operation Winter Hope white board.

"I'm sure I don't want to know," Sam had said to the lieutenant, "But just how lucrative is the sex trafficking industry?"

"According to the latest report from the International Labour Organization, traffickers earn profits of nearly one hundred fifty billion per year," McDaniel had said. "Traffickers can make anywhere between four thousand and fifty thousand dollars per person trafficked."

"Why such a wide range?" Sam asked.

"A lot depends on the victim's place of origin and destination," McDaniel had answered. "There's big money here in the USofA."

Sam asked Houston. "How much does it cost you to free Jenny a few evenings a month?"

He took a long swallow of beer. When he didn't answer, Sam tilted her head slightly, expecting an answer. "Houston."

"Up to three grand."

She leaned heavily into the table, the look on her face perplexed. "A night?"

He nodded. "I leave the money on the dresser when they come for her." He took another swallow of beer and then added, "I'll do it as long as I have to."

Sam gave him a hard stare. "Will you let me come again Saturday night?"

After a moment, he nodded.

"Then we have two days to come up with a plan," she said.

Sam was back in her hotel room, and after the late news, she was in the bathroom getting ready for bed. She had started to rinse out the commuter mug Mia had given her from *La Dolce Vita* when a thought hit her with such intensity, she had to grab the corners of the sink to steady herself.

She held the mug to eye level, turning it around, looking at it from all angles. She set it on the counter, walked into the other room and grabbed her phone from the nightstand. She looked at the time on the clock radio as she scrolled through her contacts: ten-forty-five. He was probably asleep, but she found his number and hit the call button. The phone rang one, two, three, four, times before he finally picked up, barely managing a greeting in a gruffy, sleep-filled voice.

"Houston, it's Sam. I'm sorry if I woke you, but I had to call."

"What's up?"

"You've told me you've never seen this big guy who has assaulted Jenny and the others?"

"Yeah, that's right, and I told you what I'd do to him if I ever saw him."

"But Jenny would know him."

"Of course she would, but what're you getting at?"

"Nothing, I'm sure," she answered, staring toward the bathroom where she had left the commuter mug. "It's probably just a wasted thought, and not one I can do anything about tonight, anyway. I'm sorry I woke you, but I'll let you know what I come up with in the morning."

FORTY-TWO

The moment the alarm on Sam's cell phone started to ring at five-fifteen a.m. she got out of bed, dressed and headed toward *La Dolce Vita*. She passed alongside the plaza, the trees illuminated brightly in golden light in the predawn darkness.

Mia was by a counter near the door stocking it with stainless-steel cream containers, stir sticks and a variety of sugar packets when Sam walked in a few minutes after six a.m.

"Morning, Sam! You're here early," Mia said. Sam could tell she was freshly showered; her long hair was still damp beneath her visor and she smelled sweetly of scented lotion. She had her apron on, but she hadn't tied it around her waist.

"Good morning, Mia, hopefully Amanda and her bodyguard haven't been here yet."

"Oh no," Mia said, returning the remaining sugar packets to the cabinet below. "She usually gets here between seven and seven-thirty, so you haven't missed her yet. You know how much we love starting our day waiting on Amanda."

When Sam didn't react Mia said, "Is everything okay?"

"Oh, yes," Sam said, realizing she'd have to come up with something quickly as to why she was suddenly so interested in Amanda Moore. "I have a friend in Denver and I was telling him how rude and demanding Amanda is and the size of her bodyguard."

"I know! He's the incredible hulk! Running into him would be like running into a brick wall," Mia said as she was tying her apron.

Sam followed her to the register as she said, "I thought I'd try to get a picture of him, discreetly of course, this morning to send to my friend. If I didn't see Amanda today, I'd have to wait until Monday."

"She'll be here soon, I'm sure," Mia said. "Want your usual while you wait?"

"Please," Sam said.

When she had her coffee, Sam skipped her favorite table by the window and selected another one that offered a full view of the main door. The café filled quickly and by six-forty-five, the line was nearly to the door. Sam watched as Mia, Jeff and Gigi handled every order efficiently. At two minutes after seven a.m. Sam started to look expectantly toward the door. She didn't realize how edgy she felt, hoping Amanda wouldn't pick today as a day to skip getting coffee. She couldn't bear the thought of having to wait until Monday to try again, knowing what even one more weekend meant for Jenny.

Five minutes later, Amanda Moore's lug opened the door and she entered ahead of him. He took his usual place by the door, arms crossed, sunglasses on, while Amanda took her place in line. Sam grabbed her cell phone and, making sure Amanda wasn't looking, took a handful of pictures of him in rapid succession. Relieved, she swallowed hard when he didn't seem to notice. She examined the photos, enlarging each image, satisfied they would suffice.

Sam happened to catch Mia's attention and gave her a wink and a quick nod. Mia smiled slightly and continued making drinks at the bar as if nothing had happened. Sam tucked her phone in her bag and slipped quickly out of the café.

She didn't bother to go back to the hotel; instead, she drove to the

Zia construction site and parked next to Houston's truck. She called his cell phone and he answered on the second ring.

"Do you have a second? I'm outside parked by your truck. I have something to show you."

"Be there in two minutes," Houston said and ended the call.

When he got in the car, she said, "I know I could've just sent these to your phone, but I have to do something, this wondering and waiting around is going to kill me."

"Let's see what you've got."

Sam gave him her phone and watched him as he pulled his reading glasses from his shirt pocket and put them on. He swiped through the photos, his eyes darting back and forth, up and down, stopping on one image for a moment before moving to the next frame.

"Have you ever heard of Amanda Moore?"

"Yeah. She's that personal injury attorney here with a million annoying commercials on TV every night," Houston said without looking up from Sam's phone. "What's she got to do with this?"

"Well, it's probably nothing, but," Sam pointed to a photo of the lug. "I see her every morning at this coffee shop by the hotel where she goes and that's her bodyguard. He waits by the door while she gets her coffee."

"He certainly has the size for it," Houston said. "Probably one of the biggest guys I've ever seen and I've seen some pretty big guys in the Marines."

"I bet you have," Sam said.

"Now that I think about it, the guy Jenny mentions all the time is a pretty big dude."

"It's probably not him, but can you at least show it to her tomorrow night?"

Houston studied each frame again before he handed the phone back to Sam. "Send them to me. We'll show her when you get to the room."

"Speaking of tomorrow night," Sam said. "What're we going to do?"

Houston shook his head as he removed his reading glasses and slipped them back in his pocket. He folded his hands over his lap and stared at the portable office building, seemingly lost in thought.

"Go to the same room you were in, but skip the front desk," he said finally. "I'll already have the room, so just come up the stairs. The door will be unlocked."

FORTY-THREE

The light in Jenny's room was already on when Sam pulled into the motel parking lot just before nine Saturday evening. Her room next to Jenny's was dark. Sam grimaced; she was hoping Houston would have at least turned on one light as a signal to let her know it would be safe to go inside.

She was surprised when she didn't see his truck parked in the spot below the window. It was empty, as were the spots on both sides. Sam scanned the parking lot for his pickup once, then a second time and shook her head.

She decided to wait fifteen minutes before starting up the stairs. She drove around the back of the motel. The service entrance was deserted just as it was the other afternoon she had gone.

At nine-fifteen, she checked her cell phone, but there were no messages and no missed calls. She left the car and started for the side entrance of the motel, still looking over her shoulder for Houston's truck, and trying to keep a feeling of dread from working its way in. She wasn't surprised when she pulled on the door handle and it opened with ease. "You'll get in," Houston had told her. "It's never locked. Everyone knows what goes on here."

Tepid air rushed out and fanned her face as she stepped inside and let the door close quietly behind her. The stairway glowed with neon lights, and that pungent smell of stale cigarette smoke and fast food. Sam grabbed the railing and climbed until she reached a landing. She started up the rest of the steps toward a fire door, where a narrow blue sign next to it read second floor. Slightly winded when she reached the door, she took a deep breath before pulling it open only far enough to glance down the hallway. It was deserted. She listened for a moment, hearing nothing. She stepped lightly on the carpet and let the door close, holding it with one hand so it met the threshold with a soft click.

She took three steps toward her room and put her hand on the doorknob. She turned the handle and almost gasped when it didn't turn. She tried again. "It's still locked!" she whispered. She stepped back and stared at it, cursing under her breath.

She looked toward Jenny's door, and noticed pale lighting filling the threshold. To her surprise she could tell it was open. She could feel her phone starting to vibrate in her bag and she rushed toward the fire door and disappeared into the stairwell to answer it before it could ring again. As she did, she got a glimpse of Houston's name in the caller ID.

"Where *are* you?" Sam spoke through gritted teeth, anger and fear evident in her voice. She took the stairs back down to the landing.

"I witnessed a bad accident at an intersection near my apartment," Houston said. "Really bad with three cars, wreckage and glass everywhere. Looked like lots of injuries so I stopped to call 911 and stayed until police got there. I told them what I could, but I'm on my way. Sorry, Sam. I'll be there as soon as I can."

"I tried getting in the other room, but it's locked."

"I know. I'm sorry."

"How much longer?"

"Maybe fifteen minutes away. Is the light on in Jenny's room?"

"Yes, and the door is open."

"What do you mean the door is open?"

"I don't know, it's just open with that little metal bar that goes across the door jamb so it won't close and lock."

For a moment, Houston was silent and Sam could hear the wind rushing through the cab of the truck.

"I'll be there as soon as I can," he said finally.

"Please hurry," Sam said and she ended the call.

She stuck her phone in her bag and started back up the stairwell. She pulled the fire door open slowly and took a hasty glance down the hallway before she stepped inside. She walked gingerly toward Jenny's room. Just as she reached the door, she heard, "Get away from me!"

It was Jenny's voice.

A man said, "Keep your mouth shut, you little slut."

Sam stopped, squared her shoulders and listened, her eyes wide, darting everywhere. She took a deep breath and pushed the door to Jenny's room open. It was empty, only a single light shining from the nightstand.

"Wha—" Sam blinked hard as she looked around.

Then she heard Jenny's voice again. "Get away from me! I'm not going to do this anymore!"

"I said shut up!"

Sam heard the keen sound of someone slapping Jenny. Jenny whimpered and Sam looked toward the sound of her cry and realized the door to the room directly across from Jenny's was also open partially, the same pale light filling the threshold.

In a frenzy Sam immediately lunged for the door and pushed it open with such force it pounded against the adjoining wall.

She rushed into the room and saw Jenny on the bed. The sight of Amanda Moore's bodyguard trying to straddle her stopped Sam in her tracks. It only took her a moment to process who he was.

"My god. It's *him*."

He had pinned Jenny's arms above her head and she was struggling to try and get him off her. He far outweighed her and her attempts to get out from under him were as futile as moving a mountain.

Jenny saw Sam from the corner of her eye and called out frantically.

"Sam! Please help me!"

Sam dropped her bag at the door and started for the bed, grabbing the stainless-steel ice bucket off the corner of the dresser.

"Get off her, you bastard!" Sam yelled and hit the lug against the side of his head with such force, he let go of Jenny's arms and rolled toward the edge of the bed. His knee slipped off the side and he lost his balance and fell to the floor, landing like a block of concrete that moved the room like an earthquake.

Sam raised the ice bucket about to hit him again, but he was ready this time and knocked it away as though he was swatting a fly. The bucket flew out of her hands, hit her hard on the forehead above her right eye before it careened across the room and crashed against the window.

Despite his size, he jumped to his feet with cat-like ease. Sam backed away but stumbled near the corner of the bed and lost her footing. He was at her in seconds and grabbed her by the shoulders and shoved her against the wall with such power it drove the wind out of her. She slid down the wall and slumped heavily on the floor, blood oozing from the gash on her forehead.

The lug stood in front of Sam and kicked her foot. "I don't know who the hell you are, bitch, but you're gonna be sorry you and your fat ass ever set foot in this room."

Sam tried to be defiant, but she was gasping so deeply for air, she couldn't lift her head high enough to meet his stare. He grabbed her by her shirt collar and pulled her toward him, her arms limp at her sides. He made a fist and was about to strike Sam when Houston appeared at the door.

Jenny was still on the bed when she saw him. She pointed toward them. "Houston! It's him! He's the one! Help us!"

Houston bolted from the door and tackled the bodyguard with such force they went airborne. For a moment Sam remained frozen with pain as Houston landed blow after frenzied blow on the lug, his movements too fast and brutal for her to see anything other than a blur. The men wrestled furiously, throaty growls rumbling deeply from both of them. They tussled and rolled, ending up against the wall with Houston somehow underneath. The lug managed to land a series of heavy blows to Houston's face, which was now a battered and bloodied mess.

Sam was struggling to get to her feet as Jenny grabbed the pen with the motel logo on it off the nightstand. She jumped off the bed and onto the other bed and landed in the middle of the lug's back and stabbed him repeatedly in the side of his neck with all the power and strength her slender frame could gather.

He yelled in pain and grabbed his neck, trying to pull out the pen. He knocked Jenny away, she fell backward, clutching the side of her face in pain.

Houston, his face fire-engine red, his eyes narrowed in rage, saw his opening. His small size allowed him to slide out from under the lug. He jumped on his back and with one rapid motion, shoved the pen deeper in his neck. The lug howled and knocked the pen out of Houston's hand just as he tried to stab him again. Houston quickly wrapped his arms in a death grip around his neck, uttering guttural noises as he locked his hands firmly in place.

He began to squeeze. "Motherfucker, I've waited a long time to do this."

And with one rapid, sharp twist, he snapped the lug's neck to one side. His body went limp; Houston let him drop to the floor like a felled Redwood.

Houston got to his feet and Jenny fell into his arms. He pulled her away, gently pushing the hair out of her eyes and spoke to her with love. "Are you okay?"

Jenny nodded, then pointed at Sam.

Sam was on her hands and knees, still trying to get to her feet.

"Don't get up, Sam," Houston said. He took her shoulders and positioned her on the floor between the two beds, under the sallow glow cast by a lamp mounted over the headboard.

"That's him, isn't it?" he asked. "The guy you showed me in the photos."

Sam nodded; her eyes half-closed. "Yes, Amanda Moore's bodyguard. I almost couldn't believe it when I saw him."

Houston turned to Jenny. "She's bleeding. Get me a wet towel from the bathroom, get the ice bucket and go down the hall and find the ice machine."

Sam put her hand over Houston's arm and shook her head firmly. "Houston, we can't do that. We can't make it look like I've been helped." Sam glanced toward the lug's lifeless figure. "Is he dead?"

"Yeah. Hopefully on the way to hell by now."

"You have to leave, Houston, please. Go. Right now. Call the police, I'll be fine until help comes."

Houston was reluctant to move, staying beside Sam. Jenny kneeled next to them and placed her hands over the tops of her legs.

"You can't be here when they do come because we'll never be able to explain this, so leave and take Jenny with you." Sam was more insistent now. "Go. Please. Houston, take Jenny home. Take her home. You're the only one who can." Sam looked at Jenny. "Jenny, let Houston help you. You don't have to be afraid anymore, sweetheart. These people can't hurt you any longer. Houston can tell you about your brother's affairs. He's always been here for you and he'll make sure you're safe until you can get home and see your mother again. Go. Please. Now's your chance."

Sam put her hand over Jenny's and looked at her. She could see the flecks of brown in her hazel eyes, just as she could once see in Hunter's. "Let me look at you one more time before you go. I honestly never thought this moment would come, but I am so happy to have found you. I only wish you could have met your brother. He was a wonderful young man and I know he loved you very, very much, and all he really wanted was to find you so he could tell you himself."

Houston got to his feet slowly. He pulled a handkerchief from his back pocket and cleaned the blood off his face as he dialed 911 from the motel phone. Sam could hear the dispatcher's calm voice respond accordingly as he calmly told her what had happened.

"They're on their way," he said and hung up the phone.

He reached for Jenny's hand. She got to her feet and put hers inside his. When they got to the door, Houston turned and looked back to Sam. "I'll call you when I have a chance."

She nodded. "I'll wait to hear from you. Good luck and goodbye, Jenny."

Jenny waved and Sam watched Houston check the hallway before he stepped slightly to the side and Jenny went ahead of him, his hand near the small of her back.

Sam heard the fire door leading to the stairwell close with a faint click. She stared into the hallway long after they were gone, until she heard the sounds of sirens wailing in the distance.

FORTY-FOUR

When Sam opened her eyes again El Paso Police Lieutenant Mark McDaniel was standing over her, dressed in a dark pinstripe suit and lavender tie.

The room was full with law enforcement and emergency personnel milling about. Sam saw that the lug's body had been placed in a body bag and loaded on a gurney.

"Are you back with us?" she heard McDaniel say to her. His voice sounded firm but concerned.

Sam blinked several times, still feeling a little fuzzy. The wound above her eye was throbbing; she touched it lightly only to find that paramedics had already placed a bandage over it.

"It's not too bad," she heard McDaniel say. "Good news, you won't need stitches. Bad news, the blood ruined your white shirt."

He lowered himself to be at eye level with her. "Want to tell me what happened?"

Her thoughts still felt muddled, but she forced herself to sit up straighter.

"After you came to my office, we took a closer look at the Green and Aromatherapy spas," McDaniel said.

"What about the rooms above?"

"Those, too."

"Did you decide they needed more attention on Operation Winter Hope?" Sam asked. Her voice was raspy and she had to clear her throat.

"More than that, but this motel, this cesspool," he glanced around the room. "This hellhole has been on our radar for years. Officers are out here all the time."

McDaniel waited while paramedics wheeled the gurney out of the room. He turned back to Sam when they had cleared the area. "His neck was broken. Would you happen to know anything about that?"

Sam shook her head. "I don't even know his name. I just know him from seeing him at a coffee shop downtown. I believe he's Amanda Moore's assistant. He came in with her every morning when she got her coffee. Waited by the door with his arms folded over his chest."

"Fredrick Lawrence Henderson, but he goes by, or I should say went by, Larry."

"Larry," Sam repeated. "No, I didn't know that." The fog in her brain had parted and she wanted to stand up. She offered her hand to McDaniel and he helped her to her feet. She sat on the edge of the bed. "Was he known to you, Mark?"

McDaniel sat down next to her. "A wannabe heavyweight boxer at one time as you can tell by his size, but also a registered sex offender and convicted felon, child rape and pornography, but he did his time. He's been with Moore's outfit a few years now."

"Is she involved in this, too?" Sam asked.

"We'll soon find out," he said. "Big story, as you would say, if it turns out to be true. Her face will be plastered all over TV for a different reason."

They both stared at the wall in front of them in silence. "Was Jenny here? Is that why you came?" he asked finally.

Sam nodded. "I had it on good authority she was. When I came up the stairwell and entered the hallway, I heard someone say 'get away from me.' It sounded like Jenny's voice, but it wasn't until I got in here that I saw Larry on top of her." Sam pointed at the corner of the dresser where the ice bucket had been, and where she now saw her bag. Someone must have picked it up off the floor and set it there. "I grabbed a stainless-steel ice bucket. It had a good solid bottom and it was the only thing I saw in here that might work, so I hit him over the head as hard as I could."

"And then what happened?"

"He lost his balance and fell off the bed. I went to hit him again, but he knocked it out of my hands, and that's how I got this." She pointed to her forehead. "Then he started for me and I stumbled at the corner of this bed and that's when he grabbed me and shoved me against the wall so hard I couldn't breathe."

"Where was Jenny?"

"Still on the bed. Larry was about to hit me again when I heard Jenny yell to someone else who was now standing at the door to help us."

"Did you see who it was?"

Sam was thankful for the way McDaniel phrased the question. She was worried, knowing she'd have to tell him the truth, but the truth was, she didn't immediately see Houston at the door, so she didn't know who it was.

"It was another man, but I didn't see his face."

He looked at her, his eyes probing hers as if he knew she might be holding something back.

Sam went on. "The next thing I knew, or felt, Larry was somehow being pulled off me, yanked literally. The men started fighting and I tried getting to my feet to help Jenny, but I could hardly draw a breath. All I could see was thousands of tiny black dots in front of my eyes and everything else was a blur after that."

"Jenny and this other man were gone when you regained consciousness?"

Sam nodded.

"Did you call 911?"

"No."

"Do you want paramedics to take you to the ER?"

She quickly shook her head. "My car's outside, but my head feels fine, so I'll just go back to my hotel. A hot bath will help."

McDaniel gave her shoulder a supportive squeeze. "You'll be available if I have more questions."

It wasn't a question.

"Of course."

"Be careful driving back downtown."

"I will," she said.

McDaniel rose from the bed and Sam watched him meet another plainclothes detective near the door. They talked briefly, then he turned to face her. "By the way, I called James Page and filled him in. I told him what happened but that you looked to be okay so he didn't have to worry. He wants you to call him in the morning."

"I will. Thank you, Mark."

McDaniel's stone face inched into a small grin before he followed the other detective out of the room.

Several officers remained in the room but the paramedics were gone when Sam finally felt well enough to head to her car. When she stood, she saw the pen Jenny used to stab Larry in the neck partially sticking out beneath the curtains, but she didn't pick it up. She collected her bag off the dresser, ducked under the yellow crime scene tape, which was now across the door, and took the stairs.

The cool night air refreshed her when she stepped outside and walked to her car. Given the late hour, the traffic was light as she merged onto the highway; on the horizon a waning moon was rising over a glittering city. Within twenty minutes she was back downtown and in her hotel room. Her head was spinning and every muscle in her body screamed in pain. She soaked in a hot bath for almost an hour, keeping her eyes closed and replaying the events in the motel room over and over. The only sound came from the water lapping against her body when she moved. When she got out of the bath, she turned the alarm off on her cell phone, deciding—hoping—she could sleep.

Sam was partially awake when she heard her cell phone chime with a text message. She glanced toward the clock radio, five minutes after eleven a.m. She'd slept straight through for nearly ten hours. The sun was already high above the distant foothills and tendrils of thin white clouds spread across a cobalt sky. She took her phone off the nightstand and clicked on the message she saw was from Mark McDaniel.

Watch the late news tonight.

Remembering what McDaniel had told her in the motel room after Larry's body was removed, Amanda Moore entered her mind. She responded, *You're going to make me wait until then?*

I'm not James Page. He texted.

"No, you're not," Sam said, but she texted back, *I appreciate the heads up.*

Feeling stiff with pain she rolled over and pulled the covers under her chin. She remembered the last thought she had before she fell asleep, Houston and Jenny kneeling next to her. Her first thought when she woke this morning was the both of them standing at the door moments before they disappeared down the stairwell, hopefully toward a new and better life for Jenny.

Sam called Wilson and told him everything.

"Tough stuff to witness," he said when she finished. "Are you okay?"

"I am, Wilson, because I am trying to stay focused on the last image I saw in that room."

"What was that?" he asked.

"Houston and Jenny leaving. I started to cry when I saw them hesitate only a moment at the door before they left. Jenny is finally free."

"Try to keep that thought."

"I will," she said. "I'm planning to come back to work on Tuesday, if that's okay."

"Everyone will be happy to see you, Sam."

"Everyone?" she asked with a slight laugh. "Even Nick?"

"Even Nick," Wilson said.

Then she called home and Nona answered. She talked to everyone and ended the call talking to Howard, telling him what had happened in the motel room.

"When are you coming home, Samantha?"

"Tomorrow. I want to surprise April and be with you when you pick her up from school."

"She'll be so happy to see you. We'll all be happy to have you home."

"Me, too, Howard, I can hardly wait to see everyone," she said and smiled. "There's a few things I want to do before I leave in the morning. I hope to tell a few people I'm going back to Denver. They've made being here a little more bearable."

After she showered, she examined the wound on her forehead. It was tender and starting to bruise, but she decided it didn't need a bandage. Instead, she covered it with a little of her makeup concealer. She headed to *La Dolce Vita*, though she knew Mia didn't work Sundays. She was sitting at her favorite table by the window drinking coffee when she sent a text to Sandy Petersen.

It's all over, Sandy. Be sure you watch the late news tonight.

Sandy responded immediately. *OMG! You have to tell me what happened!*

Do you have a few minutes this afternoon? I can stop by and fill you in.

Yes, of course! Come anytime!

Be there within the hour. Thanks to you, Sandy - otherwise, I'd probably still be sitting in the grocery store parking lot.

Can't wait to hear all about it!

After Sam left Sandy's house, she drove by Franklin Elementary School; the grounds were deserted on a Sunday afternoon. She passed through Hunter's old neighborhood and parked in front of his childhood home. She noticed a luxury sedan parked in the driveway at Mrs. Sheffield's house and wondered if it was her daughter visiting from Las Cruces, a busy gal like Sam, only just a little too chubby.

Before she started back downtown, she went to the Camino Rael Apartments. She entered the parking lot, looking toward the carport where Houston parked his GMC.

It was empty.

She wondered where they were now and she wanted to text Houston. But he said he'd call when he had the chance and she would wait to hear from him just as she said she would.

Sam returned to the hotel, packed and waited for the late local news to air.

The ten p.m. newscast led with the arrest of personal injury attorney Amanda Moore. Sam thought she would be surprised about Amanda, but somehow she wasn't.

Police had raided the spas and had taken the girls housed in the rooms upstairs into safety. News footage showed McDaniel standing with a handful of reporters sticking microphones in front of his mouth. He said he had received a tip about the spas and girls being held captive in the rooms above. They were believed to be involved in sex and human trafficking.

Sam could see his lavender tie loosened at his shirt collar and guessed he must have been working nonstop since he had been with her at the motel. McDaniel explained to reporters each of the girls told police the same account of being kidnapped from Mexico and taken to El Paso in a windowless van. There they were inspected by Amanda Moore and repeatedly assaulted by Frederick Lawrence Henderson.

McDaniel appeared to have a satisfied smirk on his face when he told reporters the Desert Inn Motel had been permanently shut down. "This place, which has long been a magnet for prostitution, and a thorn in our side for many, many years, is finally shuttered," he said.

A TV reporter was standing outside between the two spas in a live shot when she announced that Moore had been arrested without incident at her residence, a lavish five thousand-square-foot gated home along Scenic Drive, a narrow, winding two-lane road that skirted around the east side of the mountain.

File footage showed Amanda, leaving her Spanish-style stucco home with a dark coat covering her hands. Sam was certain she'd been handcuffed. Reporters shouted questions at Amanda, who shouted back that she was going to sue the El Paso Police Department for wrongful arrest and the television stations for slander, but police whisked her away and helped her into a waiting squad car before she could say another word.

The next day Sam waited until after eight a.m. and the morning rush for coffee to have subsided before she walked alongside the Plaza to *La Dolce Vita* for the last time. From the tall windows she was happy to see the café was empty and Mia and Jeff standing idle behind the counter. She hardly had the door open when Mia rushed to greet her.

She grabbed Sam by the arm and said, "Oh my God! Sam, did you see the news about Amanda Moore?! I couldn't believe it when I saw it. The news is everywhere and her bodyguard murdered! Oh my God! He's even creepier than I thought."

"I couldn't believe it when I saw it, either," Sam said.

"And all those poor girls, oh my God!" Mia said. "I just felt so sad hearing that news."

"It was heartbreaking," Sam said. "At least we know a few of them, hopefully all of them, will be able to go back home to their families again soon."

"Thank goodness Amanda won't be bothering us anymore," Mia said and she pulled Sam toward the coffee bar.

"You got your wish, Mia," Sam said.

Jeff was already making Sam's Americano with a big grin on his face. "Yeah, I think where Amanda's going you can bet she's not gonna get her coffee steamed to one hundred and twenty degrees anymore!"

Sam and Mia burst into laughter.

Sam stayed at the bar listening to Jeff and Mia share a few more stories about Amanda Moore before she told them she was returning to Denver.

"We hate to see you leave, Sam, we loved having you come in," Mia said. "Will you ever be back this way?"

"If I do, this is the first place I'll come."

Before Sam started for the airport, she made one final stop. She could tell when she reached the gates to Concordia Cemetery that the graves of Hunter and his parents had been decorated with fresh flowers, the colorful spray was a beacon amid the brown earth. She walked toward the headstones carrying her own fresh bouquet. When she placed hers by the other flowers, she could only guess they had been left by Houston and Jenny. On the way to the airport, she noticed the three billboards with Amanda Moore's advertising had been removed.

That afternoon, Sam was standing next to the old Chrysler station wagon, waiting under a warm winter sun for her daughter to emerge from the building. The school bell rang and moments later, a rush of students started to file out of the double doors. Sam spotted April walking with her friend Carol and brought her hands to her mouth. She swallowed back tears. When April saw her mother, she dropped her backpack and ran toward her. Sam swooped her up into her arms and they swung around together for a full circle.

When they got to the long gravel driveway, the ranch house came into view. Nona was standing on the front porch, shielding her eyes from the afternoon glare, watching the station wagon approach. Nona met Sam as she got out of the car, and the women fell into a long, silent embrace.

The moment Sam walked in the kitchen, the homey smell of spaghetti sauce simmering on the stove greeted her. A lemon cake made from scratch was on a cooling rack on the counter.

Step was sitting on the floor next to the sink. The moment he saw Sam, his tail began to whip the air. Sam put her hand out and Step didn't hesitate to come to her, his nose cold and wet in the palm of her hand.

FORTY-FIVE

When Sam arrived at the *Grandview Perspective* shortly before eight Tuesday morning, Wilson's Honda Accord was the only other car in the parking lot.

She smiled to herself as she parked her station wagon next to his.

She was so excited to return to work, she'd hardly slept. That anticipation, however, wasn't all that had kept her awake most of the night. Long after April had fallen asleep Sam, carrying the little lavender elephant, slipped into her bedroom, sat on the edge of her bed and watched her daughter. She lost track of time as she stayed next to April, who slept peacefully and carefree. She listened to the soft sound of her breathing, watched her turn over now and then, and when she seemingly sensed her mother was near, nestled closer to her.

Sam couldn't stop wondering where Houston and Jenny were in their journey. She still hadn't heard from him, so she could only hope they were safely out of the United States and somewhere deep in Mexico, closer to Jenny's hometown and the reunion with the only woman she knew as her mother.

Sam gathered her things and entered the newsroom through the kitchen, the way she always did when she came to work. Wilson had made coffee and the fresh aroma reminded her of going to *La Dolce Vita* every morning and being welcomed by Mia and Jeff.

She stopped at her desk, set her bag down and started for Wilson's office. She listened a moment to see if he was on the phone. Not hearing anything, she knocked lightly and stuck her head inside.

"Hi, here I am," Sam said.

Wilson motioned her in as he got up. He came around his desk and they met in front of it. The soft scent of her perfume followed her into the room. He gave Sam a deep hug, which she returned.

"Welcome back," he said. "It's nice to have you here."

"I didn't think I'd see you when I came in this morning. You're missing your meeting."

"I am," Wilson said. "But you were coming back today and I wanted to be here."

They stepped away from each other and Wilson pointed to one of his desk chairs and Sam sat across from him. In the moment he studied her he saw she had pushed her blonde hair back behind her ears, revealing her gold-loop earrings. She conjured a classy vibe in a polished short-sleeve shift navy dress topped with an airy keyhole neckline and matching navy pumps.

"Coming home yesterday was wonderful and I'm so happy to be back," Sam said. "Thank you for being so understanding with this whole thing."

He pointed to her forehead. "Is that from the ice bucket?"

Sam nodded as she placed her hand lightly over her wound, which she was still covering with makeup. "A small price to pay considering what Houston did to Larry. You'd never know it, Wilson."

"Know what?"

"How strong Houston is just by looking at him. Larry was massive, I mean huge, six-foot-five, six-foot-six, and well over three hundred pounds. Houston's not much taller than I am and probably twenty years older than Larry, but when he jumped on his back." Sam stopped and shook her head. "One turn was all it took."

"Thank goodness Houston came when he did," Wilson said.

Sam put a hand against her chest. "Yes, thank goodness, I'd hate to think what might have happened if he hadn't."

"Still nothing from him?"

She shook her head again. "He said he'd call when he could, and after these last few weeks and everything we did together, I'll take him at his word."

Sam and Wilson were so immersed in their conversation, they didn't realize managing editor Nick Weeks was leaning against the door jamb of Wilson's office.

"Sam, you're back," Nick said, trying to show some measure of enthusiasm.

"I am."

"Wilson told us yesterday you found Jenny."

"I did," she said. "But not without a lot of help from others. Otherwise, I would've come back empty handed."

"At the staff meeting on Thursday, Sam, if you're willing, you can give us an account of what happened," Wilson said. "Everyone has asked."

"I can hit the highlights, sure," Sam said.

"Then you're ready to get back to work?"

"I wouldn't be here otherwise, Nick."

"Great. Then I'll see you at eleven for our budget meeting and you can tell me what stories you'll have for the Friday Edition."

"I'll be in the conference room then."

Nick nodded at both of them and returned to his office.

After Sam's eleven o'clock meeting with Nick, she stayed at the conference table, her hand resting lightly over her notebook. From this angle she had a clear view of the whiteboard.

The rendering Hunter had drawn of the two of them in the Chrysler station wagon was still on the board.

Wilson was coming down the stairs when he noticed Sam still sitting at the table. He stepped inside the room considering her.

"I thought someone would have erased this by now," she said, still keeping her gaze on the board.

"There was no reason to, Sam. I told you before you left for El Paso no one was using it and when the time came and you were ready, it's something only you could do."

Sam got up and walked toward the board.

"It's time," she said. Without another word, she took the eraser and with one full swipe most of her image disappeared. She hesitated briefly, taking in Hunter's image a final time before she made several full passes over the board. In moments, save for a few blue streaks left by the marker, the whiteboard was empty.

It was after five thirty p.m. when Sam stuck her head inside Wilson's office. "Everyone else is gone. If you're ready we can walk out together."

"Give me fifteen minutes."

Sam gathered her things and shut down her computer. A few minutes later Wilson joined her at her desk and they started for the kitchen.

"How was your first day?" he asked as they began to climb the stairs toward the parking lot.

"It was so nice. Everyone was so happy to see me, well most everyone," Sam said with a cool smile.

They walked under a fading light to their cars. They stopped in front of his Accord and Sam looked down at his PAGE 68 license plate.

"Do you know how many times I've entered this parking lot and saw your plate?"

"Enough, I'm sure."

"And how many times I said to myself, 'I need to ask Wilson what that means.'"

"And you never did."

"No, I didn't, but I know what it means now," Sam said.

"After you get a little more settled, will you start reading the Big Book again?"

"Absolutely. Probably over the weekend. I just want to absorb being home for a little while. I still haven't told April that I know about you and the secret you asked her to keep."

"When the time is right," he said.

"And I'll be getting back on that exercise bike, too, though I don't think my bottom is going to be too happy about that."

They both laughed.

Sam lowered her head and kicked at a rock with the tip of her heel. "I didn't bring Jenny home, though, like I wanted to, Wilson."

"Sam, Denver never was her home."

"I know."

"Not even El Paso."

"I know," Sam said again.

"Hopefully it won't be long before she gets home."

"I hope so, too."

"But I'm glad you're back," Wilson said.

"Me, too."

"I missed you while you were gone."

"I missed you, too," she said.

"I thought about you a lot," he said.

"I thought about you, too."

A light breeze stirred between them, pushing Sam's hair into her eyes. Wilson brushed it to the side, put his hand under her chin and lifted her head toward his before he realized what he had done.

He noticed she didn't seem to mind.

Their eyes met and Sam remembered what April had told her in her bedroom the night she was packing for El Paso. How confident she seemed to be with a relationship between them, no matter their ages.

She stepped closer to him and placed her hand lightly on his chest.

"Kiss me," she said softly.

THE LAST CHAPTER

A month had come and gone since Sam's first full week home from El Paso.

The landscape was green with spring, though winter was stubborn in its unwillingness to give in, with remnants from the last snowfall still caught in the high branches and leaves of the Evergreens.

Sam was driving home from work. She had reached the turn off to the gravel road that meandered to the ranch, where she always stopped to roll down the windows and turn off the radio. She would drive the last remaining few miles to the gravel driveway and home as she always did with the wind whipping through the interior of the car and the sound of the tires crunching over dirt roads.

She had just gotten out of the car to open the main gate when her cell phone started to ring. She saw Houston Meyers' name in the caller ID, and felt her heart do somersaults. She closed her eyes and said a silent prayer of thanksgiving before she answered.

"Hi, Houston! Finally! I have been waiting and waiting to hear your voice." She was standing against the car door with both hands cradling the phone.

"Hi, Sam. How are you?"

"I'm fine, even better now that you've finally called. What happened? Did you make it to Mexico okay? Where are you? How's Jenny? Oh my gosh, forgive me, Houston, I'm rambling. Did you get her home safely?"

"Hold on, Sam, gimme a chance to answer your questions. First, I'm in Slidell now. I got back home yesterday afternoon."

"How long did you stay in Mexico with Jenny?"

"Almost the whole month. The house is so run down, I couldn't believe how much work needed to be done and still needs to be done, but there's no one there who can do it. There was a hole in the roof in the kitchen above the stove."

"A hole?"

"Yeah, a good-size hole, almost wide enough for me to fit through. I spent a few days getting materials in the city and fixing that. Jenny's mother says thank goodness they don't get much rain, otherwise cooking would be impossible."

Jenny's mother.

Sam couldn't help the tears that welled in her eyes. "Tell me about their reunion."

"I've seen a lot of people reunite after so many months and years apart, especially being in the service," Houston began by saying. "But honestly, Sam, I can tell you in all my years I've never seen a homecoming like that."

Sam put a hand over her mouth and began to cry softly.

"She knew we were coming; Jenny had called her the day before we arrived. We got there around one the next afternoon and we saw her sitting on this battered old couch on the porch waiting for us. She saw the dirt rise from the road as we approached. She's an older woman, Sam, but she literally flew off that porch and ran toward us so fast it almost looked like the wind was carrying her. I had to stop the truck because I didn't want to run over her. Jenny got out and ran to her. They met in front of the truck and Jenny just buried her head in her chest. I swear they didn't move from that spot for ten minutes.

"I have to be honest, Sam, I lost it, too, so I stayed in the truck, because I didn't want them to see me crying like a little kid."

Tears were streaming down Sam's face now and she did nothing to stop them.

"And then what happened?" she asked.

"I just stayed. I fixed the roof and repaired a fence, and would you believe they had no indoor plumbing for a bathroom?"

"Hunter always told me how poor his mother's family was. What did you do?"

"I dug a well and put in a toilet."

Sam laughed through her tears.

"I think Jenny and I must have gained five pounds each while I was there. Her mother cooked and cooked and we ate and ate. Best homemade food I've ever had—tamales, chile rellenos, pozole, sweet bread—everything from scratch. And I took way too many pictures on my phone. I've never seen Jenny smile so much."

Sam could hear laughter, hope, in his voice.

"When did you finally leave?"

"A few days ago. I'll be honest with you, I had to force myself to leave, otherwise I'm not sure I would have. I kept the sight of Jenny in my rearview mirror as long as I could. My last image of her was standing with her mother on the porch."

"Now Jenny and her mother will have the time to heal," Sam said. "How did you leave it with her?"

"I told her when she was ready to come back to the States to take care of her brother's affairs to call me and I'd come to bring her back. I know she'll call, but when, I honestly don't know. I think she's just happy to be home again. And you wanna know something?"

"What's that, Houston?"

"From the night I brought Jenny back to my place after leaving the motel, I slept. Every night for almost the last four years, I've gone to bed worried about Jenny and never slept more than two, three hours a night. For the first time, I've been able to sleep straight through 'til morning because I know she's home safe and where she should be."

"What about you? When are you going back to El Paso?"

"In a few days, but just long enough to finish the housing project at Zia Construction."

"How long do you think that'll be?"

"Four or five months, but before the end of the year for sure. I'll be back here, back home for good by Christmas."

"Your place on earth."

Houston laughed. "Yeah, it is. I told Jenny I'm going to bring her here someday. I've told her how beautiful and green everything is, not like the dry, patchy landscape of El Paso and Mexico."

"When Jenny's ready, I'll be here waiting," Sam said. "Everything that was her brother's is hers now. She'll have their parents' trust to get what she needs for her and her... mother."

"Jenny knows that, Sam. When she's ready, I'll let you know."

"I know you will."

"You wanna know somethin'?"

"Tell me, Houston."

"It's going to be strange going back to El Paso knowing Jenny's not there any longer. In some odd way, knowing she was there and I could see her made things easier for me, you know, a little less lonely. I know it was hell for her but she was always a ray of light for me, even during her darkest hours."

"You were a ray of light for her, too, Houston."

"I hope so," he said. "I miss her so much, but I can go back to El Paso for now and eventually back to Slidell, knowing she's where she should be. And when she's ready, I'll see her again."

"She wouldn't have made it through without you, and thank you for letting me in and believing in me, too. You didn't have to meet me that day at the cemetery."

"It wouldn't have been possible without you, Sam."

"I came because of Hunter. That's what he wanted, what he would have done. Take care, Houston, whenever it is, however long it is, I'll be here waiting to hear from you."

After they hung up, Sam stayed by the wagon, listening to the endless quiet that surrounded her. The sun had dropped behind the peaks, its long golden rays lighting the last of the day. She opened the gate and drove inside the property. When she got out to close it, a lone hawk flew overhead. She watched it glide silently and effortlessly through the air until it dropped down into the valley.

She drove slowly toward the house. "Hunter, I'll never be able to explain how but we did it, somehow we found Jenny," she said, letting the wind carry her words. "And she's home and safe now. She is where she should be. Sometimes there are happy endings and we can say this is one."

When Sam reached the long gravel driveway to home, she stopped and took everything in.

There were clothes on the line. After dinner, Sam would help her grandmother bring them in and they would fold them together under the soft light on the kitchen table. When Sam left for work that morning, Howard had pulled the tractor up to the barn, where it remained for some repairs. April's dirt bike lay on its side where the gravel road met the grass.

Just as she had told Wilson on her first day back to work, she wanted to become immersed in being home again and all it meant.

And she had.

Days passed simply, in quiet, unassuming ways. She embraced every moment, living and being at the ranch with Howard, Nona and April, coming and going from work and school, helping April with her homework, going to basketball games on Saturday afternoons.

She couldn't ask for anything more.

She started down the road toward the house thinking as she had all week…

When I am here, I am home.

THE END

ACKNOWLEDGEMENTS

Though I spent many hours alone writing *The Long Way Home*, it is by no means a solitary effort. I wish to be mindful, thankful and deeply grateful to those who were so generous with their time, knowledge and expertise in helping me to tell this story as accurately and as well as I possibly could.

A thank you to my editors, David and Noly, who continue to help me flesh out my stories and bring them to the next level.

I am, now and always, unspcakably thankful and grateful to my mother, my brother and my sister (in her sweet memory) and my dear, dear friends. Their unconditional patience, love and encouragement is unending and simply keeps me going.

And finally, thank you, Dear Readers, for investing your time to read my books. I hope I have not let you down and it has been time well spent.

COPYRIGHT

STAY CONNECTED WITH THE AUTHOR

Sign up for Betta's newsletter and write to her via her website:
www.BettaFerrendelliBooks.com

Follow her on Twitter: @BettaWriter

On Facebook: BettaFerrendelliBooks

Visit her author central page on Amazon:
https://www.amazon.com/author/bettaferrendelli

Write her via snail mail: PO Box 147105, Edgewater, CO, 80214

OTHER BOOKS IN THE
SAMANTHA CHURCH MYSTERY SERIES

THE FRIDAY EDITION, BOOK 1

REVENGE IS SWEET, BOOK 2

DEAD WRONG, BOOK 3

COLD CASE NO. 99-5219, BOOK 4

ON THE BORDER, BOOK 5

OTHER CONTEMPORARY FICTION
by Betta Ferrendelli

AN INVINCIBLE SUMMER

LAST THINGS

All available on Amazon

BTB

Made in United States
Orlando, FL
11 January 2022

13305121R00178